ALSO BY
MADELEINE WATTS

The Inland Sea

ELEGY, SOUTHWEST

A Novel

MADELEINE WATTS

SIMON & SCHUSTER

New York   Amsterdam/Antwerp   London
Toronto   Sydney/Melbourne   New Delhi

Simon & Schuster
1230 Avenue of the Americas
New York, NY 10020

First Simon & Schuster hardcover edition February 2025

SIMON & SCHUSTER and colophon are registered
trademarks of Simon & Schuster, LLC

For information about special discounts for bulk purchases,
please contact Simon & Schuster Special Sales at
1-866-506-1949 or business@simonandschuster.com.

The Simon & Schuster Speakers Bureau can bring authors to
your live event. For more information or to book an event, contact
the Simon & Schuster Speakers Bureau at 1-866-248-3049
or visit our website at www.simonspeakers.com.

Interior design by Lewelin Polanco

Manufactured in the United States of America

1 3 5 7 9 10 8 6 4 2

Library of Congress Cataloging-in-Publication Data
Names: Watts, Madeleine, author.
Title: Elegy, southwest : a novel / Madeleine Watts.
Description: First Simon & Schuster hardcover edition. | New York :
Simon & Schuster, 2025. | Summary: "A timely and urgent novel following a young
married couple on a road trip through the American southwest as they grapple with
the breakdown of their relationship in the shadow of environmental collapse, for fans
of Rachel Cusk and Sigrid Nunez"—Provided by publisher.
Identifiers: LCCN 2024042013 | ISBN 9781668051627 (hardcover) | ISBN
9781668051634 (trade paperback) | ISBN 9781668051641 (ebook)
Subjects: LCGFT: Novels.
Classification: LCC PR9619.4.W39 E45 2025 | DDC 823/.92—dc23/eng/20240906
LC record available at https://lccn.loc.gov/2024042013

ISBN 978-1-6680-5162-7
ISBN 978-1-6680-5164-1 (ebook)

You have gone (which I lament), you are here (since I am addressing you).

—ROLAND BARTHES

1

Fucked-Up Streets—Llamas—Swimming Pools—Window Locks—
The Hoover Dam—Speeding Tickets—Amaro with Rosebuds—A
Combination of Juice Bar and High-End Wine Store—The
Endangered Desert Tortoise—Ash on the Windshield—An Elvis
Impersonator for a Fee—The El Cortez—Unprepared Vows—A
Happy Goat—California Tofurkey Sandwiches—Magic—Seven Magic
Mountains—The Bewildering Shoots of Melon and Corn Plants

Afterwards, you told me it was part of what you loved most about those weeks. You got up every morning and you just drove, with only the vaguest sense of where we would be sleeping that night. You didn't have to make any decisions, and you didn't have to think about what you were doing each day. I sat beside you, navigating from the map on my phone even when we were out of range. My left hand nearly always held on to your thigh. I didn't know how to drive.

You collected the car. I sat on the bench in the waiting room of the airport Hertz office, listening to the final notes of *A Charlie Brown Christmas* soundtrack, then "Rockin' Around the Christmas Tree," although it was a little over a week before Thanksgiving. Six days until I turned twenty-nine, though by my birthday we'd have crossed through Nevada and California and entered Arizona, according to the itinerary. You didn't know what was on the itinerary because it had been me who planned the trip. You said you would drive me wherever I wanted to go.

When you'd collected the keys and signed the forms, we found the designated car in the lot and made our way out. It was almost midnight by my body clock, but nine o'clock on Pacific Time. I watched the city draw near in the window. The yellowy glow across the valley floor cast the big desert sky a dark purple. Las Vegas a valley of artificial light ringed by the black shapes of mountains. Billboards stretched all along the Las Vegas Freeway: Absinthe, Opium, Céline Dion, and the Backstreet Boys. "Report prescription opiate abuse," "Great cannabis deals, next exit." Palm trees, everywhere.

There's something fucked-up about Vegas streets, you said.

We'd both been to Las Vegas before, but it was the first time you'd driven a car there. I don't know now whether it was the streets that were fucked-up, or if it was the feeling you had, ever present, that there was something fundamentally fucked-up about this big South-western desert you never felt comfortable coming from.

The car came to a stop outside Malik's house and a motion-sensor light flicked on over the concrete path running alongside the bungalow down to the casita. I had supposed a casita might be cute, and more redolent of vacation than a granny flat in his yard, which is what I realized, just then, that it was. Malik wasn't home, but we didn't need a key, because the locking mechanism was PIN-dependent. The casita was bigger than our entire apartment in New York. The floors were a cold cream tile, and through the sliding glass doors we could see the illuminated brambles of a Texas Ranger, one of the few things growing in the yard's hard clay.

Neither of us had eaten on the plane. I dropped our stuff by the door, changed, and you drove us Downtown. It was the only place we knew to go. Atomic Liquors on Fremont Street was still open, and they served food late. Not much: fries and pickles, chicken wings, and curried cauliflower hush puppies. Nothing that I wanted.

Look, see, they have a whole plate of harissa carrots, you said, looking at the laminated menu displayed outside the door. You can have a big plate of carrots and a glass of red wine; you'll be happy as a clam.

We were escorted inside by a waiter and seated in a leather booth. You ordered a burger and a cocktail with gin. You knew that I would pick at your fries as well as eat my carrots, and you didn't mind. After we finished, you paid and went to the bathroom, while I walked outside to wait. Downtown was the only part of Las Vegas I was even a little familiar with because it was where your boss had previously booked our accommodation when you'd needed to visit for work. It was an extension of the Fremont Street Experience, just a few blocks away. The entire neighborhood was the target of a clean-up effort. The city wanted to do to Downtown Las Vegas what they'd done to Downtown L.A., you had told me when we'd first visited. Meaning: sanitize it, inject money into it, paint the shopfronts turquoise and rose, clear the homeless population and the baseball-capped retirees away. Make way for young people like us, and whatever it was they thought we wanted. For a couple of blocks, it really did seem as sterile and prosaic as they had hoped for. The bougainvillea that climbed the pastel walls, the wide streets, the big sky and the palm trees and the warmth. But the further east I looked down Fremont Street the dustier and more deserted it became. It was a weeknight. The population would swell over the weekend; all of the looky-loos from San Diego, or Denver, or Kansas City driving and flying in. Weeknights were quieter, and at eleven o'clock Fremont Street was almost peaceful. Small groups of young people passed by, laughing. I stood on the pavement by speakers that played tinny pop music into the open-air dining area.

Across the street I could see a woman walking alone. I saw her stumble, and hurry on. She was moving towards me from the dusty end of Fremont Street, looking not quite dressed, in flip-flops, a baseball shirt, and grubby black leggings with a hole in the knee. She was calling out, Max, come on, boy, come here, boy, looking around, trying to spot her dog somewhere in the shopfronts and patios. She gazed out into the cavernously empty parking lot across the street. A tall red neon sign skirted by a ribbon of yellow light declared it a "Motel," but there was no building which might accommodate a motel, just a lot with some inexpertly parked cars. "Llamas stay for free," the sign said beside the *L* of "Motel." The traffic island palm fronds rasped. Max, she called out into the car park. She was across the street, but I could see that tears were streaming down her face. There was panic in her voice, making the long vowel of Max waver whenever she called it out. She was still holding the leash in her hand. I watched her head turn abruptly, towards shouts that penetrated the roar of the praying mantis fire show up the street. Two men and a woman were calling out and trying to move a dark shape into the gutter from the middle of the road.

Does this dog belong to anybody?

I looked back towards the woman, still standing beneath a flood-light. I watched the knowledge hit her.

I had known such moments. The brief, quiet instant when you know the flood of pain is coming. But you are still on dry land. Wishing with all your will that you might not have to go through the ordeal of getting soaked. You try to stay in that instant and ward off the flood, knowing you won't be the same on the other side of the pain. Nothing will be the same.

Then it hit, sweeping over her face, crumpling its features. She opened her mouth and she screamed. Everybody looked. Her body seemed to unlock, and she began to run.

I'm coming, she shouted towards the lump of fur in the gutter. I'm coming!

As she ran, the leash fell out of her hand, and she did not stop to go back for it. I watched the shapes of people rush to comfort her, the muffled screams of her grief, but they were far away, and I could not see whether the dog was dead or not. I thought it was. I had heard that scream.

The tinny pop music still played, and when you came out of the bar you put your arm around me, we walked towards the car, and I didn't tell you about what I had just seen. I didn't think you could handle any more death.

We drove back to Malik's and fell into bed. I had forgotten the way it is in warm places when the weather gets cold. How those cream tiles that cool the house in mid-summer only serve to intensify the chill on late-autumn evenings. Malik had left a space heater for us in the casita, but the big glass doors onto the yard let the heat out, and in bed that night I wore two sweaters and huddled against you for warmth. It was funny, the way we had learned to sleep together after five and a half years. I was always in a sweater, under a duvet and an extra blanket, and you always in boxers and a T-shirt, beneath a thin sheet, embracing the pillows. There was barely any room for me in the bed with all the pillows you needed to get to sleep.

We drove in the morning to a coffee shop. I ordered a tofu scramble, which I ate quickly from a paper take-out box on the street, wiping my fingers on my jeans while you took a phone call from your boss. The silhouette of Frenchman Mountain was visible through the haze of Downtown. A brilliant desert sky. The old neon signs and motels gone to seed, desiccating in the wind behind barbed wire and cracked cement. "We offer affordable senior living," advertised an abandoned lot, weeds climbing towards the faded plastic banner. I felt a kind of loosening in my chest, as though the petals of a flower were easing open to receive the light. I loved it here.

We drove through the sprawl with your take-away iced coffee sloshing and threatening to spill, into flat land adorned with nothing but creosote and electricity transformers. I scanned the dial through power pop and Spanish-language hip-hop before landing on the news. Overnight the Golden Knights had beat Anaheim in the Pacific Division, there were no credible reports of election fraud in Nevada, and a former Las Vegas baker had been identified as a victim of the fires raging in northern California. The fire had by then spread to 140,000 acres, which was a number so large I couldn't quite fathom it. It was as big as the city of Chicago, of Manila, of the entirety of Malta, Barbados, and Guam. There was another fire burning north of Los Angeles. People were trapped between beach and mountain, the radio said softly, while you told me you were anxious about the emails you hadn't answered. You were worried about the tone of an artist in one of those emails, who, your boss had reminded you on the phone call, it was your job to keep happy. Neil Young's Malibu home had been destroyed in the fires, the radio reported.

Poor Neil Young, you said.

You shifted awkwardly in the seat. Are you okay? I asked.

I slept weird and now my hips are tight, you said. Which meant, I knew, that driving might be uncomfortable, that sitting down for long periods would hurt you. Our bad days often started when your hips were tight.

We don't have to go all the way out there, I said. If you don't want to.

Of course not, you said, that's the whole reason you wanted to come to Nevada.

Which was true. I wanted to see the dam.

I had wanted to drive out to see it during the last trip we had made to Las Vegas, but back then we had not thought to rent a car. I couldn't say when it was that I got into my head that the Hoover Dam—the entire Colorado River—were sites worthy of a kind of pilgrimage. I don't think, then, that I understood what it was that drew me to images of the dwindling water in this drying-up landscape. Yet for years I had been full of stories about the Colorado River. I brought it up in conversation with sort of the frequency that people find ways to mention their lovers to acquaintances when relationships are new. I talked about the streams and creeks and canals, the artificial lakes, the salty blue miracle of the Pacific edging up against so much desert. The miracle of it, and the tragedy. Long before I met you, I had read something by a writer from the West about dams in this part of the country. What I remembered was that by her reckoning the counterpoint to the dam was the swimming pool. She longed to see water under control—in a pool, in a dam—and not because there isn't a kind of transcendental power in a wild, undammed river, but because she felt in the marrow of her bones the terror of the town submerged by flood, and the terror of the tap running dry. For a while, I had thought when I enrolled in my doctoral program that I would write about swimming pools. Indeed, that was the original proposal. But my interests evolved, and now I knew I wanted to write about the River, about its imminent loss. Even though, until this trip, I had never seen it.

And didn't you understand about swimming pools? You were from the West. Like me, you had grown up in an arid place, although my place had been a eucalyptus city of tanned bodies, king hits, and Harbour views. I had never had a swimming pool as a child, but you had, at the center of the desert garden your mother had grown in your childhood yard. It had not occurred to me that the pool would be something more often observed through the glass back doors than swum in. Your parents seemed surprised that I wanted to. It had been so hot the first time I flew to Phoenix to meet your family that the sun had warmed the water to the same temperature as a human body. It felt, you remarked, like swimming in bathwater. You got out, while I stayed in, safely contained between the blue-tiled walls.

I was telling you all this, recalling to you that swimming pool in your mother's garden which I never once swam in after that baking summer, when right then you swerved a bend in the road, and ahead of us was Lake Mead, and I felt tears in my eyes. The impossible blue wonder of all that water in the middle of all that desert.

An inspection point. A ranger pulled us over. He leaned towards the driver's side window.

Jesus fuck, you said.

You fumbled at the buttons of the rental car, looking for the one to press to get the windows down. Eventually you just opened the driver's side door. The ranger was annoyed.

Every car has a window lock, bud, the officer said, like you were an idiot.

It's a rental.

What kind of car do you drive at home? Your car's gotta have a window lock.

I don't. I live in New York.

He paused a moment, then began to laugh. Okay, bud. Any fire-arms or drones?

We both shook our heads.

Have a nice day, he said, then leaned in and pointed. It's *that* but-ton. And then he closed your door.

You raced me down the stairs from the car park to the concourse, for no real reason, you said, than that it felt like winning.

I'm not competing with you, I pointed out, and you shrugged.

I turned to look out at where we were. On one side the thin trickle of blue between the steep rock face rolled on south to California. To the other, northward, lay the great stretch of Lake Mead. Red-brown volcanic rock rose up on either side of the water like a cradle, but be-tween lake and red rock there was a distinct bleach-white band; the mark of the old waterline. There was not enough water running in the River anymore.

I followed you to the left, into a low white building which looked as though it were originally meant to be temporary. An elderly woman manned a ticket counter inside, but it wasn't for the dam. What I saw through the door behind her was a kind of makeshift cinema, which housed not a screen but a diorama. The woman smiled, held out her arm, and nodded to let us know we were in for a treat. We went in. We didn't even need a ticket. We sat down, the only attendees of the diorama room, to watch the show.

Rising in the snow-capped Rocky Mountains, the Colorado River runs 1400 miles through the desert towards the gulf of California, said a great, American, male voice. The voice of advertisements for Camel cigarettes, Velveeta, Campbell's Soup. The light over the diorama brightened, a counterfeit dawn casting its sun over the length and breadth of the river system.

The voice intoned: *The Colorado, for centuries, was one of the world's wildest rivers. Melting snow in the mountains each spring swelled the River's flow, transforming it into a raging torrent. Time and again the low, flat valleys in Arizona and Southern California were flooded. Early settlers tried to protect their lands from floods by constructing levees, but levees were useless as safeguards. But flood was not the only problem posed by the unruly River. After the springtime floods, the River's flow generally dwindled, and at times its tributaries dried up completely. The only solution to the problem was to construct a dam to eliminate the cycles of flood and drought.* You shifted beside me, and I looked at you to see if your hips hurt, or you were bored. But you, like me, enjoyed the strangeness of it all. *The reservoir created by Hoover Dam is named Lake Mead. Measured by volume, it is the largest man-made reservoir in the United States, and can hold and store two years' normal flow of the Colorado River.* How current do you think those numbers are? you asked me. I shrugged. The diorama, and the audio recording, didn't look or sound like it could have been updated since the 1970s. *And so today, Hoover Dam stands like a mighty sentinel in Black Canyon, keeping guard over downstream regions. Lying calmly above the dam are the waters of Lake Mead, waters that once carried the threat of devastation, but which are now harnessed to serve mankind.*

We stayed until the show was over, when the artificial sunlight illuminated everything from the Rockies to Los Angeles, stretching out over the tamed waters. We made our way out through the door and walked out into the blinding light atop the dam. Ahead of us we could see a steady trickle of people making their way to what we could now see were the actual ticket counters.

We drifted towards them. Should we go on a tour? I asked. Isn't that what you're meant to do here?

It's weird they don't mention anything about the water level in that diorama, you said as we walked.

Well, if it was recorded in the 1970s, maybe they hadn't realized it was a problem yet, I said.

We paid for our tickets and assembled at the waiting point. When the guide arrived, he ushered a group of thirty of us to an elevator door and escorted us inside. Khaki shorts and baseball caps and sandals; we all crushed in. The elevator ascended down through the dam. My ears popped. The guide gesticulated and brushed the arm of a man beside him.

Sorry for assaulting you, said the guide. Then he laughed at his own joke.

I could feel you tense up beside me, feel you reach for your phone to start scrolling, even though there was no reception in the elevator. Just to have somewhere else to look.

Down in the heart of the dam, on the terrazzo marble floor, the tour guide collected us together. The Hoover Dam, he said, is held together by the sheer weight of the concrete. Las Vegas, the guide said, uses more power than any other city per capita, and that's where most of the electricity goes. Most of the water, however, flows on to Southern California. But don't worry, the tour guide said, none of your tax dollars are going to the dam, which is remarkable for a federal building. Any questions?

A woman piped up and asked if the dam ran on Arizona or Nevada time.

The dam, the guide said, runs all the time.

A Canadian man at the back asked, What does reclamation mean? If the dam was built by the Bureau of Reclamation?

To reclaim the land from flood and drought, said the tour guide, in a tone that suggested he might like to hold his hand over his heart. To make it useful, he clarified. I wrote the word "useful" into the notebook I had in my hand and put a circle around it.

He performed a dramatic clap of the hands, rubbing them together. Has anyone told you what our photo policy has been since 9/11? he asked.

People shook their heads.

That's good, he continued, because we don't have one! Take all the photos you want, folks, and he opened his arms to let us loose.

We wandered, looking at the machinery neither of us really understood. It's certainly very big, you observed.

Very dammy, I agreed.

At the end of the tour, back at the top, I leaned over the edge and looked down through my grubby sunglasses to the place where the waters of the Colorado spat out. I felt my heart flutter, just watching it. It was strange to imagine the River running unimpeded down below. Associations piled up in my mind, stories I'd read about this place. The story, for instance, about the grieving chief who lost his wife. A god, taking pity on him, took a ball of fire and used it to make a path to the land of the dead. The chief followed the path and recovered his wife. Kissed her, smelled her smell again. Promised that just one visit was enough. But the god didn't trust him, and rolled a roaring river down the path, a River which would overwhelm anyone else ever trying to reach the land of the dead before their time had come.

Look at the way it gushes, I said. I turned to find you.

You were standing with your phone held out, aiming its camera across the vista of the dam. You said you were sending it to your father, to say hello. Across the other side of the ravine was where Arizona began. We were so close, but it would take nearly a week for us to arrive back there.

Nearby, a long concrete bas-relief was carved into a hunk of concrete. It showed muscular, shirtless men demonstrating the many benefits of the dam: flood control, water storage, irrigation, navigation, power. The illustrative image of "power" was of a man flexing over the round curves of the cogs that controlled the dam.

They look like characters in an Ayn Rand novel, I turned to say to you, but you were looking at your phone and I don't think you heard me.

The sun was already beginning to trace the parabola of its western ebb, mid-afternoon. We drove back towards the city. The words "Pro-Gun Club" were inscribed in white paint into the rock of a hill off I-11, not far away from a PETA billboard displaying a glum-looking turkey under the words "I'm Me, Not Meat" and "Go Vegan." I was pointing it out to you when we were pulled over by the cops.

The state trooper must have been waiting there, a speed trap, knowing tourists driving back from Lake Mead were likely to accelerate a little. No cars or signs of life were anywhere around us, save the billboard. I heard you begin to panic. I heard it in your voice as you rolled the window down, the window lock right where the ranger had said it would be. You handed the state trooper your license.

You still live in Camelback Vista? the policeman asked.

You answered, Yes.

We waited in silence while the policeman called it in.

When he came back to the car he said, I knocked the fine down to $75 to thank you both for wearing your seat belts.

We drove away, and you asked me to turn the radio off. I'm too tense, you said.

Why did you tell him you still lived in Camelback Vista? I asked.

It's the address on the license.

I had never understood why you hadn't changed your license when you'd left Arizona. Sometimes I thought it might be a gesture of sentimentality, or a fealty to home. Other times I thought it might just be laziness. You had told me it was simpler that way, because you had never learned how to properly parallel park, and the fact that you'd managed it on the day you took your driver's test was a fluke. You didn't want to risk a stricter state trying to test you a second time.

I think you could have told him you lived in New York, I said. Plenty of people don't change their licenses when they move to a different state. He's just going to end up sending the fine to your dad's house.

That's okay, you said. And I wondered whether you'd ask your father to pay the fine for you.

At least it was only $75, I said. That's almost what we spent at the dam today.

We drove back to the city, and you sang a song to yourself, the words following the beat of Talking Heads' "Don't Worry About the Government." I lied to the police, you sang, I'm basically an anarchist.

We had dinner at an Italian restaurant somewhere in the Arts District. We couldn't afford it, or, I couldn't afford it, but we often did things, like this trip, that we couldn't afford. We sat at the bar, and I ordered from the bartender an amaro cocktail, which he served to me in a teacup, scattering dried rosebuds across its muddy surface with a flourish of his hand. There followed a squash pizza which we shared.

Towards the end of the pizza, you told me you wanted to buy some weed. While I paid the bill you looked for dispensaries on your phone. You found one nearby. It was walking distance, you said. We left the restaurant and, following the map, took a right. Now the sun was gone, the night air was icy. I buttoned my cardigan and crossed my arms.

I had only recently begun to notice how much more frequently you were buying and using weed. It surprised me, because when we met you did not like substances of any kind. You had never smoked a cigarette, and never been drunk. You might have had a few beers when we were out, but you never drank to extremes. Extremes simply didn't interest you. It was one of those aspects of your personality that I had come to love the most. You leveled me out. Because you had not, as a teenager, associated mind-altering substances with bohemianism or art, as I had, I who had occasionally sat alone in my teenage bedroom and drunk a bottle of cherry brandy, or port, or whatever my mother had in the cupboard and wouldn't miss, just to see what kind of poetry I might write. Instead, you had associated drinking with the fraternities and football players who dominated the social life of your college, and you associated drugs—weed, mushrooms, acid—with the most hopeless and wasted members of the art department where you were trying to be a serious undergraduate scholar. You were instead a student who listened to Gang of Four, read William Gaddis and Dave Hickey, and took off on long cycling trips on weekends. But at some point, maybe even because of me, you let go. Maybe you took a puff of a joint at a party—I can't remember, now, how it started. You began buying weed on your own terms. You found a courier in Brooklyn, who would arrive at our apartment with a box full of vials and pods and tinctures and cookies, ahead of whose visits we would need to walk up to the Bank of America ATM on Manhattan Avenue to take cash out. When your mother died, ten months before this trip, the courier began to come weekly.

I didn't mind back then, not at first. Weed helped you sleep at night. And you had so much trouble sleeping in those early months. The death of your mother was the worst thing that had ever happened to you, and us. I wanted you to be able to lie down and watch dumb television and hold my hand. I wanted you to be able to exit, if only for a few hours, the grief that crushed you every moment of your waking life, for all that time in the winter and the spring. I tried to be a comfort, as much as I knew how. But I knew there was only so much I could do. Or perhaps it's more accurate to say that I knew that whatever I did, and what comfort I provided, would never be enough. It was only after this November trip to the West that the weed began to get really bad, so bad that you would use it every night, so much of it that you wouldn't be able to remember what we'd done or what I'd said the following morning, and when I saw you take out the vape pen and start to inhale I would be overcome with a feeling of incredible loneliness. The feeling that in that intake of breath you were leaving me behind, closing the bedroom door of your attention, and retreating to a place where I couldn't follow you.

That night in Las Vegas it was still, theoretically, something fun we could do with our evening. Marijuana had just been legalized in Nevada. The billboards, the dispensaries, the sheer commerce of it all felt exciting in an adolescent way. It felt like an adventure. The warehouse you walked us towards behind the restaurant had the same ambience as walking into the car park of a Home Depot. Inside, however, it was a neon-green cavern, a combination of juice bar and high-end wine store. We were led by the employee who greeted us at the door to a glass counter, inside which the samples were lovingly arranged. There, a specialist consulted with the two of us about what we wanted. Do you want more of a sativa feel, or do you prefer an indica vibe?

Something to help with sleep, you told him. You looked at me, carefully assessing my face, and then you turned back to the specialist and added, Something to help with depression and mood, as well.

This variant was the one you were requesting for me. I understood it from the way you were looking at me, as though I were a creature that needed delicate handling. I thought perhaps that your intention was to include me in the adventure. Weed was medicine, to your mind, and I think you might have viewed it as something that could be the equivalent of going to therapy. But what did it mean, I wondered, that you thought of me as a woman depressed, my mood perilously low? You always liked me best when I was happy. Were you buying me something to help bring me up, so that I wouldn't bring you down? The specialist made some suggestions, and when you asked if I thought they sounded good I said, Sure, because I didn't want to show myself up as somebody who didn't understand the words "indica" and "sativa," and I didn't want to ask you what you meant. You took his suggestions, purchasing a vape pen, some cartridges, and several tiny pre-rolled joints. Your purchases were handed over in an opaque sealed bag.

We were back outside in the parking lot heading towards the car when I noticed you were trying to open the plastic seal.

Can't you wait until we get back to the car? I asked.

So you waited. You opened the seal in the dark of the parked car, and I watched the red glow of the vape pen bob in the darkness as you sat in the driver's seat, breathing in.

* * *

Y ou drove us to ReBAR on Main Street, where Malik had told us to meet him after dinner. Malik had lived in the city a year, maybe two. The Foundation you both worked for had experienced, three years earlier, a funding crisis. As a result, it had moved its offices from their historic home in Chelsea to Las Vegas, where the Foundation now touted itself as having found its spiritual home. The Foundation had been established in the 1970s as a kind of patronage system for land artists and conceptual artists and had become the main vehicle by which those artworks—some built on a fantastical scale in remote corners of nearby deserts—could be preserved. It made sense that the Foundation arrive here, where all those Heizers and Holts and Smithsons were being slowly eroded by desert winds, by flash floods, and that obliterating high white light. Malik was the operations manager and functional assistant to the director of the Foundation, your boss. Many of the employees of the Foundation got away with living in Los Angeles and New York, like us. But Malik had to move to Nevada when the deal was cut, and had to be on-site to assist in the easeful transfer between funding regimes, because your boss did not want to leave Los Angeles and move permanently to the desert either. I was pleased when you had told me you weren't one of the employees required to relocate. Las Vegas didn't seem like the kind of place a person should live in. It seemed a place people were forever passing through. Malik seemed to like Las Vegas, once he settled in. He lived in a house now, rather than an apartment. He spent his time playing poker and reading Emerson.

We were early. It was a bar famous, Malik had said, for everything on the premises being for sale. I ordered whiskey and observed price tags. Malik was right. A velvet painting of John Wayne was priced at $32. A turquoise condom dispenser with an AIDS-Aware sticker on its side was going for $195. You and I played Scrabble. I won the first round, so in the second round I made sure I didn't make an effort. I didn't want to compete with you.

There's Malik, you said, looking towards the door, and in the dark I could see a tall man approaching us with a short woman following behind him. You stood up and walked towards Malik, who folded you into a back-slapping embrace. He was beaming, pleased to see you.

I'm sorry we're late, Malik said, and introduced the woman by her first name, Camila.

She was a pretty, black-haired woman with a nose ring. She dropped her bag on the velveteen sofa and followed Malik to the bar. Oh no, I said quietly. Do you know who that is?

Camila Vargas was an academic, and, as it turned out, a highly sought-after recruit at the University of Nevada. Her books sat on my bedside table back in New York. You had seen me read and reread her books, seen me annotate, and pick apart her research. She wrote like nobody else and ranged across subjects, disciplines. Her work touched on cowboys, ghosts, water law, ecology, the cultural history of deserts, cults and killers and highway systems, American mythology and dreams. Most academics, I had told you a thousand times, wrote as though they hoped nobody would ever read their books. She didn't. Impossible to classify, it had been her work that had prompted me to apply for grad school in the first place. I wanted to do what she did, reach people like she'd reached me, set my mind on fire.

I had thought she had been working in Leipzig. That's what it said on the jacket copy.

Oh no, I said as we watched them order their drinks, I don't think I can cope with this. I don't think I can talk to her. I'll be too intimidated.

You can, you said, and you held my hand.

I tried to relax. Camila and Malik returned from the bar. It was confronting, and strange, to realize I was five inches taller than her. I could see her scalp through her black hair as I shook her hand and introduced myself.

Eloise, she repeated, like the children's book? The little girl who lives at the Plaza Hotel?

I nodded.

You asked about how their night had been. They had both been at an event on campus, a podcast series that had organized a special Las Vegas–themed live recording in one of the lecture theaters. The podcast series was sponsored by a local start-up, as everything seemed to be. We talked about the city and the revitalization of Downtown, which was financed, Camila told us, by the injection of hundreds of millions of dollars from the mogul of an online shoe empire, the name of which sponsored freeways throughout the city. His favorite animal was the llama, Camila told us, and that was the reason there were so many llamas in Las Vegas. There was even a kind of open-air co-working space where llamas roamed free, and sometimes spat at you. I saw something about llamas on a motel sign last night, I told her, although I remembered, as I began speaking, not to mention the dog, and realized that without the dog the story was just one in which I saw a sign depicting a llama above an empty car park, which was no kind of story at all. I tried to recover.

I asked Camila about where she was from, as if I didn't know. She told us she was from Nevada, although her hometown was Carson City. For years she had lived away from the state, studying at Princeton and UCLA, then in Leipzig where she and her husband had her son. But she had been back in Nevada nearly a year and felt now that she could never leave again. There's something about the landscape, she said. She found she could see everything with fresh eyes. She had taken to going on long drives, often with her young son in the back seat, partly to encourage her son to nap, and partly to reexperience the country. It was so easy to leave the city behind and find yourself in the middle of nowhere. That morning, she said, she had driven north out of the city on I-15 towards the Arizona border and found herself in flat creosote country in something like a trance. Then she noticed something dark and curved on the road ahead and braked, coming to a hard stop as a desert tortoise ambled across the tarmac. And as she idled, waiting for the creature to pass, she realized that this foundational experience of her adolescence—waiting patiently at the wheel for tortoises to pass—had been absent from her adult life in a way that now struck her as tragic, as incomprehensible. Her entire sense of belonging was bound up in this place of basin and range and jagged plant life and hard-shelled reptiles, and she felt, that morning, that she was finally home. The tortoise took its time getting from one side of the road to the other, moving at the slow speed of everything alive in the desert.

You told Camila, then, about the tortoises you'd had as a child. You had asked for them as a gift when you were eight, two desert tortoises, which were not an uncommon pet in Arizona. Your parents had an enclosure built by the side of the house, separated from the paved patio and the bath-warm swimming pool by a seven-foot-tall fence, to keep the predators out. It was not big inside, but big enough for two small tortoises, with a tree for shelter, and some large rocks and shrubs. But every time you had taken me home to Phoenix, and we had looked inside the enclosure, there had been no sign of either tortoise. Your mother implied, half smiling to herself, that a coyote or a snake had eaten one of them. The other tortoise was simply missing. Your parents still left him food. Sometimes he ate it. Or something ate it. I never saw the tortoise, not in all those years, and I was convinced he had died long ago. You hadn't seen him since the first summer you came home from college. You hadn't even given them names. You might have been the only child I'd ever heard of who didn't name their pets.

What did you call them? I once asked.

Tortoise, you replied, as though it were obvious.

Both of them?

Yeah, they were both Tortoise.

For all that I doubted their existence, you were quietly certain the remaining tortoise was still there, somewhere. He's just hiding, you said. And later on it turned out you were right. The tortoise would come back two years after we buried your mother. You fed him sheets of iceberg lettuce, and sent me a video of his slow, contented bites.

While you told Camila about the tortoises, I ordered us more drinks and asked Camila whether she wanted anything. An IPA, she said, and I bought one for myself as well, although I hated drinking beer. I was so eager to impress her that I would drink whatever she drank and stay for as long as she wanted to stay at the bar. When I returned and handed her the beer, she was explaining that she was very tired, but glad to be out. She did not often have the opportunity now she was divorced and it was just her and her son.

Don't ever have a kid and then get divorced, she said, and it was me she was making eye contact with. Or do, she said, rethinking her words. But know it's terrifying. Nothing prepares you for how terrifying it is to be on your own after so long, and you're barely managing, but there's a small creature you love who wants oatmeal and some juice.

I realized then that she was a little tipsy, had been drinking before they arrived. She had rediscovered freedom only a few days earlier, Camila continued, when she had driven to Corvallis to give a talk to students at OSU. It was the first time she'd been away from her son, and that first night she had felt so petrified and elated that she couldn't sleep. She had a bath and ordered room service. She watched porn and got high. She had only arrived back in town on Tuesday, after a two-day drive. And the strangest thing happened, she said, in the middle of the Sierra Nevada. The peaks were snow-capped but the ground was still warm. It was, maybe, the nicest time of the year to be on those roads. Then flakes began to fall. They hit the windshield, so she turned the wipers on. But the flakes didn't turn wet and thickly fluid on the glass like snow does. These flakes smeared the screen, turned it ever-so-slightly gray. It didn't take long to figure out that it was cinders falling onto the windshield, not snow. The smoke from the Camp Fire burning a hundred miles to the west. It had been burning nearly a week by then. The wind had picked up the ash and dispersed it over the mountains. I didn't say anything, but what she said brought to mind a smothered fear of my childhood. The looming danger of a nearby fire

I couldn't see but could smell. The fire that spreads its evidence. The guilt of finding it beautiful, even as the fire is destroying everything it touches. It is hard not to respect something that can cause so much damage, and to recognize how small and ineffectual you are out there on its periphery, subject to its haze or smoke or bits of ash on the window screen.

Camila and Malik were sitting close together, side by side on the velveteen sofa. Their legs almost touching. She pulled out a blue pack of American Spirits and texted the babysitter. She wanted to stay and get another drink. She wanted a cigarette. There was a courtyard out the back where we could smoke. We followed her. Camila explained how much she loved this particular bar, its embrace of kitsch and capital, the forthrightness of the grift. She headed straight for an egg chair, one of those white swiveling 1960s orbs with a cushiony red interior. She swung from side to side, smoking, and I watched Malik watching her. It was as though he were under a spell. He couldn't stop looking at her.

What got you interested in the West? Camila asked me from the swiveling egg.

You must have had your arm around me, perhaps you were holding my hand. I told her the truth: that it was because of you.

I had never thought about the West before we met. When you told me where you grew up at the bar where we had our first date nearly six years ago, I didn't really know where it was. I was so new to America, back then. I was twenty-three, lived in a room without windows, had a scholarship I didn't think I'd really deserved, had only flown out of Sydney three months earlier. I wasn't completely clear on the layout of everything in the middle.

It's the desert, you had explained to me. It was always hot, and you had spent your childhood inside, you joked, in the air-conditioning. It was hot where I was from too, but we didn't do air-conditioning, I told you, not in our homes at least. When you asked me why, I said I wasn't sure. Maybe we thought discomfort made us stronger.

You took me back to Arizona in the summer, and then for Christmas, the first year we were together. The place struck me as terribly strange, with tinsel-wrapped saguaro in the front yards, and those wide streets with no sidewalks, American flags the size of swimming pools waving from sky-high poles. I loved it there. I knew there was more than Phoenix, more than Las Vegas, and this trip, which we had decided to take ten months after the death of your mother, was the opportunity to see it. An adventure, I had told you, and it would benefit my research. More to the point, the trip was a thing to look forward to, and planning it had sustained me through those bad months back in New York, when you were sometimes so overcome by grief that you hit the walls, hit yourself, began to cry and could not stop.

I wouldn't mind moving out West, I told Camila. After I've finished my dissertation. But Lewis isn't sure about leaving New York. Not yet, at least.

She swiveled towards you in the egg chair and pointed her American Spirit in your direction. I think you should move to the desert for this person, she told you. Move out here, get married, settle down, you'll never find another one like her.

I know, you said. Gripped me tighter.

They're already married, Malik said. Camila looked surprised. People still were, then. We were twenty-seven when we married, a normal age by most standards. But in the circles we moved in, the fact that we had married then seemed eccentric and romantic, as though I had been a child bride.

Eloise and Lewis are married all right, Malik explained to Camila. They got married here. I was there. I was witness.

You got married in Vegas? she asked.

You nodded.

You were drunk?

Stone-cold sober, in fact. Bright and early in the morning at a little wedding chapel on Las Vegas Boulevard, which offered an Elvis impersonator for a fee. We didn't know about the impersonator, and we didn't pay for one. It was bad enough when they gave you a rose boutonniere. I haven't worn one of these since prom, you had said. It was not long after the Foundation relocated from New York to Nevada, and it was the first time I'd accompanied you to Las Vegas. We had been together more than three years, but even in the very first weeks of dating, you had mentioned marriage.

We can just go down to City Hall, you had said, back in that small Upper West Side studio you lived in when we met.

Are you serious? I asked.

Sure, you said, although I was never certain that you really meant it. Sometimes that was the way with you—everything you said was earnest, and everything you said was a joke.

I understood, though, that it was a way of saying that you were certain about me. You suggested getting married many months before you told me that you loved me. And then, once you said it—your head on my left breast, the two of us lying on your sofa in the path of the air conditioner in that Upper West Side studio—you never stopped saying it. You told me you loved me multiple times a day, when I was brushing my teeth, when I asked if you wanted eggs, when I was putting my tights on and heading out the door to school. "Love" you would text me when I was in classes. Just the one word. You loved me. We were serious. And you took marriage more seriously than I did, although I only realized it the day we actually went ahead and did it. I had grown up in a different sort of family to yours—a childhood of rattling back and forth between different homes. I had never really thought that I *would* get married. I didn't think it meant very much. Was it not just making an existing relationship slightly more official? And yet marriage kept coming up, insinuating itself into our conversations. The enchantments of security, commitment, binding ties. It was winter when we pulled the trigger. It was the same month your mother was diagnosed with cancer. We were worried. Nobody could give us a clear timeline. When to expect what. How much time: Was it years, months, God forbid weeks? We should just do it, I told you, and then celebrate later, plan a party, gather everybody in the one place. Yes, we would get married.

You told your parents. But I didn't want to tell anybody. Not until afterwards. I wanted it to be just the two of us. Our marriage would be ours alone. And it was so easy, to get married that way in Las Vegas. We were staying at the El Cortez, an eighty-year-old hotel once monopolized by organized crime syndicates and their mistresses. It was where the director liked to put up all Foundation employees and affiliates, lending to proceedings a dose of local color. The morning before we got married, I walked from Fremont Street down to one of the vintage stores on Main Street, not far from where we were drinking that evening with Malik and Camila, and bought a dress, a blue velvet thing from the 1960s, and heels. You had your nice leather boots with you, your favorite jeans, a button-up shirt you could stand. Malik went with us. While we waited outside the chapel I looked at my phone and saw a text from your mother. She had sent me an emoji of clanging bells, and several pink hearts. It was tantamount to a blessing, I supposed. When we were called in, Malik took up a spot on the side of the room and pulled out his phone to film us. Outside the window of the chapel the sky was overcast and gray. It was eleven o'clock in the morning at the end of January, and we were getting married. The celebrant was spilling out of his brown suit, with slightly tinted glasses perched at the end of his nose.

Do you folks have any prepared vows? he asked, and I remembered then that that was something you could do. Write your own vows. I hadn't thought about it. It's incredible how little thought I'd put into what our wedding might be like. Throughout the ceremony, I surprised myself at the things I had not anticipated. That we would look at each other. That we really did say, "I do." We were standing so very close. You were holding my hands and looking down at me. When the celebrant asked whether you would have and hold me, whether you would take me, you said, I do, and your voice cracked. Your eyes welled up with tears. I was humbled. I did not know until then how much our marriage meant to you. You meant it when you said those things. I loved you so much in that moment when you cried, and I was ashamed at how translucent I felt, as though I were a ghost watching myself walk through the motions of marriage. You kissed me. Now I was your wife.

We told people afterwards, of course, but we never had a party. We never celebrated. We went back to the El Cortez. We walked from the bright gray heat of the street and through the jaundiced glass doors that expelled the sunlight. Through the lobby with its stale cigarette smell, by the people at the slot machines with their ashtrays and quarters, the cling and ping of the machines marking cacophonous time, towards the elevators.

Should we, you said?

We had never gambled before, neither one of us.

You fished out a dollar and fed it into the machine closest to the elevator. I put my arm around your back, kissed your cheek. You put your arm around my waist. And then the pixelated numbers swung through the lights and the colors, and we landed something. The machine spat out a receipt for our winnings. You laughed. We had won a dollar and twenty-nine cents.

We never did cash it.

The winnings receipt was stuck with a magnet to the fridge in our kitchen. It seemed, we thought, like a good omen. We took a bet and we won.

In the afternoon you had a meeting, and you changed out of your nice shirt and boots and into your more regular clothes. I stayed in our hotel room at the El Cortez, lying on the couch in the dress I had been married in, reading *Lonesome Dove*. I was reading a scene where the party of cowboys cross a river the morning after a storm. A scream cuts the air, and the men turn to see an Irishman, in the middle of the river, barely holding on to his horse as stirred-up water moccasins swarm over his body. The screaming stops only when the Irishman slips under the water. The men pull his body from the water. They cut his shirt off to reveal eight sets of fang marks on his chest. I remember I put a hand to my throat, as though I could feel the puncture wounds in my own skin. From the window I could see west towards the red undulating rocks of the Spring Mountains. The sky was hazy, but our room was so high up that I could see right out over the sprawl and into the desert. I waited for you there in the air-conditioned hum of the room, until you came back from your meeting, and we consummated our marriage then on the scratchy sheets of that high hotel room in the early evening light.

I got up early. I boiled water for instant coffee, and through the bars on the casita's window I could see out into the clear blue sky, the palm trees still and stately, punctuating the view. I was thirsty. I had a bottle of water that I'd bought at the dam, but it was empty now, and I wasn't sure whether the tap water was safe to drink in Nevada. Hadn't they tested nuclear bombs near here for decades? I looked it up. The testing had polluted the groundwater for sure, but most of the drinking water came from Lake Mead, and was deemed safe according to federal standards. And yet, I found a notice from the Las Vegas Valley Water District recommending that nobody with a weakened immune system, nor anybody pregnant, drink the Las Vegas tap water. I left the water boiling.

I walked past you, lying in bed and scrolling on your phone, and into the bathroom, closing the door. I pulled my underwear down to my ankles, sat on the toilet seat and spread my thighs. I had felt pangs when I'd woken up. A kind of tentative cramping. I wiped, then checked. Nothing. I opened my thighs an inch or two more and moved my hand between my legs, inserted a finger. It came out clean. Some milky fluid clung to the chipped red polish on the nail of my index finger. It was the eleventh day of waiting.

It wasn't, of course, like it hadn't been this late before. Once, in our first months together, during a stressful month of study, it had been nine days late. You had waited for me outside the bathroom door while I peed on a test strip. While it processed, I sat on the floor beside you, the test on the floorboards in between us. It had been a relief when there was only one line. So, one might think, if I'd bought a pregnancy test after nine days once before, then there was no reason that an older, putatively more responsible, indeed a married version of myself wouldn't, or couldn't, have gone to buy a pregnancy test by eleven days. Eleven days was a lot of days late.

Hey, you called out from the bedroom, come out of there. I want to show you this nice video of a happy goat.

Sometimes you half joked, and half suggested, that I leave the door open when I went to the bathroom. The thing I felt pulsing beneath these jokes was this: you could not abide my closing a door on you. You wanted access to me at all times, as a child wants never to be apart from his mother. I had come to feel that it was my job to resist. I felt, without being able to explain it, that if I did not resist, some kind of collapse would take place, a collapse that was also a dissolution of fixed borders. I wanted to close the door on you. How could I have possibly explained the situation to you if the door had been open and you had been able to see?

I'm coming, I called out. I flushed. I washed my hands.

The video you showed me was of a very happy goat, leaping down a green field and head-first over a bank and into a stream.

When we got to the parking lot of the Foundation offices we were greeted by the director's personal assistant. I thought I'd come pick you up, she called out. My heart swelled. She was so bright and full of cheer and promise, tied to working for a man who I was certain, without ever needing to ask, made her professional life a minefield of transgressed boundaries and measly pay.

You had gone quiet. You always got quiet before you had to see your boss. He made you anxious.

Inside, the assistant led us along a white corridor lined with framed photographs of conceptual art pieces, down to the director's office. Your boss emerged from behind his door. He had ordered us vegan food. We already knew what we were having, because in the car on the way over you had asked me to text back from your phone, consulting on the menu. He had ordered us California Tofurkey sandwiches and chocolate chia pudding for dessert. The man was from Los Angeles, you explained in response to my eye rolling. Your boss liked to make long phone calls when he drove back and forth to Las Vegas across the desert. It was when he felt most lonely. Sometimes he called you out of the blue and you would panic seeing his name appear on the lock screen of your phone, swearing or crying out for those few seconds in between realizing what was about to happen and picking up. All those hours of small talk ahead, in which you'd need to find enough conversational material to occupy his interest until he glimpsed sky-scrapers on a horizon and felt safe again. Your boss offered to make us coffee and we followed him to the small kitchen, where a coffee maker sat lonely on an otherwise empty countertop. He made me an Americano. He focused his attention on you and asked whether you'd orga-nized everything with Kenneth. It had been over a year since you'd last checked on him in person, and since then there had been no official word on the project. The Foundation had bankrolled this piece, and while the director understood that things took the time that they took, the Foundation was within its rights to know what was going on. You said everything was fine. After Thanksgiving, you told him. You didn't think you could get access to the site, but you were certainly going to see Kenneth.

This was your big job of the trip. Seeing Kenneth, the partner of the recently deceased artist Lawrence Greco. Kenneth who was in the process of completing Greco's last major work according to his direct specifications, somewhere out there in the middle of the Arizona des-ert. Among the stable of projects for which you were responsible, I had come to understand that this one was the most consequential. That it mattered not only financially to the Foundation, but in an art historical sense. I hadn't met Greco before he'd died, but you had traveled out north and west of Phoenix to inspect the site and introduce yourself to the artist, and I had rarely heard you so excited as when you had called me on the phone the day you met him. I couldn't understand why Greco chose to work in the middle of nowhere, in a place so isolated. But you had explained to me that it suited him, because he wanted to commune with an audience best placed in an airplane overhead, or God. It was your job to make sure he finished the project he had already begun, a project the Foundation had been overseeing since the 1990s.

What had Greco been building out there for all these decades? A hole. He had been creating an enormous absence, a mathematically perfect spherical hollow in the earth, intersected with tunnels, mazes, and mirrors. There, one would have a unique experience of celestial time. Engineers and geologists had been consulted, but it was important to Greco that he build it himself, and without the hovering oversight of the Foundation. You had seen the site only that once, when it looked, to you, maybe halfway complete. with the beginnings of those mazes and tunnels gradually being constructed in the southern corner of the hollow. But this was before he got sick, and at that stage Kenneth took over communication entirely. Now the artist was gone, and Kenneth was in charge of completing the project, according to Greco's will. The ensuing alarm of the board had calmed down when it was made clear that Kenneth was more competent and communicative than Greco had ever been. But your boss was getting antsy. As the two of you spoke, I could sense your discomfort: in the way you held your shoulders, the hooting laugh you used to punctuate the beginning and ending of every sentence, a family tic which implied that no statement you made was one you were prepared to emotionally or intellectually commit to if questioned. I tried to touch you reassuringly between your shoulder blades, but not too much, unless I made you even more nervous. Satisfied that you understood what was needed of you, your boss turned his attentions on me.

And what are you doing in Las Vegas, Eloise? Just tagging along again?

I'm researching, I said.

Oh, researching, said your boss. I see. For a book?

I start working on my dissertation next year, I said.

Wonderful, he exclaimed. Clapped his hands. Reached again for his coffee.

I didn't like him, and never had. I had not told you the first time we were out in Las Vegas, when we were being put up at the El Cortez on the Foundation's dime, that your boss had put his hand on the small of my back at one in the morning, at the end of an after-party in a Downtown bar. Nor that he had suggested, with his lips brushing against my earlobe, that next time he was on the East Coast we should get a drink, just me and him. I did not think you would like it. Or maybe it was more that I feared how you might not react. That I wanted you to defend my honor. And how could you, against him, when it was because of his continued support of your employment that we could afford, just barely, to live the life we were living in the most expensive city in the country?

Well, you'll have to take in the town now, before you're handcuffed to your books, won't you? What's on the cards?

We said we were leaving tomorrow, wanted to drive out to see Seven Magic Mountains after we left his office, and would probably have a quiet night.

Nonsense, he said. Have you ever seen Penn and Teller? I bet there are still seats.

I don't know who that is, I said.

They're the longest-running headline act in Las Vegas, your boss exclaimed. You don't know who Penn and Teller are? I'm surprised. They're wonderful. Even if you're not into magic. There was this one trick they did, he said, where the men simultaneously fired guns at each other and caught the other's bullet in his mouth. Your boss had become more animated than I had ever seen him be about the art he funded. He told us that he had been, by now, to see the show more times than he could count. The show captured something for him that was unique to Las Vegas, a place that was unlike anywhere else in the world. You learn that by living here, he said.

It was a city that was built out of desire. Or dreams. Maybe both. Here in the neon garden of the desert, thousands drift. Plenty are indulging in risk, betting their livelihoods, but plenty are here for the sheer spectacle, for abundance. For *magic*.

Back in the safety of the Foundation's car park you said, We should get some groceries. Find a Trader Joe's.

I directed us. There was a Trader Joe's closer to where we were, but you had already taken off driving. I lost the turn for the nearer store, and so I directed us clear across the city, east of the airport, to a Trader Joe's in a suburban strip mall next to a Dollar Tree. We parked facing a billboard that implored us to "Donate Your Boat!"

To what? I asked.

To the boat-needy, you replied.

At the grocery store we bought junk food and snacks, the kinds of food I wouldn't eat at home. The kinds of food I would, if I ate them at home, respond to by pacing up and down the apartment, by doing star jumps and jumping jacks in the kitchen where the floor was tiled and our neighbors below wouldn't complain, or by lying down and reading but shaking my entire body back and forth, which you called "jiggling." We drove back west through the suburbs of Las Vegas by cement-poured yards, persimmon trees, canals running below the road with the tiniest trickle of water coursing through them.

And then we got onto the freeway, driving past the gates to the Desert Pines Golf Club, through which I could see vivid stretches of grass and an artificial lake. In San Francisco, the radio said, the comforting smell of campfire had quickly been replaced by a sepia pall and thick smoke. Schools were closed. The cable cars shuttered. Sports called off. It was dangerous to be outdoors, and soon the city would sell out of N95 respirator masks. San Francisco and Sacramento now had the worst air quality in the world. While the Camp Fire raged in the north of the state, surfers were delivering emergency supplies to the victims of the Woolsey Fire in Malibu. And the smoke was being funneled eastward. Particles in the air rendered the sunset we were driving towards the kind of color that seemed to augur imminent catastrophe. Everything we passed was lit in that red-gold light. A freight train progressed along the side of the road, heading back towards Las Vegas. Clouds crushed the sky. Casinos glittered along the highway, with signs for smoke shops piercing through the middle distance. The landscape was so stark that the silhouettes of Joshua trees took on the shadowy shapes of crucifixion. The sun was setting, a little past four in the afternoon, as we made our way westward.

The Day-Glo-painted boulders rose in towering totem poles thirty feet into the air. In the sunset their glow was even more intense, although Camila had told us that the coloring changed depending on the time of day. She had gone out there to visit the installation several times, particularly when they were talking about the piece as being temporary, and not a permanent piece of art, as it now seemed to be. We parked, got out. The air was beginning to cool. You pulled your jacket tight around you.

A notice on the ground nearby warned that there were venomous snakes and the endangered desert tortoise in the area, and that we should be alert, but all we saw was a pocket-sized kangaroo mouse who got up on his hind legs and then ran away as we approached.

We started by taking photographs. You wanted me to film you dancing in front of the Day-Glo boulders. I took thirty or forty pictures, but most of the videos were taken on your phone. In one of the videos I do have, you have constructed two mini towers out of rocks nearby, arranged sweetly, overshadowed by the towers behind you. You are jumping up and down between the towers, your hands in the pockets of your jeans, the cast of your face emotionless, bored, as though it's nothing at all. The video has caught the audible gust of cold, dry wind, and further behind you long white trucks move down the highway. Mountains tower above. You run out of shot, towards me. I knew my place, knew not to change the angle of the camera on my phone. I had been conscripted into these performance documentations hundreds, thousands of times. You were forever filming yourself dancing in restaurant bathrooms or distorted into an Edvard Munch scream in an elevator's ceiling mirror. I thought nothing of these videos anymore, and knew they were a game, even if it was a game you had not necessarily invited me to play on equal terms. It only takes ten seconds, and then you run back into view. You continue jumping between the towers. A family takes photographs in the background. By the end of the video—it's only thirty seconds—a car on the highway has turned its headlights on.

We walked back to the rental car, and while you checked the video on your phone you switched the heating on. We got onto the highway and drove back towards the city along I-15. The clouds were a vivid pink. I knew those sunsets from childhood fire seasons. It seemed strange that the land would burn when the temperature was so cold. Fires burning in the tail end of fake spiderweb season, fires spreading into decorative gourd season, and now fires just a week before Thanksgiving. In the spring, six months after this trip, the land burned by the fire would bloom again. Daffodils and irises would flower in patches of land that had once been front yards. Grasses would grow through cracked cement and charred metal. In the canyons there would be blazes of yellow foothill poppy, which germinates in the presence of compounds found in burned wood. There would be found, as well, the bewildering shoots of melon and corn plants, the seeds washed down into the canyon from obliterated gardens. Black oak would put out new stems, and the tufted seedlings of MacNab cypress, the seeds cracked open by the heat of the fire, would rise up bright green out of the blackened ground.

2

Leaving Las Vegas—Mr. Big Fast Car—Sand Lodged in the Pores of Tarmac—Heatstroke—Vultures—Roy's Motel and Café—Highways as a Means of Escape—A God-Haunted Desert—Simon Stylites—Madre Tierra—Palm Springs—Roland Barthes Crying in the Boulangerie—Organic Only—The Salton Sea—Tiny Bones—A Border Patrol Station—Salvation Mountain—Jesus I'm a Sinner—A Spider the Size of an Oreo—Approaching the Pacific

The border between Nevada and California was announced by the Cinderella Castle silhouettes of Buffalo Bill's and Whiskey Pete's, two casinos twinned on either side of the interstate. A cloud of dust hovered over the horizon line. There were no flagpoles, nor trees, nor anything in sight that might have indicated a wind. How strange, I thought, to be in a place so lacking in markers of movement. It was hard for me to keep clear of the suspicion that the dust cloud indicated something more sinister. Just before turning off the freeway, we passed a field of solar panels, with all their mirror-faces turned up towards the sun, appearing as we sped by like an ocean of light in the middle of the desert. The very air seemed to ripple. We slowed down, took a left, and descended through a haze of cloud into the Mojave National Preserve.

Do we have enough gas? I asked you.

I just want to keep up the pace, you said. Never let the gas tank get below half full, your mother had once chastised you from the back seat as we sat idling in a queue for the Costco pumps. It was the last piece of advice I remember her giving you.

There were three possible routes marked on the map, and I was leading us down the wildest one. We could have driven down I-15 to Barstow, skirting the edge of Los Angeles and doubling back east. We could have detoured from the interstate earlier and passed through Yucca Valley, by the enormous stone geoglyph created by an Australian, which might, if he were lucky, outlast Stonehenge. But I did not want to see the geoglyphs, I wanted to be in the desert. Google Maps said it would only take four hours. How did I know if we had enough gas?

Joshua trees began to appear in ones and twos and then, within a few miles, there were dense thickets of the imploring plants every-where we set our eyes. Ahead of us lay a vast valley where the clouds cast shadows on the desert floor. The Kelso Dunes passed by on our right, a vision of the Sahara among the sagebrush, and the road stretched out ahead of us like a long dry tongue. You were maneuver-ing the sunshade in front of your face so that the white light wouldn't blind you. You didn't seem panicked about being momentarily unable to see. I was always impressed by how calm you were when you drove. An Audi approached from behind us, overtaking and speeding ahead along the flat road.

Oooh, I'm a big, important man with important places to go, you said as he accelerated. Yes I am, oh yes I am. You spoke in the same tone of voice you might have used to indulge a toddler.

The car disappeared into the dust cloud ahead, and you kept on at a steady pace, Slowdive playing through my phone on the car's speakers.

Do you need to pee? I asked you.

I think the real question is, do you need to pee?

I need to pee.

Should I stop?

I turned and looked for a thatch of bush behind which I could squat but saw nothing promising. Where would I go?

In the desert.

I can't pee in the desert. There's nothing to hide behind.

I won't look.

What if somebody comes by?

Like who?

I hesitated. Mr. Big Fast Car?

Then I will say, drive on, Mr. Big Fast Car, my lady is peeing.

You pulled over. I walked to the back end of the car, where the Hertz sticker glimmered off the sandy, gray curve of the boot. The quiet was punctuated by nothing but the wind twisting through the Joshua trees and the dull boom of an L.A.-bound plane flying overhead. I pulled my dress up to my hips, my underpants down to my knees, and squatted low. The road was hot against the hand I put down to steady myself. I felt the grit of sand beneath my fingertips, lodged into the pores of the tarmac. I let go. That was when the bikers drove past, the actual source of the sound of the booming plane I thought I'd heard. Eight of them, in their glorious black leathers, roaring by.

Nobody honked, you noted when I opened the passenger side door and settled back into the seat beside you.

You started the car and took off again, and then a moment later you took a look at the numbers behind the wheel. Hey, I don't mean to alarm you, you said, but can you find us a gas station?

Why would I be alarmed?

We need to find a gas station, that's all.

I don't have reception, do you?

No.

I don't think I can search for one. We passed one just before, but it was abandoned.

It's okay. There'll be a gas station.

Do we have water?

I have a kombucha in the back, you said.

I remembered, then, everything your father had ever told me about driving in the desert. One summer, I had gone home with you to Arizona, and I had wanted you to take me out to see the Monte-zuma Castle Monument. You asked your father if you could borrow the car.

Your father just stared you down, before saying, Don't be a tourist, Lewis. That's how people die.

Neither of us knew how to change a tire. We had only a bottle of Poland Spring and your kombucha. It was thirty degrees outside. Eighty-six in Fahrenheit. Was thirty degrees too hot? If we broke down in the heat, out of air-conditioning, with only a couple of bottles of water between us, would we be in danger? There would be no shade. The temperature in the car would skyrocket. We would start to sweat. Depending on where we broke down, we would likely still be out of range. Getting help would depend on a passing car or on walking down the road until we found a few bars of reception. We'd drink what we had, but when it was gone, we'd still sweat it all out. Soon our core temperatures would rise. Our heads would begin to throb as we picked our way along the road. Our hearts would try to pump blood to our brains, but soon the dizziness would set in. I might faint—it would be just like me—but you'd power through. Soon enough hallucinations would begin. As the temperature rose, your organs would fail. Purple splotches appearing on your reddened flesh. You would shake. And then, eventually, you would stop moving. People die every year, within half an hour or so, just like that. That same summer I'd first gone home with you to meet your parents, a man and his grandson had died at Gila Bend. The two went hiking with no water or food, and were found dead in the July heat, only a few miles from the trailhead. Don't be a tourist, your father had said, and I knew that we hadn't brought nearly enough water with us. But November wasn't July. I had absolutely no idea if we were being stupid. The more frightening thing to me was that plenty of people die in these deserts and the landscape swallows up their corpses, leaving little trace. It doesn't take long after death for insects to colonize a body. Ants crawl across forearms. Flies move into nostrils. The gases and fluids inside the body cause the limbs to balloon. Shirts pop their buttons, bellies expose themselves, and fluids leak from every orifice. Then the vultures arrive. The beak of a vulture is perfectly designed to tear apart dead flesh. The stomach opens, and out tumble your innards. So many vultures crowd in that what once was your body is covered in black, moving feathers. They hiss at one another. Dust flies up from the disturbed ground. Shoes and socks are strewn to the side—they are not wanted, not edible. After a couple of days of feeding, the vultures have not much left to eat but a few bits of flesh on bone. Maggots consume what's left. After a while what's left of the body is so light that the birds can pick up parts and move them around, to check for any remaining meat still hanging from rib cages, from thighs, from the skull. The bones are scattered as far as a vulture can carry them. In the end, all that might be left of your body in the place where you fell might be one or two bones, the bleached rubber sole of a boot, the zipper from your jeans, the buckle of your belt.

Look, you said, a proper town is up there.

At Roy's Motel and Café, the only open business in the town of Amboy, we saw all the motorcycles of the bikers who had passed us an hour before, parked neatly by the doors. The café was just about all that was left of the old Route 66 town. It must have been such a loss, I thought, when the highway system was built. Have you ever heard the reason highways are the width that they are? I asked you as you took the hose out of the petrol pump.

You thought about it as the gas glugged in. Is it because of the police in some way?

It's because they were built during the Cold War, and they figured they'd need to use them to evacuate cities and move tanks in, in the event of a nuclear incident. They also wanted the roads to be very straight every few miles or so, so that airplanes could use them as a runway when the attack came. The glugging came to a stop with a loud click, and you removed the pump. I got my purse out and walked into the store. The thing was, I knew the story about airplanes landing on the interstates was an urban myth, and I wasn't sure why I'd told you the story as though it were fact. I guess I liked what it suggested. The interstates as analog for social psychosis, for paranoia and fear. Highways as a means of escape. As I walked back to the car, I noticed that nothing was growing on the edge of the gas station. Even the creosote seemed thirsty. As we drove out of Amboy I saw a hand-drawn sign in the yard of the only house, reading "Trump and Pence 2020." The words were written atop a painstakingly drawn red and blue ball-pointed American flag, already eagerly anticipating the showdown to come in two years' time. We followed behind a parade of slowing trucks and the revived bikers.

Turn left onto Amboy Road, I told you. And then we're on this for forty-seven miles.

While we waited to turn, I stared at the dusty white rears of the trucks.

I wonder if there's a dead woman in one of those, I said.

Probably, you replied.

A s we passed through the town of Yucca Valley, the slanting sun illuminated the crumbly shapes of the surrounding granite mountains. Up there on the hill, above the town, was a glint of white, too indistinct to make out. When we stopped at a red light, I looked at the route on my phone, following the blue dot of our rental car making our way westward. "Desert Christ Park" was the name marked on the map where, roughly, I'd seen the glint of white. I tapped the name and scanned the photographs. There's a park up there on that hill filled with statues of Jesus, I told you.

Is it a church?

No, it seems like it's somebody's passion project.

I clicked through from the map to the associated website. I read that the park on the hill was filled with white plaster sculptures depicting scenes from the life of Jesus. What I had seen glinting in the last of the light had been a ten-foot-tall statue of Christ, arms outspread and robes flowing, which the sculptor had intended to place on the rim of the Grand Canyon. There best placed, I suppose, to conquer any stray notion that down in that enormous absence lay something like annihilation. But the sculptor was forbidden from erecting the statue at the Grand Canyon, and in the ensuing argument he came to the attention of a Yucca Valley parson, who helped the sculptor bring the statue out from Los Angeles on the back of a truck, erecting it instead on the hill we'd just driven by. If human beings could not be comforted by a beacon of order on the edge of a canyon, they could be comforted on the outskirts of Joshua Tree National Park.

I did not feel comforted seeing the statue on the hill. The statue troubled me. The desert already felt so God-haunted. Even the plant life looked supplicant, holy and thorned. The statue of Christ seemed more like a gesture of empty hope before what was, in all other respects, a place where so little endured. Then again, maybe that quality of desert landscapes was the very reason so many hermits had always found their homes there. A desert was a kind of objective correlative, an easy metaphor for a struggle of the soul.

As I thought about those hermits, I remembered an evening three months after your mother died, in the spring, when I had come home from the library and you had rushed through the railroad rooms of our apartment to greet me, wearing cotton boxers and a T-shirt, laptop in hand, wanting to show me the ending of a Buñuel film you had been streaming while you waited for me to come home. The film was a depiction of the life of Simeon Stylites, an ascetic saint who lived for thirty-seven years on a platform atop a pillar erected in the Syrian Desert. You wanted to show me the moment when Simon, having been tempted three times by the devil in the form of a beautiful woman, finally succumbed. The devil appeared before Simon, all permed blond hair and naked breasts. *Get behind me, Satan*, Simon yelled, but he didn't have much of a choice in the matter. Then an airplane flew over. His pillar stood empty. The camera panned over New York City, and the music started up. Bearded men in vests and girls with cardigans were dancing to rock-and-roll music in a basement room, and Simon was sitting miserable among them.

You told me you had already watched the whole film, so the ending was all I saw that evening. It wasn't until years later, after you were gone, that I watched the film myself. This was during a period of grief when the idea of abandoning society to live alone on a treeless plain seemed maybe like the thing that I needed. I didn't know what to do without you.

In the film, in between being tempted by Satan, Simon had a vision. It was a greater temptation than all of those the devil posed over the hour of his cinematic struggle. In reality, what Simon wanted more than anything else was to descend the pillar and once again feel Mother Earth under his feet. *Madre tierra.* Emphasis *madre.* As his mind wandered, he imagined frolicking across the desert floor with his mother, who had come to live nearby so that she could watch over him and keep him safe while he dedicated himself to God. In Simon's fantasy, he and his mother chased each other across the sand, then caught arms and danced around in a circle. The pillar stood abandoned in the background. Then he lay with his head in his mother's lap while she stroked his matted hair.

Do you ever think of me, my son? she asked him.

Hardly ever, he replied.

You had not told me about that scene, I realized when I saw the film alone, years later. I wondered when I saw it why you hadn't.

You know John Ford's house is near here? you said, as we drove past the sign to Palm Desert, the night beginning to close in.

He lived out here?

Yeah, he died here. He lived in a ranch house.

Was it in the middle of nowhere?

You hooted. No, it was next to a golf club. He wasn't moving to the desert to be a hermit or anything, he was just another old rich guy who wanted to retire where it's warm. People come to Palm Springs to be rich and quiet.

You've been to his house before?

I almost went once. In college. When I was driving back to L.A. from Coachella.

With another girlfriend, I thought to myself. With a woman who wasn't me.

I woke early in the morning, after an evening of interrupted sleep. In the middle of the night, I had woken up to sounds of groaning. The groaning became louder and more panicked, as though it were really a scream that the throat was stifling, and I had shaken your shoulder to startle you out of it. Your eyes opened and your breaths quickened to pants as though you'd just finished a long run, and then you turned on your side with your back to me, and soon commenced the rhythmic sounds of sleeping. But I had lain a long while, unable to fall asleep again, staring at the ceiling until finally I got another hour or so of rest.

In the courtyard of our Airbnb I sat outside under the bougain-villea vine eating yogurt and dried apricots. A copy of the *Desert Sun* had been delivered to the doorstep in the small hours. It said that the smoke around the immediate vicinity of the fire in Butte County was so hazardous that residents who left the house without surgical-grade respirators were putting themselves at risk, and that the air quality in Sacramento and San Francisco was considered unhealthy. As a conse-quence, the Oakland Raiders had been forced to play indoors. Local firefighters were surviving on beef jerky and one-hour naps.

When you woke up you told me you wanted to make a phone call to Mariana in New York, because she said she had some time, and she wouldn't charge regular rates. Maybe you could have some privacy? I told you I would go running.

It was mild and lovely when I set off down Warm Sands Drive. I set music to play on my phone and wedged it into the back panel of my leggings. I thought I would try the side streets we had seen in darkness the previous evening, avoiding the main roads. There were sidewalks as I started, but they soon vanished. These desert towns were built for cars, or horses. I kept to the gutters when I could. The morning was steeped in a Sunday morning kind of quiet. That morning I was thir-teen days late. But there was a pain on the left-hand side of my lower abdomen, the ghost of a cramp, and that, I thought, proved that there was nothing to worry about.

I ran towards the San Jacinto Mountains. Even though the air was cool the sun intensified everything. As the music began to loop and

I settled into the pace, my mind wandered. My thoughts turned to the meeting with Camila and Malik on Thursday evening. There was something niggling at me about what Camila had said to me before we left the bar, in those moments of unspecified tension I hadn't quite understood, before Malik, carefully and deliberately, offered to drive Camila home. You had been talking to Malik about Kenneth and your boss on the sidewalk outside ReBAR, and meanwhile I was offering Camila cigarettes from the pack I kept secretly in my bag for emergencies, telling her, now that I was tipsy and brave, how much her work had meant to me.

I think it's interesting what you're doing, she had said to me kindly.

I had been telling her roughly what I was planning to write my dissertation about, and the ways in which I hoped I could emulate her work in my own. I had nodded my head as though I fully understood what she was talking about. She continued then, to tell me a story about the two years she had spent on a postdoctoral fellowship in Los Angeles. She had been living in Eagle Rock, she said, and one day when she turned the tap on to wash dishes in the kitchen sink, nothing came out of the faucet. Her first thought, she told me, was: this is it. It's finally run out. It had not occurred to her that it could be anything else. She had yelled through the house to her husband, telling him to come quickly, because the catastrophe had finally happened. Before he could reply or even reach her from the other side of the house, she had opened the front door, rushed through the yard, and raced away down the street. She inspected the windows of the other houses, searching for what, exactly, she didn't know. Signs of panic? Women in kitchens holding empty glasses? Watering systems sputtering to a drippy stop? The street looked as it always did, and she didn't see another person, nor any animal save a woodpecker in a palm tree. She went back home. And in the end, it had just been a broken water main that had affected a few blocks of the neighborhood for nothing more than an afternoon. But she thought about it often, she had told me, because she had realized in that moment that she had lived the last decade of her life with a certainty she'd never known she was so certain of: that one day we would come to the end of water.

Now as I ran—yucca, barrel cactus, pink oleander, damp sidewalk and glimmering Suburban hoods—I tried to game it out. How to build the kind of shelter that would protect everything I needed to keep safe when the water ran out. How to hold it all? The traces of loss that abide in the substrata of a life, ever present. And how was it possible to even put that feeling into words? When language is not enough, never enough. If the last year we had lived together had taught us anything it was the utter poverty of language in the face of calamity. I had gradually come to understand that you hated that I was always trying to render things into words, trying to pin things down. Because for you, once something was pinned down, the memory lost some essential essence, the event couldn't be changed. You felt suffocated, I think, by my desire to define terms and demand precision from words. Maybe it was the feeling that I was stealing your ability to move through life freely, unencumbered by narrative.

Aside from anything else, what worried me was that there was no possibility that I could elegize anything in my dissertation without my shadow falling across it. It was a risk of telling a story about anything in which I was only a supporting actor. It was something I had often thought about when your mother first fell sick. This was the winter when she was starting chemotherapy and radiation, when they'd removed her pancreas and gall bladder to stop the spread, and you were hopeful. I was not. When she was dying, I often felt like I was holding your hand inside your nightmare. You had told me, when we first started dating, that your biggest fear was that your parents would die. Once, we had taken an afternoon nap in that Upper West Side studio not long after I first met your family. In your sleep you began to moan, and then to call out. I woke up just as you began screaming. The screaming turned into sobs while I held you, spoon-wise, from behind. You told me through shuddering breaths that you had dreamed that your mother was dead. Your tears and sweat soaked through the

T-shirt—your T-shirt—that I was wearing. So when your mother really did fall ill, it often felt as though your nightmare had come to life. The only thing that made it bearable was believing she would recover. We never spoke about the thing that might lie on the other side of a Stage Four cancer. And I didn't speak about it to anyone else, not to you, nor my friends, nor my family. After all, where was my place in this story? Instead, I thought about it on my own. I read the WebMD and Verywell Health pages you refused to read, and then I bought books. I bought and read memoirs by Simone de Beauvoir and Roland Barthes and Kate Zambreno on the deaths of their mothers, by Audre Lorde on her own illness, by Susan Sontag writing on tuberculosis to evade discussing her breast cancer. I read a book called, quite straightforwardly, *Dying.* You jumped when you saw me reading that one, really jumped, as you passed through the living room to the kitchen and clocked me on the couch with my legs up against the wall, jiggling, book held over my face, the word "Dying" in large print on the front cover. I wanted to be across the literature. As though by studying the canon of death I would be able to anticipate the future, prepare a plan, and take control of the outcome. I was reading for you, for when you fell apart.

In the months after she died, when you were weeping and I was holding you and rubbing your back, I would be soothed by remembering, for instance, Roland Barthes recounting how a woman from whom he was purchasing a tea cake had said, *Voilà!* just as his mother had always said voilà, and in that moment he experienced his mother's death again as if the wound reopened afresh. From just that single moment of recognition. He began to cry in the boulangerie, and then allowed himself to sob with abandon once he got home. Like you, he seemed to suffer well—calmly—around other people. It was only when he was behind closed doors that the collapse occurred. I slowed as I reached a footbridge spanning a canal, a trickle of water running through it, and made a note to myself on my phone. I had no idea where that trickle of water was going. I stopped on the footbridge, looked towards the mountains, and took a photograph on my

phone, poorly lit, as though it would help me remember and understand something important when I returned to it, after the trip. The
heat felt atrocious, although according to the weather on my phone it
wasn't any warmer than twenty-four degrees. I was nevertheless dripping sweat. As I slowed to a walk by the rental car parked outside our
Airbnb, I noticed that across the street a set of automatic sprinklers
were watering a luridly green lawn. In the middle of the day? And with
what water? How long would that lawn stay green when the level of
the River fell below the intakes, when the water simply dried up?

W
e sat behind a fruit truck with the words "organic only" written
on the back as we sat at the lights and waited to turn out onto
the highway. You shifted in your seat and winced, gripping the wheel
and turning your knuckles white. Tight hips, I thought.

I hate it here, you said. It looks just like Phoenix.

I agreed that it did all look a bit like Phoenix, or at least the part of
Phoenix where you had been raised. I wondered if we would spend the
entire trip comparing various Southwestern locales to Phoenix.

It makes me feel dread, you said.

But I still didn't understand what you meant by dread.

Everything that looks like this, you said. It was hard for you to articulate what you meant. You cast your hand around at the mountains
and blinding sun. I just feel the same dread I did my whole childhood,
you said.

I let it rest. We drove south along the Sonny Bono Memorial Freeway, past turnoffs for Indio and Coachella, the sun beating down from
the midpoint of its arc. Signs for cannabis stretched all along the roadside—"It's just weed, old pal!" Palm trees aggrandized fat, squat buildings housing car dealerships and casinos and mini malls. Things lost
their luster and reverted to desert the closer we got to the Salton Sea,
but it was only when we were near the water that the citrus groves and
date palm farms appeared.

They can't possibly grow things around here, can they? I asked you.

This is where they grow everything, you told me. Isn't California the breadbasket? It's where all the fruits come from on the fruit packaging.

But everything is growing so close to the Salton Sea. Would you want to eat fruit grown right next to something so poisonous? I asked.

I looked out the window at the grapefruit trees laid out in neat rows, and suddenly caught a glimpse of the water ahead. Now I could smell the unpleasant odor of rotting fish, even though the windows were up and the air-conditioning on. Without my saying anything you pressed a button that stopped the outside air from infiltrating the climate-controlled interior of the car. We drove past sun-faded signs advertising water-ski rentals. It was hard to tell what was abandoned and what was simply in bad condition.

What's the deal? you asked me.

I didn't answer because I was trying to search on the map for a good place to stop. The sea glittered under the brilliant sky to our right.

The Colorado River broke through here, I said. Before they built the first dams, it burst through a canal, and it flooded this valley. It's like a pond drying up over the course of a century.

But people used to water-ski here?

I think it was nice until it got so toxic, I said. And now it's disappearing.

The problem now was that decades of agricultural runoff flowing in from all those date farms and citrus groves we'd just driven past had concentrated, year by year, in the water of the sea. In the noonday heat, algal blooms bred diseases that smothered the animals living in the water. People had eventually stopped coming to race their speedboats and sunbathe on the shore. But the animals still came. One year, I had heard recently, a flock of overwintering birds were all found dead on the shore of the Salton Sea. Their corpses were filled with things like arsenic and DDT. The birds were burned in an incinerator which had to operate around the clock to clear the carnage. There were still some fish left living in the water, but they weren't healthy either. Sometimes there were mass die-offs. When that happened, workers had to wade into the revolting water to scoop the dead fish into barrels. I'd heard that you could smell them all over the Coachella Valley.

So it's dangerous to be here? you asked me.

Maybe, I said, I just know I want to see it. I wasn't explaining myself very well.

I found a car park. Take a right here, I told you. We parked and picked our way down along the sand to the shore. It looked, at first, like an ordinary beach.

You called out from behind me, Can you still water-ski? There was a sign about water-skiing still standing by the shore. Should we water-ski?

You were joking, but I played along. I'll water-ski if you want to teach me, I called back.

I made towards the water as though I were going to dive in. Then I felt a shift in the ground beneath my sandals. Not sand anymore, but lakebed. Not sand but tiny bones. Then, a few feet from my shoes, some fish heads. The skin was leathery, mummified by the heat. There was not a single bird in sight. The water lapped at the shore's edge, leaving a faint brown scum in its wake.

Oh, it's so ruined and so beautiful, I said.

You put your arm around me and kissed me on my temple. It's like an evil mirage, you agreed. From a distance it looks like a beautiful place. And even over there, you said, pointing to the mountains. It's beautiful. But this whole place—look—we're walking on bones.

We strolled arm in arm along the beach.

As we left the car park and then drove south away from the Salton Sea, we passed a dried-up beach where a sea of RVs and concrete structures were collected like a postapocalyptic holiday community.

Then the orchards began to clear, and after half an hour, the desert took over.

A large shed loomed into view as we drove south. Oh shit, I said as I began to make out the signage. Is that a Border Patrol station?

I began to dig around in the bag at my feet for my purse and fumbled in the pockets for my green card.

It's all okay, you told me in soothing tones. Nothing to be worried about.

But all encounters with immigration made me nervous. You know, I said, these Border Patrol stations that are miles away from the actual border are unconstitutional. There was a *This American Life* episode about them. You can refuse to be checked. There are videos of people doing it on YouTube.

Do you want to refuse? you asked me.

No, of course not.

It didn't matter. We drove up to the phalanx of cameras and the man standing in fatigues by the road, but he took a look through our window, then waved us onward. Not even a word.

We're white, you said as I reached tentatively for my purse to put my green card away. That's how it is.

The further south we traveled, the more piles of scrap metal and half-inhabited ruin we encountered on either side of the road. We took a left at a brightly painted sign. "Salvation Mountain: God Never Fails." We drove along a dirt road towards the mass of color we could see ahead of us, resolving into an image that looked precisely like the photographs I'd seen online. A gift shop by the wayside sold wind chimes and dream catchers that dangled from an awning over the unpaved road, all the better for tourists like us to simply hand over the cash through an open window without ever having to open a door. We parked with a collection of other cars, all covered in dust and sand, just like ours. Ahead of us, a shrine. The mountain wasn't so much a mountain as it was a desert hillside painted in gallons and gallons of the brightest house paint. The hill was topped with a white cross, above a torrent of color tumbling down the hillside. "God is Love," the hill said. Below that, couched in the shape of a red heart, outlined in white, was written, "Say Jesus I'm a sinner please come upon my body and into my heart." In a tiny sign that I could only read as we got close to the mountain, someone had written "no climbing, stay off heart."

You couldn't climb the heart, or the words, but you could climb everything else. There were only ten or fifteen people there, but all of them were weaving up and down the mountain taking photographs of one another. I looked around and realized I had lost track of you. You had wandered, without my realizing, into the warren of hidey holes towards the right of the hill. It was hard to say what the structure was, precisely. It was man-made, and constructed out of adobe and tree branches, painted in the same vivid pinks and greens and blues as the rest of the mountain. I followed you in.

You were staring upwards at the painted walls. It was quiet in there, and smelled oddly sterile for a place so earthy. The sun had caught your hair. You looked lovely. Without you knowing I was doing it, I took a photograph, which I still have, printed out and taped to the wall above my desk. I watched you move through the space, enjoying the strange feeling I had sometimes when I happened upon you alone. I was struck by how handsome you were. Your green eyes and pale skin, your dark hair flecked with strands of gray. The strength of the muscle that filled out your shoulders and arms. You were handsome without being aware of the things that made you handsome. Even though you were so familiar to me, are familiar to me still, so that I can recall in detail the appearance of your fingers clutching the steering wheel, the faded stretch marks fanning out across the middle of your back, the twin freckles on the underside of your penis, your handsomeness sometimes hit me as though I were seeing a stranger. And so I was surprised, astonished even, that I could walk over to you and put my arm around you, because you were mine. You turned your head and kissed my temple with the audible sound of kissing, *mwa*, but you said it softly, closely, because it was a sound for kissing so saccharine that it was only meaningful when said in absolute earnest. This place is so strange, you said. The words "the holy bible" were painted in raised adobe onto the wall above your head.

We left each other's arms, and you walked back out into the light, but I stayed inside the structure. Everything about this strange place was a monument to devotion. I hadn't expected to be so moved by it. I could hear two men chatting as they entered the same half-lit cave as me, advising each other on the best positions to pose in for the photographs they were taking. I was looking away from them when the men screamed. I turned.

Is it a snake? I called out. I scanned the dusty ground but couldn't see anything moving. They moved towards me, and one of them, in a black button-down shirt, put his arm out as though to shield me from whatever it was that they had screamed at.

It's a spider, he said. A really big one.

He pointed to a dim corner. I could make out a spider the size of an Oreo cookie.

I wanted to laugh. It's just a spider? I asked. I thought it was a snake.

Black Button-Down turned to me. You're not scared of spiders?

I grew up with a lot of spiders around, I said. I'm not scared of them.

Black Button-Down seemed surprised, and stepped towards me, his chest puffed out as though he were ready to spar. But you're afraid of snakes?

Well, I've never seen a snake in the wild. Spiders showed up in my bedroom when I was a kid, after it rained. Much bigger than that one over there. Spiders are fine. Don't hurt her. Let her be, she's not going to do anything to you.

I turned and walked out the same exit you had disappeared through moments earlier. I found you on top of the mountain. You had ascended the hill of painted flowers, blue and white stripes, green fields, making your way along the yellow brick road to the man-sized crucifix crowning the edifice. You were looking out over the desert.

Did you make a friend? you asked me when I reached you.

I think I made two manly men feel bad about being scared of spiders.

There was a spider in there?

Yeah.

I wouldn't have liked to see a spider.

Well, she wasn't that big.

But I would have been afraid of a spider if I'd seen it. Was it big?

It was sort of big. Not Australian big.

Did they run away?

No. One tried to protect me from it.

You had your phone out, and raised it over our heads, pulling me in close. I liked photos where we looked like any other couple on holiday.

Hey, you said, can you go down there and take a photo of me? You pointed to a stretch of blue and white stripes undulating down the mountain.

When I got there, I realized why. From that perspective, looking up at you, you were positioned above the raised red words of "God," framed perfectly in the middle of the word. I took the picture. You followed me down the mountain and I handed you back your phone so that you could swipe through the photographs. You used your thumb and index finger to zoom in on yourself.

I wonder if anyone comes out here and actually finds Jesus?

I doubt it, you said.

I didn't tell you how being out there had made me feel. Haunted. Like I believed in God for the first time since I was a child. I suspected the way I felt was the desired effect when Leonard Knight, the man who made this place, had moved out to the desert and created Salvation Mountain. Knight was a man overwhelmed by his own particular version of the Sinner's Prayer: *Jesus I'm a sinner, please come upon my body and into my heart.* He said it over and over again once he discovered it, or so said the flyer in the box by the car park. Knight internalized the prayer so that there was no part of him that ever ceased praying. He got the taste for evangelizing. When he arrived at this place on the edge of the Salton Sea, he began to erect a monument on a hillside. Knight painted it in ten layers of the brightest paint he could come by and wrote his Sinner's Prayer right at its center. The more people read the prayer, he reasoned, the more the message would spread. I was not sure if you would see it as slightly suspect if I admitted to you that the message had affected me. It was the kind of feeling I experienced rarely now, an echo left over from childhood. It was the desire to find a church or a chapel, to get down on my knees and pray. I'm not sure what I would have prayed for. I wasn't sure if I believed in God any-more. And yet the feeling was there. We got back to the car and sat for a second with our legs held out of the open doors, letting out the built-up heat. You couldn't touch the steering wheel at the tempera-ture it had gotten to.

Imagine coming all the way out to the middle of the desert just to paint it, I said, looking back at the mountain.

But you didn't respond. You were uploading the photo I'd taken to Instagram, or trying to. Neither of us had phone reception.

There were three more hours of driving between where we were and the coast. The sun was already beginning to arc downwards, and we hadn't eaten since breakfast. Once clear of the mountain, the des-ert seemed to return to ruin, but by an old, shuttered movie theater we saw a film crew setting up for a location shoot. I supposed it was just the right aesthetic for a story about the climate or zombie apocalypse. A prairie dog darted across the road. We found ourselves following behind a truck full of onions, heading in the same westward direction that we were, towards a sign advertising date shakes ahead in West-morland.

Can we go get date shakes? I asked.

You looked skeptical. They're pretty sweet and gross.

I've never seen a date shake advertised before, I insisted. I've never even heard of one.

The shop was across the road from a Shell and a fireworks store, surrounded by a grid of numbered streets that went no further than ten. The date shake store was enormous. The smell inside reminded me of the sunbaked western suburbs grocery stores of my Sydney childhood. Shelves were piled with desert honey, local olive oil, vats of dried and fresh dates. We ordered and waited for the milkshakes, stepping back to let a middle-aged man take his place at the counter. He was accompanied by a pregnant teenage girl. She had pimples blooming across her cheekbones. She was wearing a backwards base-ball cap and a strapless tube dress in a peacock feather print. Her ankles were swollen, scarred by faded red bites she'd scratched at. The man seemed to know the woman behind the counter.

This is my daughter, he told the woman.

Then he pointed to his daughter's belly. And that's my grandson, he said.

The teenage girl smiled in a wan sort of way. She looked so uncomfortable. Too hot. She looked as though all her joints hurt, as though she longed to return to a darkened room.

Thirteen days, I thought to myself.

You were right about the date shake, it was too sweet, but we hadn't eaten, and in the heat and the dust it tasted like the most delicious thing I'd ever swallowed. We headed west. There was a little over two hours left to drive. We crossed the line into San Diego County as night began to fall. North, reported the radio, the fire toll had risen to seventy-one, with over a thousand people missing. In Malibu the fires were raging in the hills, residents cut off. Another football game cancelled due to smoke and poor air quality, but the Santa Anas blowing across Los Angeles had dispelled the worst of it. The sun was setting into an intense shade of scarlet, but we couldn't smell smoke. As the sun shone its last, we passed a fantastically old man driving an Alfa Romeo, its top down, no hair for the wind to blow through. As the ranches and citrus groves gave way to suburbs, I began to taste the ocean in the air.

I was ecstatic. We were almost there.

It's always scary driving down here at night, you said. Even when I was a kid it was scary. There are no streetlights. We're not even that far from the house. Fifteen minutes maybe, until we get there. It looks fine in the daylight, but in the dark like this it scares me.

3

Paroxysms of Love—Marry Me—Swimming in the Ocean—Blackberry—A Leopard-Print Nightdress Hanging on a Wire—William Mulholland—The Owens River Valley—There It Is. Take It—Eucalyptus Trees—The Waterless Fountains of Childhood—The House Where David Lynch Lives—Picking Grapefruit—L.A. Is Driving—The Greatest Thing—A Trip to Sprouts—Fun Beets—Trumpet Flowers—A Place That Feels Like a Record Skipping

Once, years ago, we were sitting in your childhood bedroom and going through old papers stored in the wardrobe. It was late. We had drunk two gin and tonics apiece. The papers were comprised of old school assignments and reports, photographs, certificates. That night, you found an old journal, the kind children are instructed to keep in elementary school and hand in to the teacher each morning. A substitute teacher had asked you to introduce yourselves to her by describing "The Most Important Things About You!" You had written in a spiky left-handed scrawl, *My name is Lewis. I am seven. I have two tortoises. They are good tortoises. My state is California. I don't have anything more to say.*

In the first years after we were married, I often experienced moments I thought of as paroxysms of love. These were moments when I was so happy, so filled to the brim with love for you, that I felt the emotion hit me wavelike, and absolute. Reading the assignment for your substitute teacher was one such moment. When I think back on that first year of our marriage now, those moments seem to run together like handwritten letters under spilled water. These were the evenings when we were so besotted with each other that we would do nothing much more than lie on our bed with our limbs entwined, and fingers interlaced, and you or I would say to the other, Marry me. Marry me. Even though we were already married. Because it was the only thing to say that met the magnitude of the feeling. It was the only place there was to go with all that love. I loved you for everything you were and every version of yourself you had ever been. The college student and the teenage boy and the recalcitrant child. I could discern in that journal, written when you were seven, the seeds of what formed you as an adult. You were a child who did not name his tortoises. Who refused to say more than was necessary. Who aligned himself with California rather than the state of his birth. You were declaring even then a difference from all the other children in your classroom in Camelback Vista.

I didn't doubt that you felt you had a deep connection to California. The house in Encinitas we arrived at in the dark of Sunday evening had once belonged to your favorite grandmother. I knew that she had died when you were only small, and so I suppose she had for you all the nostalgic coziness of somebody who'd provided treats and cuddles, nothing more difficult than that. Once she died, you had told me, the house sat empty for most of every year. Your father couldn't bear to sell it, and so it was re-visioned as your family's summer home. Your mother had remodeled everything; hung pieces of contemporary art on the walls, installed an induction stovetop and a sunken marble bathtub. The only thing left unfinished was the floor. Navajo rugs were splayed over the scuffed concrete underlayment. The trip we took that November was the very first time I'd ever seen the house in the autumn. Nothing looked any different, of course. No seasons in California, you told me that night, as we parked along the side of the house and rolled along our suitcases beneath a copse of sugar gums to the front door. The house was musty from being empty since July, so I opened every window in every room while you turned on the fuse box and the hot water and waited for pizza delivery. I fell asleep before it arrived. Even though you'd done all the driving, it was me who was exhausted and queasy. Morning sickness, my mother told me once, doesn't always happen in the morning.

The house in Encinitas was where we were happiest. Where we read on the balcony in the mornings and swam in the ocean in the afternoons and spent the evenings talking or watching old films on the big television mounted on the living room wall. You first brought me to Encinitas in the month of June, not long after you first told me you loved me. I had thought it was a perfect summer house. I didn't know why you hadn't wanted to live here the whole year round, or why you hadn't tried. Occasionally the town experienced extremely hot days, you explained, and on those days you felt incapacitated, because there was no air-conditioning. Back then I thought you must have been exaggerating about how ill prepared you felt for heat, because after all, you had grown up in a desert, but I learned pretty soon that it was possible to pass, in Arizona, from air-conditioned house, to air-conditioned car, to air-conditioned mall, and rarely admit to the reality of the heat that regularly killed people before the arrival of Freon. Your grandmother had bought the Encinitas house cheap in the 1970s. It was cheap because it was part of a new development built on a fallow citrus grove that sat atop a fault line. From the balcony of the master bedroom, one could see through the sugar gums the road running below the cliff. When the earthquake came, which it inevitably would, your grandmother's house would slide down that cliff like it was built on so much pudding.

I remember that during that first time you had taken me to Encinitas, when we had the house to ourselves and more space than we knew what to do with, there was a morning when I woke up before you. Down in the kitchen, making coffee, I saw there was still the detritus of the previous evening on the old Laminex kitchen table: a half-empty bottle of kombucha, the television remote, and a notebook with a pen resting in its spine. Things you'd been using after I'd gone to sleep early. The notebook was still open to the page where you'd stopped writing, two-thirds filled with your spiky handwriting. I couldn't help but read it. *Swimming with E this afternoon,* you had written. *I hated the beach as a kid. Still uncomfortable being there. But E wants me to go swimming with her, so I go into the water, and it's nice. Seeing E happy makes me happy.* Only a few years earlier, before we met, I gathered you had been unhappy. These were years you alluded to as having been characterized by a formless hopelessness, filled with a sense that you were expected to be constantly striving towards an outcome the outline of which you couldn't quite discern. You told me that these were years when you would drive south from university in Los Angeles and spend most of the summers on your own. You would stay for three full months, reading, biking, working on art projects. There was your charcoal drawing summer, your painted miniatures summer, your distorted field recording summer, and finally your internet performance pieces summer. You knew you wanted to make things, and you felt desperate to find the right form, as soon as possible. You were possessed of a creative urgency and ambition that still radiated from you when I first met you. You were so eager to show me things. You took me to Donald Judd's house in Soho, and an installation at the old Whitney where we wore sunglasses and listened to audio re-creations of sculptures we couldn't see. You arranged evenings in which we would watch, projected onto the wall of your Upper West Side studio, everything ever directed by David Lynch, and an accurately timed pirated excerpt of Christian Marclay's installation *The Clock*, from 7:30 p.m. until whenever it was that I fell asleep. You wanted me to understand the kind of art that was important to you because it was tantamount to making sense of your soul.

That first summer we were in Encinitas together, you made a video recording every morning, documenting your trip down the road to get a cold brew, the repetition and mundanity of the task seeming to be the point. Other rituals that summer were made together: the Tommy Bahama chairs set up on the sand, the spots at Leucadia, Carlsbad, and Moonlight State Beach that we preferred, the flavor of shaved ice we would buy at the beachside kiosk, the dive bar on the main street we liked to go to after swimming. We used your credit card like it had no limit and roasted chickens in the kitchen's new stove, made gin and tonics from your father's liquor shelf, and drove—me directing, you steering—up and down that stretch of coastline between San Diego and Los Angeles. I remember that there was one afternoon that first summer when you returned from the beach before me. I had wanted to stay and swim while the sun set over the ocean. It felt like a miracle to me, who had grown up on an east-facing coast, to breaststroke out beyond the breaking waves and face the sun as it aggrandized the sky in oranges and pinks. To watch it dipping into the very same water I was swimming in. Sometimes there were dolphins, their silhouettes arcing southward along the brilliant horizon. That particular afternoon I had swum until the last curve of the sun disappeared into the ocean, and then walked back to the house barefoot, dress dampening around the triangles of the wet bikini top I still wore underneath. When I walked through the door you were waiting for me. To me it seemed like something about the light, or the heat, or the house itself, caused you to walk towards me as smoothly as if you were on a conveyor belt. Hi, you said, and kissed me. I hadn't even turned the lock. Your hands went to my hips and gathered the fabric, pulled it up. Up over my arms, up over my head. Moved aside the damp triangle of swimsuit and kissed my breast, taking the nipple in your mouth. Pulled my hips to yours, against the erection in your basketball shorts. And then to the ground. On the paint-streaked concrete floor, cool against still-warm skin.

Years afterwards, when I was leafing through the books you had left behind in our New York apartment, I found in a copy of John Berger's *G* a page you had marked with an asterisk in the corner. You had been reading it that summer. The page concerned the nature of sex, and the ways in which language often fails to describe it. The writer noted that every time we have sex there is something about it, no matter how many times we have done it before, that seems as though it were the very first time. It was the quality, he wrote, of firstness. He used the example of blackberries. Berger grew up in a time before it was possible to buy every kind of fruit in every season, and so in his telling, blackberries only arrived in early summer. Upon tasting a blackberry again for the first time since the previous summer's harvest, he would experience a kind of fake firstness, stirring a blurred memory of the very first blackberry he'd ever tasted. This analogy, the writer said, went some way to explaining the single-mindedness of desire, the reason we go back to something, someone, again and again and again.

I remembered, as I read the page in your book, that there was a poem I had loved as a teenager, which said much the same thing about blackberries. The idea that no utterance of the word "blackberry" could ever be anything but a kind of epitaph to the blackberry itself. Language was never good enough. In the poem, the speaker remembered a woman he had once loved, and how holding her small shoulders in his hands was an expression of desire for her, but also a desire for so much else—rivers, pleasure boats, fish, the salt water of childhood. The body of the beloved calling into being all of it at once, as holy and unexplainable as anything said by the desert mystics. And maybe that went some way towards explaining those evenings when we would lie together, days and nights on a shared bed, with our limbs entwined, and fingers interlaced, saying *blackberry* to each other, or in other words, Marry me. *Every feature that makes her desirable asserts its contingency—here, here, here, here, here, here*, you had underlined in your copy of *G* from that very first summer. Beside it you had written a letter, in pencil. *E.* That first time on the concrete floor was not the first, not by a long shot, but it was the first time we ever fucked on the floor. Afterwards we lay there together, my bikini top still damp and pushed aside but resolutely on, semen dripping down my inner thigh, while you kissed me left to right and back again across my temple, until I laughed and asked you how it felt, after all that time, to have desecrated the floor of your grandmother's house, right by the front door.

The ocean, in November now, was not warm enough for many people to swim in. Only surfers occupied the waves. Up north, the president had visited the scenes of the wildfires, which were still out of control. He blamed the fires on radical environmentalists. The newspaper predicted that it would take twenty years for the Santa Monica Mountains to look as they had before the blaze. After I'd read the newsfeeds on my phone beside you in the double bed of the second bedroom, I tiptoed out with my shoes in my hands. I left and went running through the early morning streets of Encinitas. When I returned you were up. You'd made coffee and were sitting on the balcony that adjoined the master bedroom. I joined you. I thought it was silly that we still slept in the room you'd used as a child, when the master bedroom was much bigger, but as I walked through the bedroom to the balcony I could see in the walk-through closet your mother's leopard-print nightdress hanging on a wire. Her underwear, I discovered when you were out of the room, was still folded neatly in one of the drawers. I supposed your father couldn't bear to throw her things away. You were right. There was no way either of us could sleep in that bed, which looked on to the wardrobe filled with your dead mother's clothes.

We got in the car at nine thirty, hoping that, traffic permitting, you could get me to my appointment at the library by noon. The journey up the coast and into the city could take two hours, or four, depending on the traffic. And neither of us had ever been before to that part of the city, where a librarian would allow me access to a branch of the state university's special collections and archives room, where I would be presented with materials relating to the life and career of William Mulholland. It was temperate and sunny outside, beautiful and palm-spangled. While we inched northward on the 405 in Culver City, I emailed the librarian from my phone and asked her to please excuse my lateness, while you told me about your plans to have lunch with a college friend, Jimmy, in North Hollywood. Jimmy worked intermittently as a production assistant on film sets, and though I had met him before, on previous trips, and once had a long conversation with him about the Manson Family, about which we both expressed a kind of fascination, the amount of detail that Jimmy could recall about the deaths made me uneasy, as though he had made pilgrimages to 10050 Cielo Drive, the address in Benedict Canyon that had been the site of the first grisly murders. I was not sorry to be missing him. When you dropped me off at the university you reminded me to text you an hour before I needed you to pick me up.

The librarian brushed aside my apologies and sat me in a corner of the small timber-paneled reading room on the second floor, and presented me with the papers I'd asked to look at, along with two library-issue pencils. From the wood-laminate desk I could see across a small carpeted study space out through windows that let in a view of tidy, bright green lawns. I opened a box. My supervisor had been the one who had known about the archive, and advised me to visit while I was in California. I wasn't precisely sure what was in the boxes I'd requested, nor what I was hoping to find. Maybe something as prophetic as the line John Wesley Powell delivered in 1893 to a meeting of politicians and developers: *I tell you gentlemen you are piling up a heritage of conflict and litigation over water rights, for there is not enough water to supply the land.* I suppose I wanted something like that.

I had two, maybe three hours at most. I already knew much of the backstory, constructed from books and documentaries and the movie *Chinatown*. I knew that Mulholland was born in Dublin, a nineteenth-century city with never-ending water. He was still a boy when he went to sea on a merchant ship, and arrived in Los Angeles in the 1870s. It was not even a city back then, but a town, which had no real reason to be there, because it had no metals, no minerals, and no forests. Like most desert towns, L.A. lacked water. But it was warm, and there were railways, and the railways brought the tubercular patients westward for the sunshine that was thought to dry out their lungs. At the time, all the city had was a bunch of old waterwheels, which plugged into the ever-diminishing Los Angeles River. It was on this shambled arrangement of pipes that Mulholland first found work as a ditch digger. After digging all day, Mulholland read hydro-engineering manuals late into the evening, and taught himself to keep a map of the entire Los Angeles water system in his head. He was promoted once, then twice, and again, until at last he found himself superintendent of the city's water system. Things went well for a while. The city prospered. Citrus groves and sunshine, D. W. Griffiths and Cecil B. DeMille; people from all over flocked to the growing city of sunny days. Then came the drought. When the newcomers arrived, they discovered that they could not water their lawns, nor stroll around the ponds in local parks, because the ponds had been emptied and lawn watering prohibited. By the time the twentieth century began, the city had sucked dry the Los Angeles River. It was when the river ran dry that Mulholland decided that he would have to find a new source of water.

But where to find water in a desert? Look far afield. In this case, north. Owens Valley was hundreds of miles away from the city of Los Angeles. The river running through it was an anomaly. Bright blue and flowing through a rainless valley, it ran from the snowpack in the mountains down into a lake. The Owens River was far away from Los Angeles, yes, but it had the benefit of being many thousands of feet above sea level. If Mulholland could manage to build an aqueduct carrying the water over mountains, valleys, and desert, the water would simply arrive in Los Angeles by the force of gravity. So Mulholland stole the river.

Building began. People who had previously been farmhands, cowboys, and miners signed up to work. It took six years. The day the spillway opened in 1913, thousands of thirsty people gathered in the San Fernando Valley holding tin cups in their hands. When the water poured out of the final sluiceway, entering the city of Los Angeles, they rushed en masse to drink. Mulholland was present that day, but he was exhausted. He'd been up all night, but he felt like he hadn't slept in all those six long years. He unfurled an American flag, then turned to address the mayor. Mulholland gestured towards the stolen river.

He said, *There it is. Take it.*

Then he left. And maybe that would have been the end of the story, if the water had been enough. But it wasn't. Los Angeles just kept growing, and so did the need for water. Nowhere in the city were you not in the presence of lawns, hedges, fountains, or palm trees. Now they'd stolen one river, they knew they could do it again. People spoke about digging a pipeline to Alaska. Lassoing icebergs and bringing them down the coast. Damming San Francisco Bay. Pipelines upon pipelines upon pipelines. Mulholland couldn't have known the city would grow the way that it did, that the thirst would never be quenched, that the droughts would only get worse, nor that there would never, not ever, be enough water to firm up the future, to keep everybody safe and sound.

Only ten years after his aqueduct was finished, the city was running out of water again. Mulholland pondered new sources. He decided the only thing for it was to build an aqueduct to the Colorado River, that beautiful wild artery of the American Southwest. If they could get a hold of the Colorado, they would never, he thought, worry about water again. But before it could happen a disaster struck. Mulholland had authorized another dam, this time in San Francisquito Canyon. But he had not been thorough enough. The dam failed. The support structures turned to jelly. The water erupted. The flood destroyed countless towns and killed hundreds of people before outletting into the Pacific Ocean. Mulholland retired a crushed man, with blood on his hands, to contemplate his sins in seclusion. Upon his retirement, he got word that the Boulder Canyon project had been approved, and that the Colorado River would finally be dammed just outside the city of Las Vegas, with the greatest portion of its water promised to Southern California. That had been Mulholland's dream all along—to ensure the city of Los Angeles would never again, in his lifetime at least, run out of water. And even though I knew all of that, after an hour of paging through dull memorandum after dull polite letter, I was no closer to finding anything that I might have been able to use. Nothing I didn't already have a good sense of. After a while I put down the pencil and flipped through the photographs. There were pictures of Mulholland, but there were also many more pictures of other men, other women, whose names I didn't know and didn't need to. I took pictures on my phone of some of the photographs, pictures of Mulholland at what seemed to be various stages of the aqueduct's construction, in a car, and sitting for a studio portrait, because if nothing else they were at least evidence that I'd tried. The other photographs were meaningless to me, but it was at those I looked longest. Pictures of children by ponds, or old men posing in the middle of an orchard. I lingered over one photograph in particular. A little girl sat beside Mulholland, who dandled an infant on his knee. The old man peered down at the child he was holding as though he were afraid it might wriggle out of his grasp. There was a blur to the long, dry eucalyptus leaves in the background, as though a breeze had at that moment pushed through to break up the summertime heat. It was a photograph that could have been of my own distant family—Anglo-Irish skin prone to burning, unsmiling, posing in front of eucalyptus. The photo stirred up that shock of recognition I had first felt in Southern California when you'd brought me all those years ago. The landscape of Los Angeles looked almost exactly the same as it had in the city where I'd grown up. Eucalyptus trees were so omnipresent in Australia, so absolutely everywhere, that there was a sense of the uncanny about seeing them growing here alongside bottlebrush trees and wattles and Moreton Bay figs and Norfolk Island pines—as though I'd stepped through to some not-quite-right street in Sydney or Adelaide. I felt like I was home. And yet, when I told you about the trees, you seemed confused. You had thought that they were native to California. That confusion, I think now, was the space I was learning to inhabit, my sense of home and my experience of belonging evolving, no longer dictated by the particularities of geography, not one flag or anthem or passport, but becoming instead an amalgam— the smell of trees and flowers, the opening bars of particular songs, some foodstuffs, and all of it, all of it, was a home that you had helped make for me.

* * *

I had barely any battery left on my phone with which to ask you to come and pick me up from Northridge. It was mid-afternoon by the time I exited the library. I found you idling in a no-standing zone, swiping through photographs on your phone. I settled into the passenger seat, and while you swiped you asked me how it had gone, and to figure out how to get you back to the 101. I found a way back, south through Van Nuys and then east through Sherman Oaks, names I thought I recognized from the movies of my childhood, movies where blond-haired young people cruised in their own cars down wide streets to blasting music, movies where the material world was figured as primary colored and suggestively grotesque, movies where teens congregated in malls which always seemed to contain fountains. I had never seen a fountain in a mall. Or maybe, I reflected as we drove, there had in fact been fountains in the malls of my childhood, but like so many water sources designated frivolous, they had been the victim of water restrictions imposed when the drought got bad, and then it just happened that the drought lasted fourteen years. Maybe the waterless fountains had been there all along, and I had simply not noticed. Instead, I had grown up the kind of child—the kind of adult— who felt a spike of panic at the tap left running while teeth were being brushed, and white rage at the sight of homeowners washing down cement footpaths and driveways with a garden hose. I still felt that rage when I saw it here in Los Angeles, and likewise I was shocked whenever I saw sprinkler systems misting over bright green lawns and gardens being watered in the high heat of noon, when such activities, where I was from, had been outlawed. And the drought in this part of the world had lasted just as long, a drought with no end in sight, and was arguably much worse. Who, I wondered, was in charge? Why wasn't anybody doing something?

You told me that after lunch you and Jimmy had gone to a used bookstore on Cahuenga Boulevard, and that you had spent nearly an hour roaming the towering stacks. They had a cat, you said, and handed me your phone, where I saw a video you had taken of your hand reaching towards a tiny disembodied paw. His name was Zeus, you said.

You reached around into the back seat to retrieve your tote bag and passed it to me. I got you something, you said.

There were five books inside. Which one is for me? I asked.

The book about Charles Manson. I didn't think you had that one. And it was only a few dollars.

I fished out the soft-edged yellow-and-black paperback, where, printed on the front cover, a teenage boy who must have been a pubescent Charles Manson grinned for a studio portrait. I was delighted. No, I said, I haven't read this one.

Lovely, you said. Jimmy says it's good.

I bet, I said.

We passed down featureless streets of yellow-grassed hillsides and glass-walled offices built wide rather than high, houses swaddled by red gums and pepper trees. I know I always say this, I said, but the number of native Australian plants in this city is very eerie.

You hooted. I know, baby, you said. Do you want to steal some eucalyptus leaves to take home again?

Not just yet, I said.

It was not quite rush hour, but it was approaching that time of the day. School was out. Soon, people would start heading home from work. The light was already beginning to glow golden over the ridge that gilded the freeway, coming in at the same western afternoon angle as that which had lit the photograph I'd lingered over in the archives. We passed a sign directing cars towards Universal City, Lankershim Boulevard, and Mulholland Drive.

It's so odd, I told you, to spend all afternoon looking at the papers of somebody and then see their name on road signs.

I can imagine, you said. Does it feel like a bad sign?

No, I said. Because his name was just a name now, sewn into the fabric of the city like all the rest. I continued, It's more that I have an image in my head of what he looks like now, not just official portraits, but the way his backyard looked, and the way he held his grandchildren. The way he liked to wear his mustache.

Traffic slowed down and behind us a car began to honk, as though there were something you could do about it.

Hello, sir, you said to the rearview mirror, I can certainly hear your lovely, loud horn. Beep, beep.

Do you think David Lynch lives on Mulholland Drive? I asked.

I think he does, actually, you said.

I bet I could find his house, I said, the idea suddenly occurring to me. I bet somebody's put it on the internet.

I think I know what it looks like. It's the house in *Lost Highway*. The one that Bill Pullman lives in.

How do you know that?

I just know things. Give it a look-see.

I typed "David Lynch's address" into Google and got a return immediately. I laughed a loud, victorious laugh. I found it, I shouted. I found it. It's not on Mulholland Drive, but it's right off it. I turned the screen of my phone towards you, but the traffic was taking off again and you were driving. Shall we go find it?

Sure, you said. Got all day.

I rerouted us away from the bookstore in Echo Park I'd wanted to visit and took us off the freeway. The road snaked uphill, gilded by white wooden fences so neat they gave the impression of being picketed without really being so. The road ascended high into the hills, and yet it was so narrow, the houses so quiet, that there was, just by driving through, a sense of trespass about our trip. The light grew dappled, and the undergrowth ferned as we followed the road into a glen. There was something of the enchanted wood about it. Something to beware of. As though here Persephone would be sure to eat the pomegranate, or Actaeon spy a goddess and find himself turned into a deer. Turn left, I said. We drove up the hill and veered into a narrow street.

You pulled over. This is it, you said. You sounded awed, and pointed across the street to the angular house across the way.

Should we get out? I asked.

You nodded. We undid our seat belts and opened the doors, both of us closing them very gently so that they wouldn't make a noise. The street was incredibly quiet. We stood against the white fence of the property opposite and looked up at the windows of David Lynch's house. There were sparrows, the smell of freshly cut grass, and somewhere inside the angular house we heard the voice of a man coughing.

You squeezed my hand. Does he have a cold? you asked me.

There was no doubt in our minds that the cough we had heard had been made by David Lynch.

What do we do? I asked.

You surveyed the street, left and right. A tree within reaching distance was heavy with grapefruit. Let's pick some, you said. So I reached up into the tree and pulled down one, then two, orange-pink grapefruit. Then we got back in the car. You took the fruit from my hand and combined them with yours, piling all five of them in your lap. Can you take a photograph? you asked me. I took a photograph. Can you send it to me? I want to show Malik.

Show him what? I giggled.

All the grapefruit we have from the tree across the street from David Lynch's house.

The photograph sent, you started the car, and I rerouted us out of the Hollywood Hills. We had already lost time, and the sun would soon set. We began to descend to the lower depths, and you asked me to put on a David Bowie record from the 1990s. I asked you if you were okay with all this driving. Are your legs okay?

They're fine. This is just what L.A. is. It's driving.

But it's beautiful, I said, looking out the window at the kind of real estate we would never, not ever, be able to afford. Maybe there would be a way to live here without a car, I ventured.

Jimmy has given up driving, you replied, as the car passed between high slopes of oak trees. Jimmy had told you over lunch that he had sold his car and gotten a membership for a ride sharing app. It was a conscious choice, he had said, to do less damage. To live a more ethical life. This, I thought, did not seem precisely like the direction I had expected Jimmy's life to have moved in. Is he not into cults anymore? I asked.

Oh no, I think he's still into cults, you said, swinging the car around the bend and turning the headlights on, because in the canyon the light was nearly gone. Jimmy had discovered another favorite movement, you said, and it was on that basis he had given away the car. He has also, you told me, stopped wearing shoes.

Over lunch, Jimmy had told you that in 1948 a bearded Christ-like man waited at the stage door of a Los Angeles theater where Nat King Cole was playing, holding sheet music. When at last somebody came outside, the bearded man thrust the papers into the hands of Nat King Cole's valet and fled. Later that week, Cole sat down with the sheet music and found that he loved it. The song was sad and haunting, a song about love, loving, and lessons learned.

Cole sent his people to find the songwriter, and when they did, they found him sleeping on Mount Lee beneath the Hollywood sign. The man's name was eden ahbez. Mostly he slept outdoors and wrote songs, traveling with a sleeping bag and a fruit juicer. He liked to sleep on Mount Lee, he said, because the wind coming in across Los Angeles hit in such a way up there that when ahbez held up one of his handmade flutes, it sounded like nature itself was making music.

Ahbez was a Nature Boy. The Nature Boys, after whom Jimmy now modelled himself, wandered the mountains, grew out their hair, and shunned clothing. Proto-hippies, these men, who thought California could cure them of illnesses both physical and spiritual. Years after you relayed this story of Jimmy's, I remembered ahbez. I learned that, at the end of his life, his wife dead of cancer, his son murdered by the dealers who sold him crystal meth, ahbez walked into a recording studio and said that he wanted to re-record his song. He had come to believe, after all that pain, that a person had to abandon the idea that the world owed anybody love in return. Jimmy had not told you that part of the story, and maybe he never knew it at all.

Two hours to get back down the coast, and we were tired, but we stopped at a Sprouts before heading back to the house. We were due an especially nice meal, you argued, for our efforts. You parked, and then we walked to the queue of trolleys, and each took one for ourselves. Going to the supermarket together was one of my favorite things to do outside the city. Parking a car in the lot and taking a trolley, filling it, and then piling bags into the boot of the car, felt unspeakably extravagant to me, and slightly silly. As though, every time we did it, we were play-acting at being adults. I did not think we would feel like this if we lived anywhere but New York, and sometimes that aspect of the city's unreality was what made me want to leave.

When I caught up with you in the vegetable aisle you had filled the trolley with limes and avocados. Do we want these fun beets? you asked me.

I can do something with them, I said, and kept moving.

You sometimes still grocery shopped like a teenager, forgetting about the building blocks, and collecting instead the luxury and novelty items which never coalesced into a discernable meal. We were forever running out of basic things like salt and onions. At the end of the aisle a display of locally made raw honey ointments stood beneath a larger sign—"Have a healthy day!" Every grocery store we shopped at now wanted us to have a healthy day. Since your mother died you were wary more than ever of pesticides, chemicals, and toxins. I suppose it was natural, to be afraid, because her cancer struck so suddenly, and so confusingly, that there had to be a cause. You had started taking shots of raw ginger and sometimes ate whole bulbs of garlic. When you were high, you'd come home with egg-white puffs and CBD gummies. If it was a problem, it was only that we didn't have the money to eat that way, and it made me more aware than ever of a gulf that had formed between us. Because I tended to think that the more awful thing about her death was that there simply was no explanation. That catastrophe could not be averted, and being good and healthy would not keep a person from illness, and no matter how hard an effort was made the body could simply stop. Nothing would hold it back, and no explanation would alter the inevitable. When I located you and your trolley you were in the snacks aisle, selecting between different types of air-popped popcorn flavored with nutritional yeast. I had a chicken, and things for a salad. I put my hand on your shoulder. Let's go, I said, but you hadn't heard me coming up behind you, and you jumped.

In the morning I descended the staircase from the bedroom upstairs, to find the sky outside the window gray with morning fog. You were already up. I made coffee in the detritus of the meal from the night before—a deep dish speckled with blackened bits of garlic, lemon zest, chicken skin, fun beets. It was soaking in the sink beside the dirty plates and cutlery. Through the window I watched the flowers on the trumpet vine lift in the breeze like a chest inhaling. I could hear you in the room tucked behind the wall where the television was mounted. I was used to those sounds. I knew that behind the door you were laid out on a yoga mat wearing the cotton J.Crew boxers and T-shirt you had slept in. You were lying on the floor with your knees bent, your soles pressed together, your arms away from your sides with your palms pointing up towards the ceiling. You were moving your knees apart from each other, incredibly slowly. You were moving your knees to the point where they would get as close to the floor as it was possible to get, and then bringing them back together again just as slowly. You were waiting until the movement of your legs caught in a place that felt like a record skipping, and when you found it, there you'd stay, slowly moving your legs back and forth over that point, trying to use as few muscles as you could, dropping all the support of the thighs, abdomen, pelvis. You would be trying to release any tension in your neck and feet, breathing through it, breathing deep and loud. You'd stay there until you began to tremor, then to shake. You would twitch. The waves began in your hips. Your face sometimes contorted. Your hands became claws, half-fisted, fingers pointed, grasping in and out around nothing. Your legs would twitch, and this would send convulsions into your torso. This, you had told me, was release. Your trauma was stored in your hips, you said. You had to keep breathing with the tremors. I could not bear to watch you do it. I could hear your breathing, sometimes gasping, very occasionally a deep moaning, and because the walls were thin, I could hear what I thought might be your hands hitting the paint-streaked cement floor, the same floor we had fucked on all those years ago. I watched the coffee drip into the pot, watched the trumpet flowers heave. I moved a hand to my stomach and pressed down. Fifteen days late now. I pressed the home screen of my phone, keyed in my passcode, opened social media, and swiped downwards, double-tapping to heart photographs of lovingly made cocktails, body confident outfits, in-transit images at airports, train stations, roadside gas stations, people traveling home all over America. Captions announcing excitement about the eating of pecan pie, stuffing, and collard greens, and anticipating arguments with relatives. I scrolled, thumbing down. I poured water into the sink and watched the trumpet flowers heave. I heard, at last, the door open behind me, and you came into the room, although I didn't glance back at you at all. I felt your arms around my waist, your head settle on my shoulder, your mouth at my ear.

Happy birthday, baby.

4

A Trip to Rite Aid—Cold Swimming—Empty Strip-Mall Parking Lots—A Couple Half Wheeling and Half Carrying a Stroller—An Unhatching of Russian Dolls—A Lack of Good-Enough Words—The Sea of Cortez—Clarified Apple Juice—Four Pies—Undisturbed Packets of Beans—Fitbit—The Macy's Thanksgiving Day Parade—Elizabeth Bishop—No Coffee Can Wake You—Reminder to Move—A Waltz around the Saguaro—Anthony Bourdain

I was walking through the car park of a strip mall in El Centro when my mother rang. I held my phone in my right hand and could feel the vibration of the incoming call against the skin of my palm, but I let it ring out. She was calling, I imagined, because she had realized she had forgotten about my birthday. The time difference confused her—sometimes it was sixteen hours, sometimes fourteen—and I'd just added another three hours into the mix by flying across the continent, so how was she to keep track? You were getting pizza from a store in between a shop that sold Sketchers and an Advance America Cash Advance, and I had told you that I wanted to duck into the Rite Aid across the way. I was moving quickly across the empty asphalt of the strip mall, boxed in on all sides by squat businesses of a uniform dimension and angle, and which struck me in their sameness as conceivably malevolent. The vibrations stopped just as I got to the big blue awning and walked inside. I knew nothing about El Centro; it was a turnoff on the highway, and you wanted lunch, so here we were. I walked through the makeup and snacks and multivitamins, listening to the last song of *A Charlie Brown Christmas* playing over the sound system, looking out for pink packaging. I snatched a test, then quickly combed Rite Aid for other useful things—a packet of tissues, some hand moisturizer, Advil, a bottle of apple juice—paid, and shoved the lot in my bag, pushing the pregnancy test way down to the bottom below my purse and glasses case and book. I returned my mother's call as I walked to meet you at the car.

I'm sorry, she said, I didn't forget, really I didn't.

I reassured her. We had had a nice day, I said.

You had taken me out to breakfast. Driven me up to Cafe Topes in Carlsbad, where they served cinnamon rolls suffocating in cream cheese frosting. Then to the beach, parking behind a row of vacation rentals, and taking a steep set of stairs down to the sand. I had jumped up and down and swung my arms in circles before stripping to my swimmers and running into the water.

Yes, I told her, it was cold. Maybe fifteen, Celsius. But it was bracing.

They said that it was good for you, to swim in cold water—euphoric, and good for the immune system. I swam out until my feet floated clear off the sand, unable to think of anything, absolutely nothing but my body and the necessity of keeping it moving. Lots of people swim in waters far colder than that, I told my mother. I stood on the beach still dripping for tens of minutes after I'd left the water, looking out across the Pacific towards where I thought Sydney might be, letting the white foam of the waves wash across my feet. I had wondered whether I was homesick, or whether this feeling of birthday unease came from a less straightforward place, a veiled and ruined one. For the rest of the day I shivered under blankets, and mostly read, and mostly slept, and then had been in bed by nine, wearing three jumpers and two pairs of your socks.

We left Encinitas this morning, I said, as I saw you exit the door of the pizza place with both hands full. We're a little north of Mexicali. We can pick up Mexican radio if we want to. We'll be in Phoenix by mid-afternoon.

Is this the first time you'll have been back there since Lynda passed? my mother asked.

It is.

How are you feeling about it?

Oh, it'll be fine.

And Lewis?

He's lovely, I said, as you handed me a slice of pizza on a paper plate, and I mouthed the words "My mum" at you.

He needs to do some work for the Foundation out here, to check in on an artist, or rather, the partner of the artist, over the weekend. So we won't be in Phoenix even that long.

You nodded at what you could hear me saying to my mother and got into the driver's seat.

It will probably be very difficult for him, she was saying.

She said this to me as if I didn't know. As if I weren't already worried.

When I hung up, I opened the passenger-side door and saw that you were eating your pizza and checking messages on your phone. I told you I would eat mine outside, so as not to get grease in the rental. I put the paper plate on the roof of the car and leaned my front against its body, which felt disconcertingly warm and comforting through my clothes. The pizza had small globules of grease pooling in the crevices made by slices of mushroom and green peppers. I did not think I could eat it. It was the middle of the day. The sun was phenomenally bright. Over the roof of the car I looked out to a vista of peach-colored concrete, and lonely, strategically planted palms. It was the trees that gave the empty asphalt a function: car park.

As I stared at the carless spaces, I couldn't help but be reminded of standing in a similarly deserted strip-mall parking lot in Phoenix, earlier in the year. When, two or three days after your mother's death, we had driven to the address of the jeweler where she had, only a week beforehand, taken her engagement ring to be fixed. She had damaged the setting while she had been gardening. It's unclear to me now how she could have possibly been gardening, when she was so sick. But, then again, in the last weeks of her life she found so many urgent tasks to be consumed by, tasks she insisted must be carried out at once, enlisting our aid, demanding our attention, filling up every moment of the day so that neither she, nor you, nor I, nor your father, nor your brother, could quite get a handle on what was happening. How ill she was rapidly becoming. Afterwards, I was shocked that it hadn't been more present, in that last week of life. Shouldn't we, or I, have known she was only a few days away from death? What had all my reading been for if not to be prepared? When the jeweler called your mother's phone, we found the address written in her handwriting by the landline in the kitchen, and we went to collect the ring.

I stood outside by the car while you went in to explain the situation to a man behind the counter. I remember how incredibly cold it was in the shade of the awning, and how warm in the sun when I stepped into it. I stood there waiting for you, pacing a little, looking out across the parking lot, with identical empty car spaces and strategically placed palms. As in El Centro, so in Phoenix. Down Scottsdale Road I could see several other strip malls. I could see signage for a furniture showroom and baby supply store. I watched a couple exit the baby supply store, and half wheel and half carry a new stroller out to their car in the lot, discussing something between themselves. The woman was blond and heavily pregnant. Their car was small, and the stroller wouldn't fit neatly into the boot. Her husband—I assumed her husband—was attempting to fold down the back seats. She was smiling as she looked on. Maybe I was too far away to really see her face, but it seemed to me like she was smiling. I could tell even from all that way across two parking lots and a four-lane road that she loved him, this man who was folding down car seats for her. The kind of love that makes you say *Marry me*, even when you're already married. And in that moment, of one thought turning into the next, I remembered why I was there, pacing in front of a jeweler in a Scottsdale strip mall in the middle of a desert winter. I realized right then—and it hit me with the full force of a cinematic premonition, a flash-forward from the frame of the present moment—that one day you and I would be buying a stroller when I was heavily pregnant, and you would be folding down the back seats, and I would be smiling, unable to help at that stage of advanced pregnancy, and maybe we might even be performing the scene in some place like this one, if we ever left New York, and that when that moment came, there would be an absence. The idea hit me with a sudden queasiness: that the child I knew we would one day have would be without a grandmother. She would just be a story we would tell them. It strikes me now as an odd sort of mourning— grieving a future I didn't know I'd even been so certain of. And yet it was the first thing about her death that struck me as directly, indisputably personal. As though I could feel her reaching inside me, into the future-child which would one day pop out of me, women nesting inside women inside other women like an unhatching of Russian dolls. I felt myself approach the edge of tearfulness. I sank my fingernails into my palms and pressed down until the red shapes of half-moons appeared in the flesh, and that was how you discovered me when you exited the jeweler.

You hugged me, I hugged you, and with your face in my hair you told me the jeweler had said, I'm so sorry for your loss.

It was one of those things that people did say. We had heard it so many times by then, and would hear it many times more. I understood that it was beginning to frustrate you even though you knew it was simply the thing that people say. But it was so polite, and so banal. Where was the howl of rage and pain to equal the thing that you were feeling? Where were the good-enough words? I remember that it was as we broke our hug that you took the ring box out of your jacket pocket and showed it to me.

I don't know what we're meant to do with it now, you said.

Her engagement ring? I asked.

Then you opened the green felt box with the sapphire ring nestled inside it, and you held it out to me so that I could see. Like you were proposing. Do you want it? you asked.

I stepped back and looked you in the eye.

Seriously, you said to my silence. You should take it. Nobody else is going to wear it.

I don't think you expected me to sob. Nor really understood why. But it was the ghostly symbolism of it that made shards of me. The sense that I was being offered the kind of trinket that causes the downfall of the fairy princess in a children's story. The fear of putting on my finger the ring I had seen on hers only a week beforehand. And then, even though it was the week of your grief, not mine, I burst into tears, and you comforted me.

Back on the road the desert seemed obliterated by the bright green, perfectly square fields of alfalfa, lettuce, and sugar beets, all growing on irrigated water. That was all I knew about the Imperial Valley: a lot of agriculture grown on piped-in water, and a lot of prisons. Toxic air, poison dust, a dangerous fungus stirred up by dry winds blowing over turned soil, spores floating through the air and into the lungs of hundreds of thousands of people locked behind razor wire. The land we passed through was flat, dull, long, fifty-one miles to Yuma, 296 to Tucson. It was the closest I had ever been to Mexico. The number plates of cars were nearly all the white of California or the purple of Arizona, but there were some that I'd never seen before, plates from Sonora and Baja California. I was scanning the land out the window, my head swiveling around. What are you looking for? you asked.

Somewhere near here must be where the Colorado River, or what's left of it, passes into Mexico, I said. I could see on the map on the phone in my hand that we were passing north of Mexicali. Won't we see it? you asked.

I think by the time it gets down here, I told you, it's basically a trickle. Or it's all just kind of divided off into canals and ditches to take it to San Diego, or to irrigate all of this lettuce. Is it lettuce?

Looks like lettuce, you agreed.

I looked south across the flat sandy plain speckled by creosote and tried to imagine the land deluged by the River. I had heard of floods before the time of dams which had broken the levees and sent people fleeing in the night to whatever high ground they could find. Houses swept away on the tide. And a former mayor of Yuma, so overcome by panic he collapsed from heart failure while trying to restore order.

Before the River was dammed, it snaked down the border of Arizona and California then crossed into Mexico and kept going, emptying out into the Sea of Cortez at the place where the Baja Peninsula reached down from the continent like an arm bending at the elbow. When the waters of the Colorado were divided up, they recognized the water rights of seven states, but not Mexico. And then, the joke of it was that their math had been wrong—the years used as data points were the wettest since the 1400s. There had never been that much water in the River again. Since the time our parents were children, the River rarely made it to the sea. There was a bridge across the border called the Puente Rio Colorado. Motorists had to pay a toll to cross this bridge over the River, which, when I had once dropped a pin on Google Street View and dragged the cursor to achieve a 360° view, I had found spanned nothing but mesquite and sand.

You know, I said to you, breaking my silence, the Sea of Cortez is where it's meant to go, the River. But it doesn't. So the sea down there is saltier now than it ever was, because there's no fresh water from the Colorado flowing into its mouth anymore. It's hard for anything to survive in all the salt. The vaquita are on the verge of extinction.

What is a vaquita? you asked.

A dolphin, I think. Or a porpoise. Or, actually, I'm not sure what the difference is. They're very small, I remember that much. Very cute.

Like you could give one a hug?

Exactly, I said. I tried to find you a picture, but you couldn't look, you reminded me, as you were driving. Can we get date shakes? I asked.

That does not sound good to me at all, but if you can find a place to get them, we can. It'd probably have to be in Yuma, if you can see somewhere there.

I tapped out of our route and searched the map for date shakes, rerouting us to a farm only a little off the highway. When I looked up, the road was bending around the outskirts of Yuma, and I could have missed it, but I clocked the sign. "Colorado River." It was only a couple of feet across, but there it was.

That's it, that's it! I cried out. Can we stop?

We're in the middle of the highway.

We can't stop?

If you can find me somewhere to pull over, we can stop.

We crossed the state line into Arizona.

You sighed. Well, here we are.

We didn't make it back to the River. Instead, we drove to the date farm at the end of a dirt road, nested between carefully manicured patches of palms. You parked, and I told you that I needed to pee, so I would meet you by the Spanish-style fountain near the doors to the store. I took my bag with me. I found the bathroom, opened the door, walked to a stall, and latched it shut. I sat down. I examined the scratches in the stall door above the bin for used feminine hygiene products. I held my bag in my lap, so that I would be saved from having to rest it on the floor, which was wet with what I assumed was someone else's urine. The walls of the stall were free of any graffiti, any warnings about bad men, confessions of wicked thoughts or sexual infraction, professions of friendship forever. I reached into my bag and felt around for the cardboard shape of the pregnancy test. It felt damp. Everything felt damp, in fact. My glasses case, and my purse. The pages of the right-hand corner of my book had turned wavy. I extracted the book and fanned the pages, catching the smell of clarified apple juice. The bottle had leaked. The test box was wet, as though it would tear if I applied the slightest pressure of my fingernail. How could I possibly get a correct result from a test in a wet box? I thought. It's useless now.

I didn't think it through further than that. The test, of course, would still have been usable. Perhaps, though, that was what I wanted: to continue to suspend myself in the amber of waiting. And after all, hadn't I done my due diligence? Hadn't I tried my best? I stood, pulled my jeans up, flushed, and undid the lock.

I tidied my hair in front of the murky glass of the mirror. I looked pale. I had dark circles under my eyes, although it could have been the poor light reflecting off the grimy cream tiles. When I walked through the door and back out into the garden, you were sitting by the fountain holding a date shake. You handed it to me as I walked towards you. Got you this, you said, and stood up, putting an arm around my waist and kissing me.

Thank you. You didn't get one?

Too sweet, you said, as we turned and walked back to the car.

We drove down the dirt track towards the road that would lead us back to the highway. You know, you said, as though you'd been thinking long and hard, I've always been terrified of what would happen if I ever got lost in the wilderness and had to drink my own piss. I don't know that I could do it.

I laughed. I doubt that it will ever come to that, I said. I shifted in my seat. Another ghost cramp, I thought.

You don't know, you said. Anything could happen.

We passed gradually from unpeopled land into the outer exurbs of Phoenix. In no time at all, saguaros became the dominant feature of the roadside landscape, crowding around the concrete edges of dusty lots trying to return to desert, their branches beckoning upwards to the untrimmed palm trees. On the outskirts of the city where the desert met subdivision we passed a pop-up Christmas-themed amusement park, a banner facing the highway saying, "Elves at Work." The shapes of three reindeer and one Father Christmas, all in outlines constructed out of fairy lights, hung between the ticketing office and the stables.

Look up Pie Snob, you told me. That's where my dad wants us to go to pick up the pies.

Pies plural?

I guess so.

We need more than one pie?

Of course we do.

I rerouted the map to Pie Snob and got us off the freeway. We passed a bail bondsman, a Panda Express, Arthur Murray Dance Studio, Diablo's Mo' Money Pawn—"Arizona's Largest Pawn Shop!"—and then over a canal carrying a foot or so of water somewhere, somehow.

We have to get there before they close at six, you said.

It's four thirty, don't worry.

There's traffic, though.

There's always traffic.

You sighed. This is awful, you said.

I know, I said, and I reached across to put my hand on the back of your neck. We sat idling in traffic on East Indian School Road behind a beaten-up black Nissan, a sticker on the bumper that announced "Self Made" in big silver letters. Do you think he is? I asked.

Oh yeah, you said, real bootstraps kinda guy. I'm sure the system's working out well for him.

See, you can still joke, I said. But your face was a rictus. You were clenching your teeth and looking straight down the road with both hands on the wheel.

All of the weird artificial things here are what feel comforting, you said after a pause.

Huh?

The artificial things.

What do you mean, I asked, as you pulled off into a car park and spun the wheel hard left into a parking space.

The grass and the malls and the palm trees and stuff. All the things that shouldn't be here. The stuff you're always noticing. I just mean that I know that it shouldn't be here. But that it's what's comforting. About being here. Like, it's *that* stuff that feels like home.

We were already unstrapping our seat belts and opening the car doors, and I could see that there was a line of people waiting for their pies. But I felt a crushing sadness about what you had just said. I understood that in some way you were trying to defend yourself from an attack you thought I might make on the city. A defense of whatever sentimentality you might be about to feel, regardless of what you so often said: *This is awful*. And, after all, it made sense. I loved Arizona. I loved it for its beauty and its strangeness and its perseverance despite the sheer impossibility of its continued existence. It felt very far from my home. But it was yours, and there was never any way you could disentangle a whole childhood—first day of school and first lost baby tooth and first kiss and first heartbreak—from the vision of paradise on the brink I was nearly always describing back to you.

Do you know what's been ordered? I asked you.

No clue, you said, pushing open the shop doors. You told the woman behind the counter, once we reached it, that you were picking up an order under the name of Carl.

You're Carl? she asked.

My dad.

Okay, so we got here: one pumpkin, one chocolate pecan, one apple crumb, one caramel apple pecan, that right?

Sure.

We headed back to the car, and I sat with the pies piled on my lap. You didn't need my help directing from there. The sun was dimming. A big moon was already low in the sky as we headed north and then curved left, continuing along the same road as it changed its name and entered Camelback Vista. Convertibles with their tops down sped by. A big desert sunset hung over the road as we drove, smoke-infused, huge, violent, pink, and orange. The red of the mountains redder in the light, and every sidewalk a parade of paloverde, citrus, and oleander, bougainvillea climbing cream- and terracotta-colored facades. We followed your way home. Past the median strips planted with the artificial saguaro that were fitted with speed cameras, conspicuous for being so neat and uninhabited by birds or bats or lizards. Palm trees waving over the canal, past the golf course, and then a left, your street, first house on the right, and we parked by the garage door. It was with your house the way it was with all those houses: nobody but the mailman ever went in through the front.

* * *

I had expected the house might look different without your mother. But it looked, eerily, the same. The cleaners still came once a week, and the landscapers, and that had lent everything a sense of continuity. The only thing that was different was the food. Or rather, the difference was that there had been so little turnover, such that I walked into the pantry that evening at your parents' house and felt there what one might feel in a morgue. It seemed like nothing had been touched. The pickles and relishes, the packets of spices and nuts and dried fruit, they were all exactly the same. I had always loved that pantry—the fact that you could walk inside it, the variety and quality of shelf-stable goods, the sense of comfort and plenty I had from being in the presence of food, which I rarely experienced when actually eating. The woven basket that held the packets of Rancho Gordo beans that your mother received bi-monthly by subscription was exactly as it had been since the winter, and I knew, because I had rifled through them back then, and had thought about taking with me a pack, and then felt that to do so would be pilfering from the dead, and so had put them back right where they were now. Even the jar of jam in the fridge, when I checked, was the same jar of jam—nobody seemed to have touched it since I last spread some on my toast. Your father, I realized, was living off a lot of bagels, a lot of omelets, and ordered-in Italian food. He was treating your mother's collection of heirloom beans much as he was treating her leopard-print nightdress hanging on a wire in the walk-through closet. As relic, as monument.

For that reason, I suggested we get take-out, and you consulted with your father, settling on an order of pizzas and salad before driving to the restaurant to collect it. The three of us sat at the dining table in the open-plan living area, with a space open at the end of the table where your mother might once have sat, but which now operated as an interrupted sightline towards the wall-mounted television, which was playing the Phoenix local news with the volume down, but not off. In between bites of food and pauses filled by the news reports on that year's turkey sales and what we could all expect from tomorrow's Macy's Thanksgiving Day Parade, you caught up: your father's practice (going well), repairs needed on the house (minor, constant), your job (good!), your own art (yeah, okay), our downstairs neighbors (high-strung), and your brother (well, you know what he's like). There was a particular quality to the way you spoke with your father, and the way he had spoken to your mother. You were a family who spoke without ever telling an anecdote. No characters were described, no scenes set, no stories told. It was as though the general feeling among you was that to communicate in stories was gauche, somehow, and fundamentally unserious. Conversation was an exchange of information, ideas, a space for polite debate about current events. Reports on the weather and films watched, restaurants eaten at, chores that needed doing. I sat quietly, still not precisely sure of what I should say to make conversation, but knowing quite well by now what I should not.

There's a letter for you here, your father told you. From Nevada. Did you get a ticket?

You explained that you had. You told him about the speed trap, the cop outside Hoover Dam, that the fine had been knocked down because we were wearing our seat belts.

So you're going to pay it? asked your father. The tone of his voice implied that he was, of course, joking, and he issued a small hoot of laughter like yours, and your mother's. We all knew you would not be paying it.

You know you put over $2,000 on your credit card last month, your father said then.

Oh yeah, sorry, you said conversationally. I got a new desk chair.

Why did you need a new desk chair? You have that one from, what's it called, Design Within Reach?

It was hurting my legs, you explained. The one I got has back support, it's much easier to sit at the desk all day. And we didn't throw out the DWR chair, you hastened to add. Eloise uses it now.

In fact, you had asked me to sell my old, remaindered library chair, with its scuffed legs and paint splatters, in order to take your old one, because your mother had bought it for you, just like most things in our apartment. The library chair had been one of the few things in our apartment that I had bought for myself.

How much is the fine? your father asked.

I'm not sure, you said. Is that okay?

Yeah, sure.

It was the first time that I'd been present when you asked your father for money, and I supposed that it made sense that the request itself was only uttered in so many words, a sort of gesture understood by you both. It was all there in the pivot from one question to another: *How much?* to *Is that okay?*

We had never spoken about what would happen to the way we lived if we no longer had access to your father's money. I said nothing while you spoke about the fine. Instead, I watched the television, where the residents of a Sacramento suburb were putting aside their own Thanksgiving plans to serve meals to the hundreds of refugees from the wildfires, their houses having now burnt to the ground. They're going to be loved on and spoiled, a woman was telling the camera. I put my knife and fork down and poured myself another glass of wine.

When are you leaving? your father asked you.

But it was me who answered. Saturday, I said.

I'm meant to have a meeting, you explained. I have to go see Kenneth Eder.

That's that artist?

His partner.

It's that thing, right? The what's it called? Negative something?

It's called *Negative Capability*, you said.

Your father laughed to himself, very quietly—was it meant to be some bad joke about physics? There was nothing your father found more ridiculous than laypeople who did not display an adequate and logical understanding of scientific principles. You laughed in turn, and so I smiled.

Lawrence Greco named it after an idea of Keats', you explained. Negative capability was a quality that Keats believed the best artists possessed: the ability to stay open to doubt and uncertainty. To be receptive, negative of self, and therefore open to experience. And this was the quality that Greco hoped visitors to the work would develop. It was also a nice pun, you explained, because the process of building the work involved removal more than it did construction. It was sort of like negative digging.

You so wanted your father to understand what was special about Greco, about all the artists that meant so much to you, and which had played such a foundational part in your own self-conception. If you had not loved your father as much as you did, you might have smarted when he responded by saying, But it's just a hole in the ground, right?

You laughed along. Yeah, you said. A really big, and expensive, hole in the ground.

That night, after we'd eaten, you sat on the couch in front of the living room fire, discreetly vaping from the pen in your pocket whenever your father was not looking. The television was turned to a recently released Coen Brothers omnibus, a series of tales on Western themes. I stood washing the dishes. It felt so strange to be watching television. To be suddenly so domestic in this suffocating, open-plan house, after so many days on the road. It was only for a little while, I told myself again.

I plugged the sink and sunk in the wineglasses, the wooden salad servers, the knives too good for the dishwasher, and turned the faucet on. Out came the water. Water that had started as snowmelt in Colorado, slid down the mountains and over state lines. Water that had been brought to a standstill at Lake Powell, then Lake Mead, and then Lake Havasu on the California border, where it was sucked out into a canal. The water was pumped thousands of feet in the air, over mountains and buttes, pushed through tunnels that plowed right through the foundations of sandstone peaks threaded by feldspar and mica, re-emerging out of the darkness and into the sunlight, and finally arriving in the north of the city, where canals and pipes fed it into the suburbs, flowing underground below the roads and houses, beneath the saguaro security cameras and the golf courses, plugged into the house, and out of the tap. 190 miles of travel. It would take over a week just to walk it. I washed the wineglasses and knives, emptied the sink, and then turned the faucet on again, to clean it of soap suds. While I was tipping vinegar into the dishwasher to combat the chalky residue left by hard water—as your mother had taught me—your father came into the kitchen and began fiddling with something in the drawers beneath the bench where the landline telephone sat. Eloise, he called out. Do you want this?

What is it? I wiped my hands on a dish towel and walked over to him.

It's Lynda's Fitbit. He held it up to show me. She didn't have it for long, he said. She got it just before she—

I remembered. I remembered when she'd bought it, four or five months before she died. How she'd told you about it one day on the phone, explaining that it would be useful at the gym when she wanted to keep track of calories burned, and when she went hiking and wanted to maintain her heart rate, or the next time your dad and she went on a cycling vacation, so she could keep track of her pace. I remembered the way it had looked, all black and bulky on your mother's spindly arm when she sent you a photograph. You had told her that sounded like a great idea, and I did not mention what I was thinking, which was that your mother could barely go for a walk around the block with all the chemo she was going through, so when would she possibly be able to make full use of a Fitbit? It seemed too cruel to point it out.

You should have it, your dad said, placing it carefully on the edge of the sink. It still works, and it's just being wasted here. I think the charger is in the drawer.

He turned away to rummage, and so I picked the Fitbit up from where he'd put it down to rest. Here you are, he said, handing me the cord. It's fully charged. He looked down at the gadget in my hands, and a devastatingly sad expression crossed his face. The date and time are still correct, he said.

I thanked him.

Later, when the Coen Brothers film had finished and your father had left for bed and I had cleaned up the last of the dishes, you ate an edible and went to brush your teeth. I sat on the edge of your childhood bed under the shelves which displayed a poster of Louis Armstrong with his trumpet held aloft and the "Lewis Rd" sign you'd stolen from a nearby street corner as a teenager. I listened to the running faucet, and I fiddled with your mother's Fitbit. It was all still there. Records of her steps taken, the pace of her heart, her calories burned. It was all there. All the data of her body. How intimate, how awful, what bizarre things we now leave behind when we're gone. I did not tell you about the data, because you came into the bedroom and smiled at me.

I'm glad you're wearing it, you said.

The Fitbit?

You nodded. You looked at it in my hands, and smiled. It makes me feel close to you, you said.

So I didn't tell you. I put it on. My steps, my heartbeat, my calories, taking up where your mother had left off, adding to the data collection.

The next morning when I got up, the television was broadcasting the Thanksgiving Day Parade to an empty living room. A float bearing a police dog from *PAW Patrol* was followed by a turkey on a float sponsored by Ocean Spray, followed by a reminder that *Mean Girls: The Musical* was coming soon to Broadway. Your father was nowhere to be seen, but it occurred to me that he had become one of those people: someone who left the television on all day, no matter where he was in the house, just so that he wouldn't think about the silence, forget his loneliness.

While I waited for the coffee to drip into the pot, I padded barefoot across the tiles into the sitting room behind the kitchen. I opened the door of a closet, and immediately knew whose books I was looking at. Your mother had often told me how she couldn't take novels seriously. What your mother liked was poetry. I crouched down. I passed over well-thumbed collections by Sharon Olds and Ted Hughes, until I found something that looked so pristine and resolutely unthumbed that I could assume these were volumes she'd never read: books ordered from independent stores in L.A. and Portland, shipped to Phoenix and unboxed, then banished to the closet unread. I didn't want to risk finding a penciled note or a strand of her hair. I took a still-plastic-sealed volume of Elizabeth Bishop, closed the wardrobe door, and walked back to the kitchen as silently as I could, aiming to get out into the yard before your father noticed I was awake. I did not want him to see that I had taken off the Fitbit and slipped it into the pocket of my dressing gown.

I passed the door to the tortoise enclosure and veered to the left, where a lounge chair faced the house and was situated, at that time of the day, in full sun. The lounge chair I'm talking about was the same one I sat and read on every morning during those weeks when your mother was dying. It was the only thing in the house that felt even a little bit like mine. Every morning of those weeks before and after she died, the only time I was ever alone were the minutes and hours before you woke up in the morning, when I could sit on the lounger by your parents' pool and read. I read with an absorption and fervor I'd rarely felt since being a child, because for the time I was reading I was incapable of hearing the thoughts in my own head. And even though it was colder back then, in February, I did not mind being outside, because I was always left alone. For all the work they did in the garden, for all the money they paid the landscapers, I never saw your parents sit in any of the many loungers or chairs, nor saw them swim in the pool, nor bar-becue. And I suppose you followed their lead. Eventually, during the mornings of last February, you would wake up and come to find me out in the yard on my lounge chair, but only to give me a hug and say hello. You would never stay to read on one of the other lounge chairs. But then again, I don't recall you ever reading when your mother was dying.

There was a knock-knock-knocking that sounded from above. I looked upwards to the palm tree growing next door. A woodpecker was gripping the rough bark by its feet.

I felt so foreign, all of a sudden. So absolutely not at home. I wanted, in that moment, the familiar, harsh shriek of a lorikeet or a cockatoo, something that would signal to me that I was in a place where I was legible, and which was legible to me.

The book I had chosen collected previously unpublished drafts and unfinished work written by Elizabeth Bishop before her death, an-notated with explanations by the editor. I read the introduction, then skimmed, reading several poems before happening upon the one that stopped me. It's strange to think of it now. As though the poem I read that morning were some sort of warning, which I should have recog-nized at the time. I suppose it's always easy to see signs everywhere in hindsight. The poem was only short; a longer annotation followed. The poem was concerned with a great tragedy.

The tragedy was this: in the early 1950s, Elizabeth Bishop paid a visit to a landscape designer she'd met once in passing, Lota de Macedo Soares, and discovered that Lota was the love of her life. Bishop moved into Lota's Rio de Janeiro house. There they were, for the most part, happy. Life idled along for over a decade until the prob-lems began. Under pressure from a project on Guanabara Bay, Lota's nerves began to fray. Bishop, in turn, began drinking, and commenced sleeping with a pregnant girl more than thirty years her junior. When Lota found out about the affair she fell apart. She was hospitalized, and Bishop escaped to New York. They wrote to each other. Sometimes

Lota pleaded with Bishop and begged her not to let there be any more secrets between them. Bishop wrote her every day, calling Lota her honeybunch. But she was also afraid. Lota wrote to say that she hoped Elizabeth believed, as she did, if either of them were to lose the other there was no wealth in the world that could make good the loss. Eventually Lota booked a flight to New York. Bishop picked her up at the airport. In Lota's bags were twelve bags of coffee beans and grubby copies of Bishop's own poems, which Lota had been reading on the plane. They had dinner, went home, had two small glasses of Dutch beer, and went to sleep. When Bishop woke at dawn, she found that Lota had taken ten Valium. A short while later, she was dead.

Bishop returned to Brazil but found herself banished by all their friends, who blamed her for Lota's death. She did not help matters by moving in, shortly thereafter, with the girl thirty years her junior and the girl's new baby. Bishop insisted it wasn't her fault. But she couldn't write any new poems. She drank. And eventually she admitted that the past could not be banished. In a letter to a friend, Bishop wrote that she missed Lota more with every passing day. After breaking up with the young girl, Bishop began to plan a sonnet sequence she would write about Lota. She made notes for the work she called "ELEGY poem," composed of different sections, sometimes lyrical and sometimes anecdotal, of Lota's childhood, her skin, her pride, her tiny feet. Bishop would write of her own guilt. The nighttime horrors. And yet when she tried to get it down, she couldn't. Everything she wrote was a jumble, she couldn't get the words right.

And wasn't she responsible? Wasn't it, in the end, her fault?

She struggled on but found that other people had articulated her loss much more precisely than she was able. There was the poet Miguel Hernández, who wrote of wanting to dig up the grave of the beloved and kiss its skull. And there was her friend Robert Lowell, who asked whether, after decades of loving, forgetting was a choice. She tried, for the rest of her sad, sodden life, but Bishop could never bring herself to finish the elegy. The closest she got was a howl of a draft, the one collected in the book.

The poem was called "Aubade and Elegy." In a typewritten litany she wrote of Lota's death as a wave beneath which she was constantly sinking, slashing through the "you" like she couldn't bear to even conjure the second person.

It was a draft full of dirt and hands, "ten" times for the ten fatal Valium. Those twelve bags of coffee in the suitcase. The terror transmuted into endless repetition. There was no amount of coffee in the world that could restore her to life.

There was something about the lack of punctuation, the staccato pace, the ~~you~~, that rendered me blank and shaken. The closest to breathless that I could be while sitting still and reading. The poem seemed to issue from the raw origin of consciousness, where thoughts are never coherent, the fragments before thought.

I read the poem again, trying to get to the bottom of it. Who was erased in that struck-out "your"? Was it the beloved? Or was it the poor husk of the person left behind, rendered suddenly second person? What consolation could Bishop have possibly expected from the poem? The consolation of being alive? A body, drinking water, putting socks on, breaking a fingernail, eating blackberries. Wrecked and shattered, but still sensate. Was that consoling? When I first fell in love with you, I knew for the first time what I was truly capable of feeling—the heights of the pleasure and the depths of the pain. This ability to feel, to me, seemed like the major measure of my humanity. The poem made me imagine, for a moment, the kind of howl I would become if I lost you. The cataclysm. And did I want to be as human as all that?

I sobbed for some time, out there on the lounger, until I began to feel a vibrating in the pocket of my dressing gown. I reached in, thinking it was my phone, before feeling the smooth rubber of the Fitbit's straps. I pulled it out. "Reminder to move," read its screen. I sighed, and looked around the yard at the still, blue swimming pool, and above to the palm tree, where the woodpecker was still knock-knock-knocking. I wiped my eyes and closed the book, strapped the Fitbit around my wrist.

Later that morning, once you were awake, you and I together took the turkey out of the fridge, placed it on the kitchen counter, and prized it open. I remember that you put your hand inside the cavity of the turkey, and out of its insides slipped a block of bloodied ice. You dropped it in the sink, and I watched it melt as I peeled parsnips, chopped carrots, and smashed garlic. You covered the turkey's flesh in butter and thyme, then slotted it into the oven. The house filled with the smell of cooking. Your father drifted in and out of the kitchen like a ghost, washing up, moving a paper or a mug from one surface to another, but never saying much, except that the food smelled good. I did not think he was being rude; I wondered how many years it had been since he had last spent Thanksgiving without Lynda. In the mid-afternoon your brother Brandon arrived, and as the sun was setting, your father's bitterly divorced sister. When it was time for the meal, we ate mostly in silence, while the television whispered quietly on the living room wall, streaming *American Water* from Apple Music, your choice. The four pies sat there on the kitchen counter, pastry crumbling into congealing filling, barely touched. When it came to it, I found I could not stomach any pie.

I didn't realize how much you had been vaping—all day, since we arrived?—until afterwards, when I suggested that you and I go for a walk.

You had been drifting off into other rooms all day, but only as we set out with torches in our hands did I realize how far gone you were. You began to giggle. You were looking up at the bright full moon, which shone over the branches of a saguaro strung in fairy lights across the street.

Are you high? I asked.

Very.

How much did you have?

I don't think that much. Or maybe. But wow, you said, taking my hand. I've been trying to hide it in front of my dad. My shins feel like hands.

You're okay, I said, I have your hands right here.

I giggled. I was not sure whether you were performing your high as I used to perform teenage drunkenness after one Smirnoff Ice, or whether there was in fact something about the strangeness of being home that had sent you more quickly into a peculiar place.

We passed into the windy streets behind your house, walking in the middle of the road, torches shining in front of us because there were few streetlights. I'm glad no one is around, you said, I don't want anyone to see me.

I was taking photographs as we walked: a palm tree bathed in full moonlight. That moon looks like a movie poster, you said, pointing at it.

From which movie?

I don't know.

We passed Christmas decorations and trickling water features in yards, families silhouetted around tables though big windows, eating the same version of the meal we had already consumed. Even without you being as far gone as you were, it would have felt like we were outsiders, delinquents. In the middle of the road the sound of our footsteps took on a weightier dimension. It was not the dark that was unsettling, so much as the things we couldn't see. The scorpion fixed motionless on the gravel drive, the rattlesnake coiled tight behind the pool pump, the hidden water dropping away, the sense that there was everywhere an enormous absence of presence. Eerier was the sound of a strange feline barking, somewhere beyond, or inside, the canal. The odd stillness of the darkness eroded my sense of direction, and I couldn't tell where it was coming from, nor how far away. The effect of all of this can't be understood without being there, neither the loveliness, nor the sense that time had snapped loose from its familiar chronology.

I stopped by a saguaro crowned with a five-pointed star. Do you want to dance? I asked you.

Yes, you cried out, as though you'd been impatient for me to ask.

We waltzed as best we knew how in a circle around the cactus, giggling and breathing hard from the effort. The saguaro hummed a tune, the torches whistled, and in those moments, while we waltzed, I suddenly knew the steps to every dance, and believed that I knew my way back west through the desert to the sea. That finally I had come home. All our friends and family waited for us in every house along the street, and the River ran full and wild beneath the asphalt, as dizzying as it felt when you spun me out, my skirt lifting high at the peak of the twirl, and then falling as you pulled me back.

Wait, you said, suddenly stopping. I have to do something.

You took a step forward into the road and straightened out your arms. You paused for a moment. Then you began to click your fingers, to the left and then the right, like you were a greaser in a 1950s musical. Then you stopped, pivoted, leaned backwards, and waved your arms to the side as though you were possessed by a wave. It was a slow dance, completely silent, and nearly beautiful.

I clapped for you when you finished.

You walked back to me, took my face in both your hands, and kissed me. You're my family, you said.

How did you get so high? I laughed, still not quite sure how seriously to take it.

You looked worried all of a sudden, genuinely so. Am I too much for you? you asked.

I love you, I answered without answering. Who else would I dance in the street with? I said.

We turned and walked back towards the house, the torches lighting the way. Don't let go of my hand, you said as we approached the shadow of the palm tree in the yard next door to your own. Don't let go of my hand. If you let go, I'll feel too far away. I'll disappear.

No you won't, I said. I have you.

When we walked through the back door your father was just finishing doing the dishes, and if he noticed that we were giggling and sweaty he did not say anything. He asked whether you wanted to watch something. You nodded, your eyes set wide, afraid to say a word, I think, in case you began laughing again.

While your father sat in the armchair by the fire, we two settled on the couch. You sat upright for a moment, and then fell towards me, tucking yourself into the fetal position so that your head lay in my lap. Your father asked what we should watch, and I suggested Anthony Bourdain's *Parts Unknown,* which I told him we often watched before bed back in New York. He scrolled through the episodes available on Netflix, before asking whether we'd seen the one about Antarctica.

That sounds good, I said. I wonder what kind of food they have in Antarctica?

I felt you stifle a giggle in my lap. You looked up at me and mouthed, No jokes.

In the episode, the camera panned over vast vistas of sky and ice, horizonless. *It is no short hop to Antarctica, and no easy thing to see it the way it should be seen: the last unfucked-up place on earth,* said Bourdain's voice-over. Despite the snow and ice, the place was technically a desert, *The highest and driest on the planet, a frozen desert holding sixty-one percent of the entire world's fresh water. It looks like nothing lives. You won't see a single plant, a single leaf.* But the ice was on the move, said a glaciologist over dinner. They were trying to formulate a reliable forecast. There was talk of sea level rise. The climate apocalypse. A fetishistic shot of fresh vegetables in a station kitchen. Edamame salad with cranberries and carrots. A meditation on facts, and the crisis of truth. *The world is increasingly hostile to everything you're all about.* Big questions. *Where do we come from? How does it all work? How far can we go? What are we, as sentient humans, capable of? And what, what's on the other side?*

When we turned off the lights in the living room and went to bed, you couldn't even manage to brush your teeth before falling into bed. I undressed, turned off the lights, took off your mother's Fitbit, and got in beside you. You began to giggle. I pulled the duvet up so that it covered our heads, and we were safe there under the blankets, in the darkness. You put your arms around me. Do you think he could tell how high I was? you asked.

No, I said.

It was so hard not to laugh.

About what?

The South Pole, you said, and began to laugh again. I didn't know it was so funny. There's so much ice! It's a desert, but it's also water. It doesn't make sense.

I smoothed your hair over your forehead. Go to sleep, I said.

You turned around and pulled my arm around your waist, big spoon to your small spoon. You love deserts, you said into the dark of the bedroom. And you love water too. So it's like it's for you. It's all for you.

5

Boys on Motor Scooters—Angel Food Cake—The Watching of Gentle Television—A Badly Made Cheese Crisp—A 1989 Cabernet Sauvignon Gone Bad—A Goodbye—Broken Earrings—Lilies in a Vase—A View of the Continent—Lightning—A Cry like a Baby Mountain Lion—Dinner in Old Town Scottsdale—Nightshades—A Phase Angle of Two Point Five—Barry Goldwater's House—The Loss of a Nintendo & Noise-Cancelling Headphones—Wattle Tree

W e passed an AZ-Tex Hats selling boots and Stetsons, a See's Candy, then an illustrated cowboy holding a lasso up high around the words, "Welcome to Old Town Scottsdale." This is awful, you said.

We had just driven past a man on the street dressed as an Elvis impersonator. He had the same black quiff of hair as Elvis, the same kind of swagger and bell-bottomed trousers, but strapped around his waist was a black support brace.

On the radio the headline story was what to do if you had a Mexican vacation planned but were worried about the border being closed. *Have a different route planned, and make sure you have all the right travel documents*, they advised, but don't go so far as to cancel. *If you're a citizen, you'll be A-okay*. Fleetwood Mac was playing next week at Talking Stick Resort Arena, *only a few tickets still available, get them while you can*. A syphilis outbreak was sweeping the state. ICE was abandoning undocumented immigrants at the Greyhound bus station in Phoenix and driving away. Churches and volunteer groups had stepped in to provide housing for the immigrants and were pleading with the public for more help. A black Labrador named Max who had disappeared in 2013 had been found in a local car park; a lesson, the radio said, in the importance of microchipping your pets, because the dog had since been returned to her owner. *Broga! It's yoga for the boys.*

We passed a jewelry store called Crazy Horse, where a group of retirement-age people had stopped to stare at the turquoise bracelets in the windows. They loitered under the awning dressed in outfits of beige and cream, in golf shirts and linen, boat shoes and cork wedges.

Everyone we had passed was, without exception, white. They're all so old, you said.

Those two aren't, I said, and pointed to a pair of teenagers racing along the edge of the road on rental motor scooters. They dodged and swerved fluidly around motorists, pedestrians, and parked cars.

I fucking hate everyone, you said, and gestured to the teenagers. Especially them.

Like, fuck your joy, so much, you shouted.

The windows were up. In the car, only I could hear you. At the bottom of the ramp into the parking garage, we could see the boys cruising towards the elevators. I bet there's a fucking app or something, you said.

Probably down here is where they have a station for the scooters, I said, scanning the rows of parked cars to try and find you an empty spot.

I hate this place, you said.

We had already spent hours in the car that day, driving out to the arboretum near Superior with your father. The photographs I took at the arboretum are nearly all of the small signs behind the plants describing their scientific names, common names, and natural habitats. The saguaros are endangered because they're fertilized by bats who are dying off. A jumping cholla is a nuisance because the arms fall off and the needles will go straight through your shoes. Cottonwoods always grow near water. You took one photograph of me that day using my phone. I'm wearing a big red cardigan from the 1980s, a scarf in my hair, a tote bag from the *Los Angeles Review of Books* over my shoulder. I'm standing next to a sign that reads, "Australia in Arizona? Absolutely!" and pulling a skeptical face. Behind me there's a pittosporum. You can see the groove in my teeth I'd carved from grinding in my sleep.

We were meeting your brother at an organic restaurant at half past six. Brandon wanted to eat early, you had told me, because he said that it was important that he had enough time to digest his meal before he slept. The restaurant advertised itself as serving exclusively healthy food, to complement an anti-inflammatory diet. They printed the calorie content of the meal on the menu. I had already looked online and knew I would be having the Tuscan Kale Salad (350 cal). My understanding was that your brother had been into this kind of thing for a few years. What "that kind of thing" was, was amorphous. Mostly what I knew was that your brother spent a lot of time at the gym.

When we were first dating and you told me about Brandon, you'd said that he lived alone, and that when he wasn't at work he was working out. He was an assistant real estate agent and sold protein supplements on the side. You told me that he would come home on weekends and close the door of his air-conditioned house and turn on his video game console, and sit there playing, regardless of season, weather, or incident, from Friday morning until the end of the weekend. Sometimes, when you had visited, you had gone over to his house and heard him, through the parchment-thin door, swearing over the gunshots. Once you told me you had not heard the video game, but instead the song "Don't Speak" by No Doubt playing very loud, your brother singing along in a voice that was both doleful and remarkably good. You told me you thought that perhaps this is what happened when a man stayed single, in the same city he'd been born in, lacking curiosity or ambition.

But I had noticed the evening before that he seemed to have attained a new kind of upbeat glow since we had seen him last, which I thought was curious for a son still in mourning. Judging from the enormous size of his arms and thighs, his gym attendance had accelerated dramatically. The previous day at Thanksgiving dinner he had eaten only dry turkey breast, and had left after an hour.

"Rockin' Around the Christmas Tree" played on a recessed speaker in the arcade into which the elevator let out. The sunset was wildfire red. That morning when I checked the *Guardian*, I had read that the smoke from the fires had spread all the way to New York. There was a very slight burning smell, they said, and asthmatics in all five boroughs were encouraged to stay indoors. You dawdled two steps behind me, texting your brother, trying both to figure out where he was vis-a-vis the restaurant, and to figure out where the restaurant was vis-a-vis our location. I think it's going to be bad, you said.

Seeing your brother will be bad?

No, the restaurant. They put edamame in the guacamole. Hang on, I'm calling Brandon.

While you called your brother, I walked further into the green, towards the water feature at its center. But when I got closer, I saw that there was a blue sign nailed to a pale-pink adobe bench, which said, *Due to water conservation and budget efficiency initiatives this water feature is no longer operational. The City of Scottsdale Parks and Recreation Department appreciates your consideration and support.* Nearby, a man and a little girl were throwing a Frisbee to a dog. The dog, a sandy-colored rottweiler, darted between Frisbee and owner, throbbing with pleasure. The little girl threw the Frisbee, missing her aim, and shouted, Max, bring it back! Max bolted. I remembered that first night in Las Vegas, standing outside the restaurant on Fremont, and hearing the woman across the street call out. I remembered the way she had frozen in that intake of breath, that caesura between wondering and knowing, and the sound she had made before she began to run. Max ran back with the Frisbee in his mouth, and the little girl lifted onto the balls of her feet, grinning. Good boy, Max, she said, and patted him soundly on the head.

Come on, you called out to me, he's running late but it isn't far. He's coming from the gym.

The big one your mother went to? The one with the juice bar and the Olympic-sized pool?

It's not *that* big for Phoenix, but yeah.

We walked towards Stetson Drive and crossed the road, passing stores selling kachina dolls and pottery, a children's party center, a clothing store selling cactus-themed candles and doormats, everything still open and ready for Friday evening business. We passed Cartel. We passed the store with the dream catchers hanging from the awning. It was all so familiar. It was like rewinding old videotape and pressing play. Like reliving those days when your mother was dying, and we had come to this stretch of shops in Old Town Scottsdale every day, parking outside Cartel to buy a single matcha latte with vanilla syrup. When your mother was dying, she liked to eat only three things. She liked those matcha lattes from Cartel, she liked the angel food cake they sold at Sprouts, and she liked broccoli and cheddar soup from Panera Bread. When we had last been in Phoenix, I remember knowing things were bad when nobody picked us up from Sky Harbor; we took a cab from the airport through thin February rain. When we arrived at the house we came in through the garage, dragging our roller bags up over the door ledge and into the kitchen. Your mother was sitting at the dining table facing us, as though she were waiting. Her completely bald head was covered in a baseball cap. You had prepared me for that, had told me that she had texted about her decision to shave off what was left of her hair.

She gestured to her head. It looks good on me, huh? she said.

Then her face collapsed into tears, and she began to cry.

We hadn't even said hello.

I felt that I should go to her, hug her, do something, but I was not sure what my role was in this house, in this family. I looked to you for direction. You were stock-still, staring at your mother. You looked petrified. But when you spoke you betrayed none of what your face had suggested.

I think it looks pretty good, you told her, and then you issued a hoot of a laugh, exactly like hers.

Then she got up from the table and walked quickly into the back of the house, past the Yayoi Kusama cushion display in the sitting room, and down the corridor to her bedroom, as though she had forgotten something. From behind, I could see for the first time how small she'd become. How birdlike her bones. She disappeared and did not come back. We were still standing there beside the kitchen counter with our roller bags.

We set about being useful. You drove and did chores. And she had so many chores that needed doing. She wanted the laundry done, she wanted a planter moved, she wanted a picture framed, she wanted to get the oil changed on the car. You laundered, you moved the planter, you drove to the framers, you drove to the mechanic. When Brandon came over, the two of you set up a hammock in the yard, replaced the gas cannisters in the barbecue, and drove your mother to the jeweler, and Costco, and Home Depot. She had elaborate plans for renovating Brandon's kitchen, and wanted the yard completely rearranged.

I took responsibility for the food, and for cleaning. I made muffins. I tossed salads. I roasted chicken. I washed dishes. I cleaned surfaces. I swept. For the first and then the second night of our stay she sat with us at the dinner table in the evening, her baseball cap low over her eyes. The television on the wall was always on, playing something that nobody ever watched. Whatever it was that I had prepared—and there was always a lot, whatever she had suggested might interest her, shrimp risottos and chicken dumpling soup and Irish stew—she'd have a few bites and then say it didn't taste right. Not that she couldn't eat it, but that in fact there was something wrong with the food. The list of things that tasted right grew smaller and smaller, and so we made trips to buy whatever she asked for, for the broccoli cheddar soup and the angel food cake and the matcha lattes. On the third night she did not want to come out. She wanted to stay in bed. She never ate dinner with us again.

Sometimes she might wander into the kitchen, silent and conspiratorial, taking a scoop out of the Sprouts box of angel food cake with her papery fingers before drifting back down the hallway to bed. The fridge was filled with half-eaten broccoli cheddar soups, half-drunk orange juices, and dried-up English muffins on plates, one solitary bite missing from their corn flour–caked edges, around which I had to find space to store leftovers. Never throwing away her muffins or half-drunk juice because the sense was that they should remain there, in perpetuity, in case she wanted them.

I mentioned nothing. I tried to move through the house invisibly and silently. I had a horror of being in the way, of being a bother of any kind. Because my role, whatever it was, was to be helpful, and need nothing.

In the evenings when we were in bed you perched a laptop on either one of our bellies and we watched gentle television where people were nice to one another, and only good things happened. This was often the only time, in those weeks, that I remember you crying. When a particularly challenging cake had been pulled off. When a man in Georgia had been encouraged to love himself. When a fish dinner had been cooked for a whole Dorset village. I'd look over and see the tears welling up and put my arms around you while they trickled down your face. When the show was over, we would close the laptop and lower it to the floor, and you would turn over on your side. Hug me, you would ask, in a small, plaintive voice. And I would. I would hug you, big spoon to your little one, until you were breathing deeply. You fell asleep under the influence of ZzzQuil syrup or a dropper full of melatonin. You could not sleep without them. I can't remember, now, how I was sleeping then.

It was during that week that I began sitting on the lounge chair by the pool in the mornings, with the wind chimes tinkling in the paloverde and a cup of coffee balanced on my stomach, reading dense theoretical books on the fallacy of the human-nature dichotomy, and books that coined compounds like "thing-power," or had subtitles like "Philosophy and Ecology after the End of the World." Once, your father came out into the yard and hurried over to the lounge chair, addressing me in the most desperate tone I'd at that stage heard him use. Do you know how to make a cheese crisp? he asked.

What's a cheese crisp?

He laughed bitterly, and then shook his head. Welcome to the Southwest, he said.

I found out, when I looked up a recipe, that a cheese crisp was a flour tortilla grilled with butter and cheddar cheese. That was what she said she wanted. Your father had made one for your mother in the toaster oven, delivered it to her in bed, and she had spat out the single bite she had taken right onto the back of his hand. He hadn't made it right, she had said, and he needed to do it again. But your father said that he didn't know how to do it any differently; he thought maybe I would know how. All she wants, your father said, is a cheese crisp.

Your father, I could tell, was making every effort to appear cheerful, and the effort was taking every ounce of will that he possessed. One evening as I was preparing dinner, he told us that when you'd been born, your parents had bought a particularly good and expensive bottle of wine to commemorate it. They'd been saving it for a special occasion.

We should have drunk it when you got married, he said. But I guess you didn't have a wedding. I'll see if Lynda wants some. He disappeared into the sickroom and came back with his shoulders slumped. She didn't want any.

Let's open it anyway, your father said. It was a 1989 cabernet sauvignon, from the Gundlach Bundschu Winery in Sonoma. He used the electric bottle opener to uncork it. The cork emerged crumbly and damp from the green glass bottle. I'd never drunk wine that old, and so I wondered perhaps if that's what happened to cork over time. But when he poured it into glasses, toasted us, and I drank, I knew immediately that the wine had gone bad. I looked at you, for your reaction. Your face was expressionless. So was your father's. The three of us sipped the vinegary wine and sat down to dinner, finishing the bottle without any of us ever mentioning the taste.

We established, a few days before we were due to leave, that you would not be taking the return flight back to New York with me. You would be staying. But I had classes, and I could only miss so many. That you were staying in Phoenix was the only way we really had of acknowledging that her days were numbered. She must have known it as much as we did. I remember that the day before I left we drove her to her doctor's appointment, and how odd it was that she sat in the back seat of the Suburban while I sat beside you in the front, as though in that arrangement we were asserting that her place in the car-seat pecking order had been diminished, that she no longer had the authority of an adult woman, but had been rendered weak, or a child. She had already, by then, begun to wheeze, but we didn't notice. It is hard to believe that we didn't notice, neither the strange sounds she was making, nor that she was having trouble breathing. If the doctor noticed, he said nothing to us, instead shaking your hand when she introduced us in the waiting room. This is my youngest son, Lewis, she said, and his wife, Eloise.

The doctor asked us whether we were in town for long.

They're flying back to New York tomorrow, Lynda said.

Eloise is, you said to the doctor, but I'm going to stay for a while.

No you're not, Lynda said. Don't be stupid. There was an uncomfortable silence before she said, again, You're going back to New York. I'm fine. I don't need you here. You're just wasting your time.

We'll talk about it later, you said.

We got back in the car, and I remember using the side mirror to look at your mother in the back seat, tiny in her big puffer jacket, looking out the window as the February desert rain drizzled over the city. She issued directions without looking at you: drive to Costco for gas, it was cheaper there with the membership. It was out of the way, and there was a long queue of cars waiting for the pumps when we got there. Never let the gas tank get below half full, your mother chastised from the back seat. It was the last piece of advice she gave you.

The next day I went, for the first and only time when she was still alive, into your parents' bedroom. You were outside, putting my bag into the boot of the car, the flight leaving in two hours. She got up when I knocked at the side of the door. I was taken aback. The sour smell. The sweaty sensation of the air. The leopard-print linens on the king-sized bed conjuring sleaze, sex, and the unsettling sight of your mother rising up from them, her hairless head and the bird-bones of her wrist where the bulky Fitbit was fastened. Eloise, she said. She'd never before said my name with so much emotion, or affection. Then she began to cry. She was wearing sweatpants and a long-sleeved top that swam around her collarbone. She put her arms out to me, and I put my arms out to her. Her head was stubbled with fine white hairs which brushed my jawbone as I lowered my head. I have never felt another adult so fragile, so tiny in my arms. She only came up to my chin.

Thank you so much for coming, she said to me through tears. I'm so sorry, she said, and again, I'm sorry.

It's okay, I said to her, afraid of hugging her too tight lest I cause irreparable damage. She was breathing heavily, and the tears streamed down her cheeks. I'll see you soon, I said. Don't cry. I'll see you very soon.

I was a coward.

Shouldn't I have taken the moment to speak? Promised her all the things you promise the dead? Said, I will keep him safe. Said, I'll look after him. Said, I'll take good care. I promise you.

I let go of her, abandoning her while she was still crying, by the leopard-print bedclothes in the sour, damp room. To where you were waiting by the car, to drive me to the airport where I would imminently be leaving you behind to face all of this alone.

At Sky Harbor I progressed slowly up the escalator towards the Delta check-in counter, and then fumbled towards security. I stood in line to put my bag on the belt, and at the moment that it became obvious to do so I took my shoes off, unsheathed my laptop from its case, emptied my pockets of coins and phone. I felt around my person for anything that might set the metal detector off—earrings, belt buckle. I took them off and placed them on top of my folded winter coat in the plastic bin. Off they went down the conveyor belt into the X-ray. When the TSA agent on the other side of the scanner motioned with his fingers I stepped through, put my feet in the foot-shaped spaces, held my hands over my head, waiting until I was cleared to move forward. I looked to the left to see the scanner's screen update, with a red patch highlighted right between my legs. I was invited to step to the side while they procured a female security guard. The woman was forceful, her hands working up into my crotch and instructing me not to move, as though I were squirming deliberately, just to spite her. I kept my eyes ahead on the belt, where other passengers who did not have red patches between their legs were collecting their things. You can leave, she finally said. I went quickly to the plastic tubs. I put laptop back inside laptop case, and belt back around my waist. One earring was in the tub on top of my coat, but one was not. I checked the tub, looked down at my shoes, and then further along the ground, back towards the start of the belt. The earring was in pieces, glinting gold beneath the X-ray. The rolling cylinders of the conveyor belt it had fallen through had destroyed it. I got down on my knees.

Hey, what are you doing? a security guard shouted in alarm. Heads turned. I stood up.

My earring, I said, it's broken.

I'm sure it can be fixed, the guard said, standing beside me now.

Then I burst into tears. It was my mother-in-law's earring, I lied to him. She's dying. She has cancer. And she gave me these earrings. They can't be replaced. They can't be fixed. I began to sob.

The guard looked stricken. Is there anything I can do? he asked.

Nothing can be done, I sobbed. I walked away, the pieces of my earring in my hand.

I could not have told you why I lied. The earrings weren't your mother's. They were large 1970s-era hoops I had bought myself from Etsy. They were nothing like any jewelry I had ever seen your mother wear. But the lie felt right, and I let myself sob. They couldn't be replaced. Nothing could be done.

* * *

In the morning you messaged me. You had woken up early, you said. Your mother was asleep. Earlier, she had asked for an English muffin and orange juice. You'd made it for her, but she said it tasted wrong. Now, you were going to do laundry. I looked out the window of our Brooklyn apartment at the storm-tossed trees and decided not to go to class. Instead, I cleaned the bathroom. Then I worked systematically, cleaning kitchen, living room, office, bedroom. I mucked out the oven, scrubbed mold from the grouting between the tiles in the shower, and pulled all the shelves from the refrigerator to disinfect and wash them in the sink. When there was nothing left to clean, I transferred money from my Australian savings account to my American checking account, left the apartment, and went to the grocery store— the extravagant one on Manhattan Avenue—and returned home with $200 worth of things: Lebanese tahini and date syrup, kimchi, crispy chili in oil, the finest grade maple syrup from Vermont, organic udon noodles from a factory in suburban Ballarat, thick pappardelle from Puglia, fresh berries, coffee beans, kale, fennel, and bright red tomatoes. I bought lilies and put them in a vase on the table in the living room. When the light began to fade, I took the red cast-iron pot from its cupboard and put it on the stove. I chopped vegetables. I cracked the kitchen window open, and through the crack I could hear the wind rattle the naked branches of the maple tree in the yard below, a horn blowing from a boat on the East River, ragtime jazz being played at the restaurant on the corner. I stood at the stove, barefoot in my tights, stirring. Rice, wine, butter, onion. Tomatoes and zucchini and cheese. The smell of the cooking food mingled with the lavender of the cleaning products and the lilies in the vase on the table in the living room. Everything was in order, everything still. The plates were stacked in order of size, the glasses were nested inside others of their own kind, the spoons and forks and knives all had their places. I fell asleep early, soundly. So soundly I didn't hear the vibration of my phone when your messages came in.

Your father had awakened you in the middle of the night, your messages said when I read them in the morning. You said that he shook you awake and told you that your mother was not breathing. You drove her to the hospital, where they looked her over in emergency and determined that your mother, dying of cancer, had contracted pneumonia. I responded as soon as I read the messages. And you wrote me right back. You said she had just been moved into her own room. You had called Brandon, and you were waiting for him to arrive. You said she was attached to machines. She wasn't speaking, but she was making sounds. I tried to slow you down, to soothe you. I told you that I loved you.

I'm here. You'll be okay.

I kept messaging as I got out of bed and walked into the spotless kitchen to grind beans, brew the coffee, spread butter on toast. I carried them with me to the chair by the window in our bedroom. It was quiet, a clear, cold morning, and across the street I could see a rugged-up man and a heavily pregnant woman pushing a stroller down the sidewalk.

You said, She's dying.

I know, baby, I said.

I had thought in that moment—when you were looking at her tiny body attached to monitors in a hospital room—that you had finally realized what the end of the story would be. But I was wrong. The end was already here.

She's dead, you replied.

I flew back to Phoenix six hours later. I left a key under the plant by the front door for a friend. Take all the food you want, I told her, there's lots. I knew the lilies would rot, so I threw them in the trash. I filled the bag I'd just unpacked and arrived at JFK for the flight at four. The plane climbed up over the water, nosed south, and then turned west into the waning sun. I sat by the window and watched as New Jersey became Pennsylvania became Ohio and Indiana. The land below was endless towns and suburbs, small and less small cities, chemical plants and industrial farms, warehouses and logistics centers. The woods were the bleached brown of winter, the grasslands yellow, snow-speckled. America lay fallow. The setting sun caught the snow, tinging its outline red and gold, and as the cars turned on their head-lights, I could see them flowing down the highways, along all those roads bisecting the land like a vast circuitry of veins. I saw tractors stalled in fields, and it was impossible to tell for how long they had been idling, whether moments or many months, or whether they were an ancient artifact waiting for examination by some future civilization. I could not see a single human being. Only the things they had made. I could see the cities they lived in, the lights that illuminated their windows and roadways, the pumps and cylinders, pools and drums of their industry, the cars in which they moved. But no people. Their presence extended across the face of the continent, into Illinois and then bending south over the Missouri line, connected by networks that extended far beyond what I could see, to mines in South Africa and Mongolia, to cargo ships cruising across the Atlantic, to the dis-orientation of the shearwaters and the plastic bottlecaps in the belly of the whale, to the uncontrollable division of cells beginning to grow, metastasizing, breaking loose and entering the bloodstream. The dark came in and the threads of light grew fewer as the plane crossed the hundredth meridian into the West. Somewhere near there, over a cor-ner of Kansas or Colorado, or maybe the Oklahoma panhandle, we encountered a storm. The plane flew smooth and untroubled, but up ahead I saw a flash of light, and then another. It was a lightning storm, and we were heading right towards it. I had never been eye level with lightning at its origins. I thought I could perhaps make out the top of the bolts, could see them long and deadly in their fullness as they struck towards the earth. I repeated your name like a litany to myself, under my breath, as though it might protect me. As we approached, the plane rose higher, gained altitude, and we passed clean over the storm. It must have raged beneath us, made children whimper and caused dogs to bark down below, but from the vantage point of the plane it didn't make a difference.

You were there with your father to pick me up outside the arrivals door at Sky Harbor. You were in the driver's seat, so it was your father who got out to help me put my bag in the boot of the Suburban. The first thing he did was hug me.

Thank you for coming, he said into my ear.

I am certain, though I can't be sure, that it was the first time your father touched me.

I'm so sorry, I said.

A few days later when we were at the funeral home, trying to make a decision about what arrangements should be made—she'd left no instructions—I sat alone with your father across the table from the funeral director. He was being presented with a folder filled with pictures of coffins in laminated plastic sleeves.

What does a nice coffin look like? he asked, issuing a small hoot of laughter. A moment later he began crying. You were outside, in the parking lot. It was just me and your father and the funeral director, and when he broke down, I reached across and put my arm around him, just as I always did with you. I didn't say it was okay, I didn't say anything. I already knew there was nothing to say. I just held my arm around him, steady. Your father, tear-stained, reached up to touch my hand, and brushed against your mother's engagement ring on my wedding finger. He took hold of my wrist. And he just held on. By the time you'd come back, he'd composed himself. I don't think I ever told you.

When we got back to the house it was dinnertime, but nobody spoke of dinner. You and I went into your childhood bedroom and closed the door. Without speaking we lay on the bed. I was big spoon to your small spoon. You began shaking before the sobbing started. I felt the shaking all through my own body. I held you as tightly as I could. I curled my head against your shoulder. You sobbed and shook and shouted, a ravaged animal sound I had never heard before. Like a baby mountain lion, or the last thylacine. I held you tighter. Then you turned around, quite suddenly, towards me, and put your arms around me. You listed, so that soon I was beneath you, supporting your weight, constricted by it. You hid your face in my hair. The hair muffled the sobs. I kept my arms tight around you. I stroked your back, my lips pressed into your shoulder in one limitless kiss. I didn't say a word. I remember that outside the window I could see the garden lights, hear the wind chime tinkling in the paloverde. It was cold. I wondered what we were to do now.

When we got to the restaurant that night after Thanksgiving, Brandon was already at the entrance, asking for a table for three. Brandon had never had a girlfriend in the time you and I had been together. He didn't want to be tied down, he said. As ever, he was wearing shorts. He had a thick, trimmed beard which covered teenage acne scars. His facial hair was of the same texture as yours, but his was a dark blond instead of brown. His father's background was Scots Irish, whereas yours was the son of Lithuanian Jews, and it was in this way, despite your physical similarity, that the difference first showed. We were escorted to a table in the middle of the room, the fourth place cleared, and offered a drinks menu. Your brother wasn't drinking, but I was. And that in itself, I suppose, was a choice: to continue to live suspended in the amber of waiting, the caesura between the intake of breath and whatever came next.

I sipped my wine while the two of you caught up. It was the first evening that you'd spent real time with him since your mother's funeral. How was he doing?

Amazing, man, amazing. Kitchen's getting renovated, which is a nightmare, but going to be great in the end. I got this awesome water filtration system installed the other week. It's going to save me so much money. This system, it's a hybrid system so it softens the water as well as taking out all the shit the government puts in. Arsenic. Mercury. Cost me a bomb but it's worth it.

Your brother said he was trying to diversify some of his assets. The protein supplement game was over. He had invested in Bitcoin, but he was also interested in more cutting-edge stuff. It troubled him that the monetary system, as he saw it, was built on life insurance. We have a monetary system built on death, he said, which is, obviously, fueled by fear. And guilt. If we let go of all of that, we can create a new monetary system that's built on life. Because we now know, scientists know, that the biggest, most resilient form of energy on the planet is biology. It's us. So what we need is a biologically backed currency.

I don't think either of us had heard him speak like that before. He seemed to glow from within with a kind of contentment and certainty. I drank a second glass of wine. Brandon wanted sustainably sourced salmon, but no nightshades. He wasn't doing nightshades.

What's a nightshade? you asked your brother.

I jumped in. They're, like, tomatoes, peppers, eggplants, potatoes. They all have alkaloids in them, and they might cause inflammation, I said.

You raised an eyebrow at me but said nothing more.

It's not bullshit, said your brother, clocking your eyebrow. There's so much about plants we don't understand. Did you know that plants love music? If you play a tree Mozart or, like, Steely Dan, it's going to be a happy tree. They have an energy field just like our energy field. But that's why we have to treat them with respect, you know. The government puts all these gene-editing tools into our vegetables, and antibiotics in meat, and it's so bad for our energy, for our gut health, for our immunity. Think about how much of that garbage Mom had over the course of her life. No wonder she got sick.

The salmon arrived, with your poke burger, and my Tuscan kale salad. While we ate, Brandon asked us about our trip. Why, exactly, were we going to keep driving, and all the way back to Vegas at that?

Eloise is studying the Colorado River for her dissertation. We're visiting some of it.

Oh, really? You know a lot about it? Brandon asked me. He asked with the skepticism of somebody who supposed I wouldn't know what the hell I was talking about.

I'm trying to learn, I said.

About what?

Well, one thing I'm interested in is the fact that the River was apportioned out to all these states, with the expectation that there'd be enough water. But there never was enough water, not even when they allocated the water back in the 1920s. So now every year there's a greater need for water as cities like Phoenix and Vegas expand and farms keep growing, but there's less actual water to go around. With climate change. There's less water every year. It's like the Southwest is a paradise built on quicksand.

Brandon nodded. Well, I'll give you this, Vegas is insane, it just should not exist, it should be left to disappear into the desert. But, like, Phoenix is fine. Because there's the Salt River, and the aquifer is full—

Actually, I interjected, but the waitress was bringing my third glass of wine and Brandon carried on.

The thing is, the water in the Colorado belongs to Arizona, he said. There was a battle when I was a kid, you know, because California and Nevada were trying to take our water. Goldwater was amazing, you know who Goldwater was? Such a great guy, I met him once. Goldwater went to Washington, and he fought, and he got us our water. So, sure, maybe back in the 1920s there might not have been enough water, like you say, but there's nothing to worry about now.

You met Goldwater? you asked him. I never knew you met Goldwater.

Yeah. His house is real close to Mom's, you know?

Is it? I knew it was in Camelback Vista.

Yeah, it's like, so you know when you're driving towards the gym? You go the other way, and you take a left, and then there's this other road off to the right at the top of the hill, and there's a dead end. At the end is Goldwater's house. I went over there once when I was working for this caterer in college. Really nice house. Great guy.

It was only indirectly, towards the end of the meal when the check had been requested, that the two of you spoke in any way about your mother.

It really woke me up in February when Mom died, your brother said. That's why I've been working out so much, looking out for my health. You know about phase angles? I'm trying to get mine tested. It measures how healthy you are. A healthy body measures out at between ten and thirteen. The thing I found out is that cancer always occurs at around four to five, and death occurs at two point five. There is no disease that has ever been able to attack and conquer a healthy human cell. You don't get disease with a phase angle of thirteen. If you're at thirteen, and I wish I knew this when Mom got sick, I wish I could have told her, then you're so resilient that you can repair faster than any disease can even imagine itself. You're really in the quantum state of energy at that point, where repair is instantaneous because it's all built around the coherent waveform of energy.

You think Mom would have got better? you asked him.

I don't know. I think maybe. I just know that now, right, I feel like I could fight anything. Nothing can touch me. Like, *I'm* alive right now. Humankind may decay, the earth may collapse into a sixth great extinction event, or whatever, but *I'm* alive right now. And I am going to participate in that. I'm not going to be dragged down by this, I mean, this intense fear and guilt paradigm.

As he said this your brother looked at me, as though it were me who was the engineer of this vibe-killing paradigm.

Outside the restaurant the sprinklers had turned on and young men in polo shirts were weaving in packs down the street. We lingered there. Your brother seemed to want to stay with you. Hey man, did I ever tell you about the time that I hung out with Sugar Ray? They were in Phoenix doing a show, in, like, '97, '96, and they had a free night when they were just going to crash. I found out because my buddy Jason was helping them load their gear after the show. And we said, come see Phoenix! Phoenix is a great city, come hang out with us. And they did, man! They came over to Jason's, and a bunch of us went over, and we sat in the garage and just, like, jammed all night. They were such nice guys, such, such nice guys. And you know they said it was one of the best nights they'd had on tour, because they just got to chill.

I think I've heard that story about Brandon meeting Sugar Ray like fifty-nine times, you said in the car.

Do you think he believes what he says? I asked you.

About the health stuff? I don't know, you said. You were silent for a moment as we took a left onto Scottsdale Road. When you spoke again, you sounded frustrated. Every time he talks, you said, what I hear him saying, what he's really trying not to say, is that it doesn't matter how healthy you eat, or how much you work out, it's all just senseless. You'll just get cancer, and you'll die.

Do you think that too?

Oh, I don't know.

On the way back to your father's house you suggested going the other way, up to the top of the hill.

To see Goldwater's house?

Yeah, you said, turning the steering wheel hard.

Why do you want to see Goldwater's house?

Curious, you said.

We drove up a dark street of Pueblo Revival mansions, recessed behind thatches of saguaro and palm trees, enormous brick driveways, not exactly unwelcoming but not welcoming either. It looked like the rest of the neighborhood, but it also looked statelier. The house was shielded by trees. In the darkness we could see a closed gate, a spot-lit American flag flying high on a pole, some garbage bins set out on the road. Nothing more. Do you think it's weird to get out and look? you asked me.

I don't know what you'd see. Goldwater's been dead a long time, hasn't he?

You didn't respond. We sat there a few moments longer with the car idling. What an asshole, you said suddenly.

E arly the next morning, we fought. I can't remember what the fight was about. Only that I was wearing your mother's Fitbit. That in the aftermath, in an exhausted pause, sitting on the edge of your bed, our stuff still scattered around the room, an hour late on our planned departure time, I idly looked down at my wrist and noticed my heart rate was as high as it might be if I were jogging. I laughed.

Look, I said, you can see on the graph when we began fighting. It looks like I went for a run, but I've just been sitting here. I'm in the "Fat Burning Zone."

You were quiet. I'm sorry, you said. I know this isn't sustainable. I know that it's hurting you.

It's okay, I said.

You said you wanted to cry.

I can't remember if I hugged you. I should have. I know I was still angry when I began loading our things into the boot of the car. Walking through to the garage I noticed that on the kitchen counter there was a notice addressed to you from the Nevada Highway Patrol, left where we would notice it. Your father had written the word "paid" in capital letters at the top of the envelope.

When I'd packed my bags into the car and cleaned it out of popcorn packets and empty plastic water bottles, I came back inside to hear you crying. I thought perhaps you had been dwelling on what I'd said about my heart rate, dwelling on what was unsustainable and what was hurting me. I followed the sound of your voice. You were shaking. Your face was bright red. You looked up and saw me behind you in the en suite bathroom mirror. You told me you had just discovered that you had lost your noise-cancelling headphones, and your Nintendo. They had been in your bag, but they weren't anymore. You had checked everywhere. They weren't there. You might have left them in Encinitas. You might have left them in Palm Springs. You might have left them in Nevada. You didn't know. You weren't sure.

I tried to hug you. They're just things, I said, putting my arms around you.

My mom bought me the headphones. She bought me the Nintendo.

I know, I said.

You shoved me away. You leaned over the sink and sobbed into the mirror. You wouldn't meet my eye. I put a hand on your shoulder, but you wouldn't be comforted.

I went back into the bedroom. Silently, I began to pack your bag. I listened to you weeping in the bathroom. When I was done, I walked out and opened the sliding glass doors and stepped into the yard. I walked past the swimming pool and my lounge chair, past the tortoise enclosure and the barbecue, to the far side of the garden where your mother had erected raised beds for herbs. I lit a cigarette, the cigarettes you didn't know I sometimes smoked, that I had in the back pocket of my jeans. I stood beneath a tree and gazed upwards, to the blue sky between the leaves. That's when I saw the blossoms. The small yellow baubles of flowers. It was a wattle tree. What you would call an acacia.

I reached out to the flowers, broke off a stalk from a branch, and brought it down so I could smell the yellow blossoms and the oil from the leaves.

That smell of home.

I held on, with one hand on the wattle tree trunk, the cigarette burning down in my right hand.

6

Spilled Coffee on a Couch—The Mom Spot—Two Water Signs—
Nightmares—The Five Stages of Grief—Enter Sandman—
Ghost Town—Sedona—The Pleasures of Domesticity—Broken
Technologies—What's Wrong with Route 66—Flagstaff—An
Abortive Hike in Kachina Peaks Wilderness—What Dogs Can Smell—
Freight Train—A Cry at Dawn—The Problem of Photography—
Katie Lee—Ruins—Invitation to a Burial—The Heavens Falling Down

During the summer, you had taken to wearing your noise-cancelling headphones in the house. When your mother had first bought them for you, you would wear them only in cafes, or on the subway, or to take long phone calls from your boss so that you could tidy as you talked. But after a while you began to wear the headphones at home. You would wear them in the bedroom, in the kitchen, in the bathroom, even when I was there. If I wanted to say something to you—ask, for instance, whether you wanted sweet potatoes for dinner, or if you knew where my running hoodie had gone—you wouldn't reply. Because unless I was squarely in front of you, you didn't know that I was speaking. The headphones were notionally to stop you being disturbed by the ambient noise of our street, which had begun to trouble you more and more. You told me that the sounds of the ragtime jazz played by the restaurant on the corner rendered you unable to think, and the sound of the toddler playing with his grandmother next door had made you bang your fist against the shared wall. I'm going to kill that kid, you said more than once, and seemed astonished when I told you that I rarely ever noticed the boy next door. You surmised that it was because you were home so much more often than I was, and so perhaps I wasn't there to hear the worst of it. The headphones helped. And even though I never made much noise, you preferred to keep the headphones on in case I did. As a consequence, sometimes when I came home from the university or the library and opened the door, and you were there, somewhere in the apartment—in the bedroom, perhaps, folding laundry with your back to me—you couldn't hear that I had come home. I'd attempt to call out to you, attempt to make a noise that the headphones wouldn't cancel out, but it rarely worked. And so, when my shape eventually made it into your line of sight, or, God forbid, if I made the mistake of trying to lay my fingers gently on your shoulder, you would shout in such shock, and sometimes jump, that it would make me jump in turn.

One Saturday morning, four or five months before we set out on our trip through the West, I had been reading and drinking coffee on the couch in the living room, after leaving you sleeping in bed. When you eventually got up, you walked from the bedroom into the living room wearing your noise-cancelling headphones, saw me sitting there drinking coffee and reading a book, and you screamed. The jump-startle of an animal. As though you had forgotten that we lived together. As though you had forgotten that I might be in the apartment at all. And because you jumped, because you screamed, so did I. The coffee in my hand spilled out of the mug, onto the pages of my book, my leggings, and onto the gray fabric of the couch. That's what started it.

You shouted my name, and you swore. Then you rushed to the kitchen and brought back paper towels and dish cloths, handing them to me and telling me to soak up the coffee as quickly as I could. I crouched over and dabbed. You got on your knees and watched me do it. The thing that you couldn't say, of course, was that I had spilled coffee on the couch your mother had bought for you, a couch *she* had picked out. That the couch had to be looked after, as did everything she had ever picked for you, because she would never, not for the rest of your life, help you pick out anything ever again. But because it was the thing you couldn't say, we argued about couches, and we argued about money, which was a shorthand way of arguing about mutual respect, and once the coffee had been sopped up, we kept arguing. And so after we had been arguing for hours—truly hours—and I was so confused and beside myself, crying, with the spilled coffee chilling across the crotch of my leggings, not knowing how to end the argument, not knowing how to leave the living room, not even knowing what we were arguing about anymore, you said that it was really important to you that I go to the healer.

You called her Mariana, her name, not "the healer," or "the body-worker," even though that's what she did. You said that if I wouldn't go to therapy—another thing you had been asking me to do for some months—then I could at least take your place at your appointment with Mariana that afternoon. Would I go? Just this once. You would pay for it, and you would text her now.

I think now that you viewed it as a form of trade. You would sacrifice an appointment with somebody who gave you solace, so that I, your wife, might also be reimagined into somebody who didn't ruin your couch, or make you scream. So that I might be someone, once more, who gave you solace.

I acquiesced. If nothing else, it ended the argument.

So later that afternoon I took the subway to Park Slope and found my way towards the address you had given me. The office was above a Caribbean hair braiding salon, up a flight of stairs that smelled, on one floor, like cloves and cumin, and on the second floor, like the lemon verbena all-purpose cleaning spray sold at Whole Foods. It was dim in the hallway as I pressed the bell beside the office door. I don't know what I had expected Mariana to be like—older, perhaps? Wearing hemp? But when she opened the door, I realized that she was only three or four years older than me and looked like somebody I might ordinarily be friends with. She was wearing a strappy summer dress, no shoes, and her hair was tied back in a braid that thudded against her back when she moved. She hugged me after asking if it was okay to do so first. She led me down the bookshelf-lined hallway as she explained that these were her parents' offices—one was a psychiatrist and one a psychoanalyst—but they let her use their workspace on weekends for her own practice. I'm not sure that she explained what she did. I didn't really know what she did. When you started going to her, not long after your mother died, you told me it was because your boss had recommended her during one of those long phone calls when he was traveling to or from Las Vegas. You were experiencing pain in your lower back and hamstrings, and your hip bones were so tight that you could barely bend your legs. The pain was probably, your boss told you, something to do with grief. He said that Mariana was not only a healer, but she was also a gifted art-ist, whom he had met at the opening of a new show of a Foundation artist in West Hollywood. She had recently gone through a divorce and moved back to New York, to be near her parents. You had looked up some of her drawings, which, you said, were close studies of moss, and the fact that you liked her art seemed to make you more confi-dent in her abilities. By that summer, you were seeing Mariana once a fortnight. That was on top of two therapy sessions a week, monthly acupuncture at a man's apartment in Williamsburg, and occasional cupping appointments in Chinatown. I didn't ask what happened in sessions with Mariana, and you didn't tell me, only that afterwards you felt infinitely better. It had been Mariana, I knew, who had told you that the hip bone was the "mom spot"—the place where trauma about the maternal was stored. You brought this piece of news home to me in the spirit of revelation. It all made so much sense. Of course your hips were tight, of course your lower back was in pain. It could all be traced back to your mother. And maybe it was around then that you became convinced of the idea that I needed healing just as much as you did.

Mariana led me down the hallway into a large sunny room with a view across the road into Prospect Park. It was high summer, and the light that penetrated the room was of a brilliant green. She sat me down first on her father's sofa and asked me for two pieces of informa-tion: the story of my birth, and my full horoscope. She also told me that she had a professional code of practice, and that she and the room were a safe space. Nothing I told her would get back to you, and vice versa. I told her that I was a Scorpio, Leo moon, Aries rising. Was it possible to be alive and young in Brooklyn and not know those three things about yourself? She said that mine was a particularly *intense* horoscope, and that moreover it was interesting that I was married to you, because you were, of course, a Cancer, and two water signs together in a marriage was oceanic. I didn't know what you had said to her in your sessions together. I didn't know whether "oceanic" was something she was implying might be a problem.

Our water signs were in the room, and your presence hung over the entire session.

Once I had explained the circumstances of my birth, she asked me to move over to a massage table. I needed to take my shoes off, and I could strip to underwear if I wanted, but it wasn't necessary. She only asked that I take the belt off which cinched in the waist of my dress, so that she could more easily flip up the skirt to address my stomach with her hands. I suppose I had never thought before about the intimacy of these sessions, nor the fact that every time you came back from seeing her, Mariana had been touching you. I wondered, briefly, whether you ever got an erection when you were lying on the same massage table that I was now lying on. And then again, would I have minded if you had?

She told me to bring my awareness to my breath. As I inhaled and exhaled, she held my rib cage, pressing my tailbone down to the table with one hand, holding my middle as it expanded and contracted. She told me to relax my jaw, let my tongue hang heavy in my mouth. Then she moved to the top of the table, rubbed her hands with a CBD balm, and began with my shoulders and neck. Eventually, she worked her way along my entire body, right down to my feet. She was, she explained, feeling for shifts in the fields of energy my body produced. Throughout the session, she talked to me. She asked me questions: What was going on with me lately? I found that as I began to speak, my perception that this was all a bunch of bullshit began to melt away. Something was taking place, although maybe it was as simple as being asked about what was going on with me lately. I'm not sure I'd given much thought to it myself. As I spoke, she dug into muscles, smoothed them out, and felt for the way my body changed as I spoke, as though it had the ability to express more than my words could. Mostly, I spoke about you. About how death-haunted our lives had become that year. About grief. About hours-long arguments. I told her, for instance, that my mother had observed during a recent phone call that, from what I had told her, you did not seem to be moving through the five stages of grief at a clip that she found satisfying. Or rather, that you seemed to move on to one stage, and then move backwards. You'd be in a fit of depression, then you'd move back to anger, then to denial. I repeated this not because I believed what my mother said was true, but because I found it so difficult to know what I felt without bringing in words of others; without, in a way, footnoting my own thoughts.

There's no right way to grieve, Mariana said gently.

And I knew this, obviously, because whenever somebody says there's no one right way to do anything it's nearly always true. But what I was trying to get at, I said, was that I felt like I had no scaffolding. I didn't understand what was happening to you, and, by extension, to us. If I didn't have stages of grief, then what did I have?

She said, You should forget about them.

The stages of grief weren't even anything to do with grieving. Not originally. She told me that the woman who invented the stages of grief in the 1960s and 1970s, a Swiss doctor in Chicago, had pioneered the language of denial, anger, bargaining, depression, and acceptance to talk about the dying. The stages were originally meant to describe the experience of those, like your mother, who are barreling slowly but consciously towards death. The stages were never meant to be a road map for the grieving.

I didn't know that about the five stages, I told Mariana. So how was I meant to think about grief, I wondered, as she kneaded the muscles in my calves. If there wasn't a narrative container, it occurred to me that there may not be an actual end to your grief. And this realization frightened me. I asked Mariana how it was that the Swiss doctor's lectures had come to be misunderstood.

They weren't exactly, she said. The Swiss doctor fell out of public view for a while, but then re-emerged when she had a series of strokes and announced that she herself had started dying. The television crews got word, and an interview with a prominent daytime television program was arranged. In the interview, the Swiss doctor sat crouched in a chair, chain-smoking Dunhills.

And what stage of dying are you in? the television host asked gently.

I am angry, angry, angry and enraged, spat the Swiss doctor.

It was only in those last months of her life that the doctor wrote another book, this one about grief. In it, she used the same five stages she'd standardized, but this time to describe the course of grief for those left behind. As though, from the depths of her anger about her own imminent death, she was hopeful that the fury of what she was feeling could be seeded in everybody else, and would no longer be hers to bear alone. So, she wasn't entirely misunderstood, Mariana said, but she was dying herself when she wrote the book. You can think of it as an act of spite.

But why, I wondered as Mariana smoothed my calves down with her CBD balm, would one want to make a grieving person feel all the terror of the dying?

Well, Mariana asked, have you ever had a dream you've woken up from screaming?

I told her—and perhaps this was overstepping the boundaries of the therapeutic relationship—that *I* hadn't, but you had. You often had screaming nightmares. I knew that sometimes this happened when you dreamed about the morning of your mother's death. You dreamed about those last awful hours when I was not there, when it had been you, and your father, and her, alone. And I knew that I could not possibly know or ever understand what had gone down in those moments, nor what it had been like. You dreamed about her all the time.

Nightmares don't necessarily make sense, Mariana said. That is, if you think that the human organism is self-interested, pleasure-seeking, always looking out for itself. Why put itself through something frightening night after night? But we do. Nightmares serve some kind of purpose.

What does that have to do with the stages of grief? I asked.

Well, it's the nightmares themselves, she said. Why would you have a recurring nightmare, for instance? She thought that perhaps it was because, for some of us, it's preferable to hold on to the memory of the nightmarish thing. Because worse than the nightmare itself would be to forget what had happened. The only place that the dead exist is in our memories. When we forget them, we lose them for good. An attachment to suffering, therefore, might be a moral mode of witnessing. I could think of a nightmare as a way that a person might keep the dead alive.

Had I possibly expected her to say something so profound when I walked up that staircase? I absorbed what she said, and contemplated your dreams, the elusive stages of grief, the dawning realization I was having that I wanted and needed you to come out of whatever nightmare it was you had entered that year because I often felt I couldn't find you anymore, and it was while I was letting my thoughts drift over topics I ordinarily found too frightening to even articulate to myself that Mariana wound up the session, with what she said she thought I would find the most profound and meaningful part of the experience.

This was because she was going to read me a poem. Oh no, I thought, but did not say. I wished that she would not. This, I thought, was the sort of thing I had been prepared to roll my eyes about.

She had many favorite poets, she said, but the poems were chosen to be meaningful for the specific patient. She often read to you from Mary Oliver, she said, but she felt that I would find substance in Rumi.

She sat on a chair beside the massage table and read to me. I was looking at the leaves moving in the trees across the street in Prospect Park, and the incredible green flooding through the window. I was thinking that I should like to go across the road and into the park, lie down, and drown in all that green. I wanted to drown in all that green more than I wanted to walk to the subway and get the G train all the way back across Brooklyn in the high, breathless heat to return to a home that had you in it.

A s we drove out of Phoenix I saw eucalyptus trees growing by the entrance to Wet 'n' Wild in Glendale. Billboards along the interstate pleaded with Phoenicians to "Vote 1" for Republican candidate Martha McSally in the 2018 midterms two and a half weeks ago. A notice on the side of the road warned of burros for the next twenty miles. Is a burro a horse? I asked you.

I think they're donkeys, you said.

But then why would there be a sign? Are there donkey herds?

Maybe they're wild? you said.

We spoke as though we had not fought. You had not recovered the noise-cancelling headphones or the Nintendo, and when I had returned from the backyard smelling of cigarette smoke you had said nothing about it. You no longer looked as though you'd been sobbing. We drove through dense patches of saguaro, tall and erect like human bodies supplicating themselves to the sky. We had the local radio station on, one that played "golden hits." Sometimes Ike and Tina Turner. Sometimes Nirvana. As we passed the sign towards Arcosanti an old heavy metal song began to play. You turned it up.

Get out your phone, you said. I want to make a video for Brandon.

What song is this, I asked.

It's "Enter Sandman," you said. Quickly, do it now.

I held my phone up and turned the camera on. In the video you are driving along a barren desert road with the sun angling down into the car. You're wearing your Ray-Bans, and the insignia is bright in the glare hitting your face through the windscreen. You drive facing the road, both hands on the wheel, with the long guitar solo soundtracking the drive. For the first ten seconds you're looking at the road. Then your head turns, for a second, to gaze at the camera. Once. Another ten seconds. Then again. I can tell, watching you, that you are trying not to giggle, the twitching around your lips a giveaway. The video lasts for forty seconds, Metallica playing all the way through. Did you send it to Brandon? you asked.

I will, I said. I was trying to toggle between different apps, trying to get a hold of the directions so we wouldn't miss the turn off. The last saguaro grew outside of Flower Pot, and from there the landscape became foreshortened, shadeless. You asked me to check how long it would be until we got to Jerome.

Not long, I said. You turn left when you see a McDonald's. Do you want to stop there for long? The land was dull—thick grass studded with thistles and mesquite, low hills, a palette of green and brown and yellow.

No, you said. I just think you'd like it. It's ghosty.

Are you sure we should go? I asked.

Yeah, it's not far. I should just really make sure I get to Sedona in time to meet Kenneth, you said. We said we'd be there at 3 p.m. Did Brandon reply? you asked.

Not yet.

I had never met Kenneth before, only heard about him from you. From the way you'd spoken, he seemed like he might well be one of those human products of the twentieth century who had managed to live their lives *as* art. You had implied to me that Kenneth had come from money, some sort of erstwhile European dynasty who had prospered at the dawn of the twentieth century. He had ended up a kind of muse and caretaker to Greco. I could not imagine the intensity of the pressure he must feel he was under, having to complete the enormous half-finished void his partner had been creating in the Arizona desert for decades. Along the side of the road, we passed a teenage boy walking moodily beside the interstate, like it was any other suburban street. As we entered Jerome, we were informed by a road sign that there was a high fire danger.

Do you think Kenneth is mad about having to finish the project? I asked.

You laughed. No, you said.

As I directed you to take another left, you told me that there was something almost evil about Lawrence Greco. You said that his work, his whole worldview, had an apocalyptic character. Which was what made him so brilliant. That was why he had moved out here, you thought. It wasn't just the scale—far bigger than a gallery could ever allow—that the landscape offered. It was also the loneliness of the desert, the fact that you could go days, weeks, months, without seeing another person. Moving out here when you were cool and young in the 1970s and saying goodbye to hanging out at Max's Kansas City with Andy Warhol and whatnot, that's surely a rejection not just of the city but of people. You thought Greco was interested in nature, and in the power of the individual—of the artist—to shape nature and create something from it. But he wasn't so interested in people. After all, for the most part these artworks—earthworks in remote places few people are ever expected to see—exist only in the mind. Or in photographs. *Negative Capability* had been puttering along for decades, funded by the Foundation, with only a handful of people ever actually seeing it as it progressed. So much of its power was conceptual. And to that extent, it didn't matter if you or anyone else ever saw the finished project, although naturally your boss and the board did not see it like that. What they were hoping for was another *Sun Tunnels* or *Double Negative*, something to reward their generous decades-long patronage. Which was all to say that it didn't matter that you wouldn't be seeing the project, that it would be lovely just to see Kenneth that afternoon, and no, you didn't think Kenneth ever minded; he had loved Greco too much to ever mind.

We drove around the bend and into the center of Jerome. I want lunch, you said, do you want to go get something to eat? I was ravenous, I realized. I found you a parking spot where you wouldn't need to parallel park.

We walked past a Ghost Theatre, a Ghost City Inn, and a Haunted Hamburger before we arrived at a Mexican restaurant. In the shopfront window we passed a piece of paper stuck at eye level, in large type, reading, *California Fire Victims NEED YOUR HELP! Fires raging through the state have decimated towns, ruined livelihood, and injured pets. Victims are in serious need of donations.* I expected that they would be collecting to aid injured people, but as I read on, I saw that they were not interested in the human. *We need your help sending animal supplies,* the flyer said, and asked for donations of kennels, leashes, dog beds, collars, medicine, and treats to be brought directly to the Embry-Riddle Aeronautical University Lower Hangar in Prescott.

I must say this is very populated for a ghost town, I said.

Inside, you found a booth below a mirror, which reflected the blue-and-turquoise Laminex floor. Thanksgiving decorations were still strung up across the doorway. "Gobble, gobble," said the cartoon turkey. A terrifically thin woman in her seventies brought us a bowl of chips. Before she left, she leaned down to you, whispering, I won't charge you for the chips this time. They taste good but they look real ugly.

When she brought us our food, the vegetable soup I'd ordered had greasy chunks of beef floating on the surface. The sight of those globules of fat, the scrim of animal, the slight taste of dish soap on the rim of the spoon; all of it turned my stomach. I excused myself and rushed to the bathroom, bent down over the grimy toilet, and puked. I got vomit on my jeans, and I tried to wash out the splotchy patches of bile and cream cheese by the sink, but I didn't tell you what had happened when I came back.

Did Brandon reply? you asked. When I checked, he had sent the word, Amazing!

I wasn't sure whether that was the reaction you were hoping for.

As we left, another couple were settling into a booth. Passing by, I heard the waitress say, I won't charge you for the chips this time. They taste good but they look real ugly.

I wanted to change clothes when we got back to the car. I checked that there were no day-trippers wandering nearby, then pulled clothes from a bag in the back seat and shimmied out of my jeans. You rolled your eyes. You just want to be naked, you said. You just want to have people see you.

Do you want to do something else in this town? I asked.

You shook your head, then said, I like it here now a lot less than when I was a kid. There's something horrible about it. I looked up from the back seat I was emerging from, to find you looking at an elderly couple walking by, wearing outfits of beige and cream, in golf shirts and linen, boat shoes and cork wedges.

Are you sure? I asked. We haven't even seen it except to drive through and eat lunch.

Let's just get going, you said.

We followed along the road through Cottonwood behind a truck with Oregon plates and a MAGA bumper sticker, watching sprinklers arcing water high into the air right off the highway. Signs as we got closer to Sedona advertised various holistic and spiritual services. We passed World of Jerky and a vendor of crystals and fudge, the Cowboy Corral and a statue of Sacajawea in the plaza of the entrance to a mall. You told me that I should find somewhere to get coffee, so that you could tell Kenneth where to meet us. He'd be on his way by now. I opened Google Maps and clicked around on nearby icons until I found a diner a few blocks west.

It was the afternoon by then, but the diner was full of families, more than you'd expect even for a Saturday. The post-Thanksgiving holiday had dissolved the bounds of regular mealtimes. A turquoise Navajo cross hung on the wall, against a lurid mural of Sedona's red rocks and desert skies. As we were led to a table for three, I heard one man explaining to another how beautiful Jackson Hole was at this time of year. We were seated at a table near a family—two sons, a wife, and a father wearing a Yellowstone T-shirt. You sat nearly back-to-back with the Yellowstone dad, and you texted Kenneth to tell him we'd arrived. I was starving, having puked in Jerome, and I told you I wanted break-fast for afternoon tea.

I'm glad you're so hungry lately, you said to me, before you caught sight of Kenneth, progressing towards us though the diner in a pristine black-and-white Adidas sweat suit and a red-dusted pair of Nike Gore-Tex running shoes. He moved slowly, as though there was a stiffness in his hips, but he walked with his hands clasped behind his back in a way that suggested he possessed an inner calm, like a perambulating philosopher. I had not expected that he would, despite his outward frailty, speak with such a resonant voice. A voice so high-pitched that I'd have thought it was a woman's voice had he not been there. But clear as a bell, loud without shouting, projecting itself across the room. He shook my hand and told you he was glad to see you again after so long, and sat, gently unfolding his napkin over his knees.

I come here often, he said.

Behind him the wife of the Yellowstone dad raised her voice. You always have your phone out when we're eating, she said.

The eldest son laughed. I wish I'd recorded that, he said to the table.

I cast my attention to the scene playing out behind you and Kenneth.

The Yellowstone dad continued to look at his phone. Instagram told me to post, he said in his defense.

His wife's voice grew louder. You have children here, she said, you're not present.

Maybe I don't want to be present, he said.

The waitress arrived and I ordered an avocado, cheese, and mushroom omelet with hash browns and a biscuit. The biscuit was served with whipped butter and little packets of Smucker's strawberry jam. I slathered the butter over the biscuit as the Fitbit began to vibrate on my wrist: "Reminder to move."

Do you mind us eating? you asked Kenneth. He just had a cup of coffee.

Of course not, he said. At my age I don't have much of an appetite anymore.

I'm starving, I explained.

Kenneth asked you where we were going on this trip. You explained where we had been, then turned to me. Eloise knows the rest, you said.

We're going to Flagstaff tonight and we'll be there for a couple of days, I said. Then on to the dam at Glen Canyon. Up into Utah, back east through Bears Ears and Canyonlands and then St. George, and from there down to the Grand Canyon. And then we take the car back to Vegas, fly home.

That's a complicated trip, he said.

There are things I want to see.

He nodded. Your heart is in the desert, he said matter-of-factly. I didn't know mine was, either, until I came out here.

When did you come out here? I asked.

Oh, 1974, or thereabouts?

Where did you grow up?

Connecticut, Kenneth said. God, I haven't been back to Connecticut in a thousand years. He said that back in 1974 he had never thought about leaving the East Coast. Then one night at Max's Kansas City he had met Lawrence. The artist had a reputation for being difficult—for being an asshole, in essence—but Kenneth found that it wasn't as simple as that. Lawrence was a man who knew what he wanted, who put his work above all else. And he was gorgeous, a vision in black jeans and cowboy boots. Kenneth fell in love that weekend, and a month later he followed the artist out West, to a bungalow in the middle of nowhere a little under an hour's drive west of Sedona, where Lawrence had set himself down and where he worked.

At the time Kenneth came to live with him, Lawrence was abandoning painting altogether. For hours he would sit in his makeshift studio, tormented by the very gesture of the paintbrush. Lawrence detested the idea that, as an artist, he was required to make "imagery." It seemed ridiculous: the idea that whatever the artist did could be read as *something*, whether a mesa or a snake or the levitating skull of a bighorn sheep. It was nothing more than some kind of overblown inkblot test. What was important in art was physicality. Presence. Lawrence began wanting to carve away at space and reveal *the thing* itself.

Often, Lawrence would leave Kenneth in bed and spend his mornings in utter silence, trying to turn the entire question of artmaking on its head. If the studio didn't work then he would leave and take off into the desert, coming home dusty, vivid, summoning Kenneth back to bed. He always wanted to fuck after he'd been out there a long while. They had a happy life together. A domestic life that ran counter to the expectations Kenneth had formed for his future. He had not allowed himself to imagine such companionable everydayness. Had not thought there might be something beautiful about a life of toast and coffee at the breakfast table, of laundry, of waking up every day beside the same person and watching the way their face became more itself while they slept. And I didn't say so, because it was wonderful to hear him speak, and I didn't want him to stop, but I knew what he was talking about. How surprising it is, how surprising I had found it, when I found myself unaccountably happy in domestic life.

I had always thought of myself as somebody who could never settle. I had assumed that I would never be content with interminable mornings of coffee and toast, and never happy with the same person every morning of every year of my life. How incredible it was to find the story I had told myself all wrong. And how almost unbearably happy I had found myself sitting across a table from you in the mornings, inventing this thing called having breakfast together. This intimacy felt like a miracle. Reading in the evenings, long walks after dinner, you running me a bath, me buying day-old bagels on the way home, you locking the doors at night, me watering the plants. Habits and rituals. I understood what Kenneth was saying because I couldn't imagine a life anymore without you in it, or didn't want to. And so, when Lawrence got sick, they didn't tell anybody, because their world, after so many decades, had whittled away to the immensity of their relationship. The artist stopped being able to work. His body, which was once so strong and full of energy and life, just shriveled. He had to be driven to chemotherapy appointments from the ranch, where he would lie in the reclining chair while the chemicals drip-dripped into his veins, headphones on, playing *Impossible Princess* from an iPod Mini.

The Kylie Minogue album? I asked.

Kenneth's face lit up. Oh, I should have known that you'd know, being Australian. We both just love Kylie Minogue. Do you think it's silly?

No, I said, I still listen to Kylie Minogue when I'm feeling down.

As Lawrence ailed, she was one of the few things that kept his spirits up. He got so thin. Papery skin and rank breath. His hair started falling out. Kenneth would find it on the pillowslips and in the shower drain. Kenneth took him to the healing springs and the pain relief wellness clinics at the Creekside Whirlpool, just a little out of Sedona. They hadn't worked. Lawrence was very slowly slipping away.

One night they were watching TV together. Kenneth had looked over at Lawrence on the other end of the couch, his feet resting on an ottoman. He was unrecognizable from the tanned, naked Adonis standing at the foot of the bed in 1975 and telling Kenneth to take his pants off. How was it possible that this shriveled man in piss-stained trackpants and a Diamondbacks sweatshirt was possibly composed of the same flesh as the man he had first loved?

There must be something we can do, Kenneth thought, to try and protect ourselves from the tyranny of illness. From all these in-built endings. It was that evening that he raised the question of what they might do.

Kenneth had recently picked up a book from one of the "Take a Book, Leave a Book" shelves at a coffee shop. It was called something like *The Anthropocene Cosmos* or *The Anthropomorphic Cosmology*, something new age-y and entirely forgettable. The book meditated on the ways in which information processing was increasing exponentially over time. The authors believed that in the not-too-distant future, computing power would become so sophisticated, and artificial intelligent life would improve so much, that we would reach something they called the Omega Point. This was a point of runaway intelligence more powerful than everything in the universe, and what would be beyond that point they called "the singularity." Such an event would, among other things, allow future societies to resurrect the dead.

They discussed the matter. Kenneth noted that they had been born into an age of technological miracles, and who was to say, really, what miracles were to come? When they evaluated their radio childhoods and their Alexa-aided old age, the future Kenneth had read about didn't seem particularly outlandish.

The body, the book said, is a broken technology. Surely, Kenneth reasoned, scientists have all the tools now to move beyond it. And isn't our only hope our technologies? What bad luck, he thought, that they might both surrender to their internal clocks just a little too soon. Lawrence agreed. So he started looking around.

Kenneth found an organization in Scottsdale. There they would keep you until science had caught up and figured out how to sustain life beyond the poor stopwatches of our natural lifespans. The men made arrangements. They set up direct deposits through their life insurance policies. An annual membership fee, so to speak. But it was nothing like what we were thinking. Heads in glass cases, the stuff of bad science fiction. No. They keep the brain inside its skull. It's a ready-made case, after all. It keeps the brain safe and sound during the period of time that it's preserved. Ideally, you die in a regular way—no car accidents, no wildfires. Cancer was ideal. With cancer, they can keep you on the machines afterwards. Because of course you think that death happens when the heart stops, but that's not true. Death happens after that. It happens when the cells and the chemicals in your body begin to break down, and that might happen fully ten or fifteen minutes after the heart stops. That's when the people from Scottsdale arrive and start cooling you down, and that's what they did to Lawrence.

I said my goodbyes, Kenneth said, and they drove him down to Scottsdale. And that's where I'll be going too, when I'm ready.

Nobody is sure of course, Kenneth said. But it's got to be worth a shot. I know it might sound crazy. But it makes me feel hopeful. I don't need this body. They might be able to do something with electronics one day, you know. To upload our minds to the internet, the way they do with the cloud. When your computer breaks you don't just lose everything anymore, do you? You get a new operating system; you get new hardware. And both he and I will be there for it. We won't lose each other. We'll see each other on the other side, even if we look like something none of us here can even imagine. As Kenneth spoke, I couldn't help but remember things I'd read in books about the history of the American frontier and the history of the Colorado, of which this place, this state, was its apotheosis. Belief in technological ingenuity having the capacity to break new ground, a refusal of endings or of boundaries or of volume. And all playing out across this land bearing the scars of so much violence and wanton destruction. I did not think I had ever in my life as an immigrant in this country heard something that sounded so decadently American as what Kenneth had just told us. So fearsome and optimistic.

Later, I wondered whether you had recognized in what Kenneth told us the simple, painful truth of what he was saying. That we are all trapped by death, knowing an end is coming, if not for the world, then at least for us. For the "I." For one's own cherished, singular life. And technology was slick and weird and gross, but it was also the only thing we seemed to have at hand that might possibly redeem us. To figure a way out of that intolerable state; of being human.

And how funny, to be in that diner in Sedona, stuffed with more lunch than I'd thought I had the capacity to consume. Cells dividing, placenta growing, uterus expanding, eyelids forming, webbed hands and webbed feet, a raspberry-sized cluster of tissue. All body. As maximally human as I had ever been. While you and Kenneth talked, wrapped up, ordered the check, walked to the door, I was dawdling slowly behind, building another human being inside my body. We are mad, I thought as I crammed the last crumbs of jammy biscuit into my mouth, and maybe our madness is precisely because we are animals who cannot accept the fact of our own animality. The biscuit stayed down.

The two of you were speaking, standing by Kenneth's dusty Ford pickup parked in the lot outside the diner. I sloped up behind you, half-hidden behind your shoulders in a way that made me look, deliberately, supplementary to the conversation. Barely there. I heard you discussing something to do with the Foundation, and telling Kenneth not to worry, and that the support was there for as long as the project took. That we would see him again soon. You reached out and held his shoulder, and he in turn reached out to hold yours.

We drove north. We passed a store selling "Indian Garden Jewelry," and a rainbow trout farm along the side of a creek hugging the road. Red mesas loomed overhead. I spotted the sign from the window as we drove by: "Stop in for pain relief and relaxation at the Creekside Whirlpool!" That's the wellness center, I said, pointing back at it through the window. The one Kenneth said they went to, the one that didn't work.

There's a lot of that around Sedona. Hey, Slide Rock! you exclaimed. I've been there! It's like a little waterslide. You can slide on it.

The creosote and live oak had made way for pinyon pines and juniper. Black maples planted along the highway were flushed in the red and orange of autumn. The radio played "Panic" by the Smiths and I sang along. But halfway through Morrissey imploring the listener to burn down the disco, the radio reception cut out, and the road began to wind uphill through towering ponderosa pines. At least the road is paved and there's a safety barrier, you said. I have a suspicion we're going to encounter some roads that have neither in a day or so.

What did you think about what Kenneth was saying, I asked you.

I think he's lonely.

You don't think it's some sort of con being pulled on him? These Scottsdale people?

Do you?

And when I thought about it, I supposed I didn't. He seemed in full grip of his faculties. He also seemed like he was grieving. But what does that change? He sounded as though he had found some comfort in locating a possible solution to his grief.

It sounds like a very complicated relationship between the two of them, I said.

Kenneth told me that when he moved out there, when he wasn't sure, he had a horoscope done for the both of them in Sedona. And that's what convinced him to get through the hard stuff.

A horoscope?

Yes. Like, done by an astrologer.

I was silent. I looked up to the silhouettes of pines on the ridge. Mariana said you and I are very compatible, you continued.

She said that? In what sense?

I don't know. Just that we were.

Because we're water signs?

No, more than that. The other stuff. Other planets.

Would it matter to you if we weren't? Astrologically speaking?

But we are.

We entered Flagstaff on the remnants of the old Route 66. I couldn't see much in the dark, but ahead there was an old diner, the word "Restaurant" lit up in red neon over a rock-stucco wall. Can we have breakfast there in the morning? I asked as we drove by. It looks like something out of David Lynch.

You prevaricated. It's just a stupid Route 66 thing.

What's wrong with Route 66?

It's just tacky.

But I've never been here before, I explained. I don't know what's tacky about a Route 66 thing.

You'll see, you said.

The Airbnb we'd booked was out on the edge of Flagstaff, on a street with no lights at all. The night was extremely cold. The temperature monitor on the dashboard read thirty-two degrees, and when I got out of the car I could hear ice in the grass crackle beneath the soles of my shoes. The air was thick with woodsmoke. A sign in a front yard across the street read "Vote No on 418." We unlocked the safe by the fence using the pin we'd been provided, inside which was the key to the cabin, and I shone the torch of my phone over the lock while you opened the door. It was an A-frame house, with wooden walls and doors and sidings. Somebody's family vacation home, slung up on Airbnb for the off-season. The whole place, I thought, would have gone up in flames when the fires came through in the summer. It must have been luck, pure luck, that the winds hadn't pushed the fires this way. You went in search of the panel which would turn the heating on, while I looked around and opened drawers, searching for blankets. In the living room I opened a drawer to find that a shotgun was locked up inside. Seeing the gun gave me chills; the old Chekhov problem. I didn't tell you it was there. As I closed the drawer, I heard the heating system turn on, creaking and cracking from a ventilation square in the middle of the floor.

T he next morning, we drove into the mountains. There was already snow dusting one of the peaks to the north of Flagstaff, and as we gained elevation the autumnal trees shed their leaves and winter began to set in. I had found the hike by searching online and had picked this one for the descriptions of the picturesque, white-barked aspens that reviewers uniformly spoke of in reviews. It became clear that we had missed the last of the autumn leaves, at least in these mountains, which were some of the highest in Arizona. Kachina Peaks, I told you as we drove, like kachina dolls. The Hopi deities were said, in ancestral tradition, to live in these mountains during the summer, and depart when the rains came, moving down to the red mesas way beyond this landscape of pines.

As we climbed the crumbling, twisting road up the mountain we saw that the forest had been completely burned out some months before by summer wildfires. The charred tree trunks had collapsed and rolled down the slopes, crashing into one another and sending other trees falling like ninepins, and where there ought to have been canopy there was nothing but clear blue sky. The mountain had a graveyard atmosphere, and I began to feel increasingly afraid. I knew that the forest had the ability to regenerate, and that a landscape that appears charred and blackened is not dead, per se. I knew it wasn't a graveyard. But I did not want to be in a place so devastated, so burned. I found it hard to explain the panic I felt. I held on to the hand rest on the passenger-side door and gripped it tight. A sign on the road advised us to beware of falling rocks and dead trees and flash floods, and the fear began to spike. Jesus, I muttered to myself.

We're safe, you said very calmly. I trust that the rocks won't fall on us.

You were driving along the cliffside of the road, and it was me, on the passenger side, who could see the sheer drop we would tumble down if your driving didn't hold up, if you miscalculated and overshot a turn. I became certain that we were about to skid on the gravel and fall right off the mountain. What do we do if another car comes past? I asked.

We just hope that one won't, you said.

It must have taken us nearly an hour to drive up that mountain, and when we arrived, we found the aspens had indeed lost all their leaves. We were the only car parked in the car park, which seemed to suggest something ominous about the trail, because didn't people always hike on Sundays, no matter the weather or season? The wind up there seemed to gain a dimensionality, a sound, that I had never encountered before. I heard the knock-knock-knocking of a woodpecker. He was leaping up, a foot at a time, along the trunk of a ponderosa pine, as though sounding out the best spot. It was the only other living creature around us. At that elevation, in that much isolation, I suddenly saw how immensely silly I appeared. I was wearing jeans, an old cardigan, and the running shoes I went jogging in every day. You were wearing an outfit much the same. We both had tote bags, one bottle of water each.

Oh look, you said. I turned to see where you were pointing.

Bears, you said.

You were pointing to the sign by the trailhead. It was a warning put up by the Arizona Game and Fish Department, taped to the official Forest Service information board. The warning said "Living in Bear Country" over a picture of a black bear salivating. I approached the information board so I could read it. If you encounter a bear, the sign said, never approach one. Stay calm. Yell, make loud noises with whistles, blaring music, or pots and pans. Raise your arms, stand up tall, and appear dominant. Don't stimulate the bear's instinct to chase by turning and running from it. Slowly back away. But if attacked, fight back. The board behind the bear warning advised us to use common

sense. Over a hundred people needed rescuing from Arizona's wilderness areas a year. Hikers accounted for the vast majority of those needing rescuing. I read the warnings and then reread them, thinking about
our stupid shoes and our New York tote bags and how neither of us had
any phone reception, nothing warmer to wear, no whistles or pots and
pans. You made to enter the trailhead, telling me to come on.

I'm scared, I said. I don't want to see a bear.

You hesitated.

I'm really scared, I repeated.

You walked back from the trailhead entrance towards me and put
your hand on my shoulder. Okay, you said calmly, let's rationalize it.
You probably won't see a bear, right? If you do, they'll have seen you
first.

That's what scares me, I said.

Come on, you said, You're a nature person now, you like deserts
and mountains and oceans. Wouldn't real wilderness people just jump
right in?

But that's the thing, I said, I'm not. I read about the wilderness,
but I don't know what to do in it.

I'm sure it will be fine, you said. Also, it's totally okay if you don't
want to go. We can drive back into town. We can go have a nice dinner,
get massages or something.

I stood still and undecided for a moment, and then nodded my
head. I felt terribly ashamed.

But you put your arms around me and kissed my forehead.

We drove back to the A-frame, and while I changed you said you
knew a bookstore I might like, because you'd been to Flagstaff
all through your childhood. For ski trips.

You learned to ski here? I asked.

Yeah, you said. There's snow, isn't there?

But that much of it? To ski?

Well, there *was*. They use snow machines now, I think. It doesn't get so cold.

We parked and set off, past juice pubs and craft cocktail bars. It struck me that the town, with its old brick buildings and narrow streets, could have been one of the small towns we'd occasionally passed through in the Catskills. It looked utterly unlike anything else we'd seen on this trip. We took a right at Babbitt Brothers—"Ranchers, Merchants & Indian Traders"—then a left, and there across the street from a smoke shop was the used bookstore.

Inside, an old man sat behind the counter with a small dog in his lap, training a new employee who was so nervous that I could hear his voice breaking as he tried to explain away his shelving mistakes. I found a hardcover edition of the first volume of the *U.S.A.* trilogy, and a memoir by a woman I'd seen interviewed in documentaries about the damming of Glen Canyon. When I came to the counter to pay, the man's dog leapt from his lap and made towards me, stepping up on his hind legs and digging his face between my thighs. This was embarrassing but suggested something more significant. Dogs always got interested in what was between my legs when I was bleeding. With a familiar sense of alarm, I recalled all the dogs I'd had to discourage and avoid during every period of my adolescence, the excruciating embarrassment of the time a high school friend's new poodle had excavated a used tampon I'd deposited in the trash, and carried it around in his mouth like a prize. I tried to push the dog away as the bookseller apologized for its behavior. I gave the dog firm pats on the forehead, pushing him away as much as I was offering affection.

Katie Lee, the bookseller said as he evaluated my purchases. That's a name I haven't heard in a while. You know she lived near here, in Jerome? She died last year.

I didn't, I said. We drove through Jerome just yesterday.

Tourist trap, he said with a note of disgust. The dog stood on its hind legs and once more attempted an exploration of my crotch.

Max, shouted the bookseller, stop that!

The light was already fading from the sky as we left the bookstore. You put your arm around my waist and led me to a restaurant you had already located on your phone—we never did go to the neon "Restaurant" on Route 66. Instead, a meal of butternut squash soup, fish, and potatoes, with apple cheesecake for dessert. Two cocktails for you and three glasses of red wine for me. All on your credit card. Afterwards, we went to a bar next door. We sat in a booth by the window looking onto the railway tracks that lined the highway. In the corner, I spied a photo booth. I convinced you to come in with me, and before the flashes began you fished my sunglasses from my bag and put them on. When the photos spat out, you took them and showed them to me. I look so good in your sunglasses, you said.

When we left the bar and walked out into the woodsmoke-cold night, two freight trains were roaring along the tracks, one heading west to California and one heading east to New Mexico. We waited there at the crossing, watching the trains go by for something like ten minutes. There were carriages moving freight containers marked with the logos of Amazon, FedEx, and Intermodal, and flat-bed cars that held John Deere mowers, military-grade Jeeps, plastic-shrouded boxes holding refrigerators, and washing machines. While the trains sped by, I looked up at the night sky, and through the cloud of my breath I saw the one-two-three of Orion's Belt. I could not recall ever having noticed a constellation before, could not remember how I came to know about Orion's Belt and what it looked like. But there it was.

I wonder where they're going, I said. Chicago?

I think Texas, you said.

We didn't know, and we'd never find out.

When we got back to the cabin the waning moon was bright overhead, illuminating the shapes of the mountains behind the A-frame. There was the distant sound of horses sputtering as they settled into their stables for the evening, and I was almost surprised, when I heard them, that I knew that they were horses. How was it that I knew what horses sounded like in the evenings? We had left the heating on, and the house was warm. I took my shoes and socks off by the door, and you put on an album by Arthur Russell and let it play on speaker mode from your phone, balanced in an empty water glass to amplify the sound. I poured red wine into Airbnb mugs, and as I handed you your drink, you kissed the top of my head. It's been a really nice day, you said.

Despite the failed hike?

That's not important. It's just nice to feel so close to you.

We took the wine into the bedroom, climbed under the covers, and undressed piece by piece. I burrowed down and took you in my mouth, the soft earthiness of your smell, but you stopped me before you came. You had me lie down on my back, and kissing me, you used your fingers, and maybe it was because of the four and a half glasses of wine, but I remember thinking, as it began to peak and shoot down my spine like a rush of hot honey, that it was the first time I could remember having an orgasm in months. When you pulled your fingers out, you noted that there was a little blood on your fingernail. Maybe your period is starting? you said.

I went back down beneath the covers, and you came in my mouth. As you did, I watched your toes curling in and out, in and out. How incredible to know another person so well, I thought. To know exactly how much pressure and friction was needed to hold you off, to know about the way your toes contracted in and out when you had an orgasm.

Love, you said to me, and pulled me back up into your arms.

In the morning I woke up before the sun had risen, just as the sky was lightening. I shook you awake. We took the blankets from the bed, put socks on, and opened the French doors of the bedroom to the balcony, which looked up to the ponderosa pines that grew sheer up the face of the mountain. We looked east as the sunrise came over the hills. The air was icy in my lungs, and our breath rose in clouds of mist above us, but we huddled together. Roosters crowed. Something howled.

Is that a coyote? I asked.

I don't know, you said. We heard the howl again. Maybe it's a wolf, you said.

Are there wolves in Arizona? I asked.

Not many. You paused again, to listen. It's probably dogs, you said.

But it sounded wilder than a dog to me. A sound that could only be produced by something undomesticated, something that had come down from those mountains. I asked you again whether it was a coyote.

I don't think so, you said, as the howl sounded again.

I've heard that the howls of coyotes' sound like the crying of human babies, I said as the sun breached the crest of the mountain.

You were due on a Foundation call at ten, but we still had not bought any food and had nothing to eat, so you drove us to find breakfast early, before you needed to be on the phone. Our bottles of water had frozen in the car overnight, and I put them between my legs to try and melt the liquid. We drove to a coffee shop you'd found, which turned out to be in an arcade with a plastic Christmas tree set up in its center—"sponsored by SouthWest Bank!" We waited for your guacamole-less burrito by the station with coffee lids and water jugs. The jugs were filled with a green liquid, and a small sign explained that the green substance was chlorophyll, which the café added because it aided digestion. While we waited, we talked about what you expected from the call. The call was routine, but you knew that among the talk of upcoming exhibitions and commissions, funding, outreach proposals, and acquisitions, you'd be called upon. Malik, you knew, was keen on trying to partner with the National Parks Service to do something outdoors, in California, and he would be called on too.

I wonder if that's a bad idea, though, I said, and scrolled until I found a *Guardian* article I'd read a week earlier, about the crisis Instagram was causing in the National Parks system. Obscure landmarks in the middle of the desert had become famous via geo-location tags. The article told stories about traffic pileups caused by visitors trying to get good photographs of bison herds, and men falling to their deaths trying to get good shots from unstable rocks. You sighed, and said that it reminded you of what you'd been saying about photographs the other day. So much that the Foundation was responsible for was only known to the public through photographs. But what had changed in the last decade was the fact that it was simpler, now, to travel to the remote locations where works like Greco's could be found, easier for people to take photographs for themselves. To post them online and geotag them. It made every photograph an advertisement for a certain kind of art-adjacent lifestyle, and rendered all those pieces of remote land art no better than a stop on a tourist trail. There was nothing you or anyone at the Foundation could do about it.

I think now that the way you thought about photographs and their ubiquity was what brought about the biggest change in your own art. It was what was impermanent that was interesting to you. Or that's how I understood it, to the extent that I ever did understand. Your work now was made in manic bursts, and nearly always completed on the same day you started it, as though you had no ability to think through a piece over days, or weeks. Most of what you made you posted to Instagram Stories, because however long the story became, sometimes thirty or forty connected videos and images, it would disappear after twenty-four hours, like it never existed at all. A rebuke of the whole documentary impulse. Thinking about this, about your own artmaking, about where you'd expected to be in your career as an artist by now versus where you felt you were—working in an "art world" you hated and loved in equal measure—seemed to make you morose.

When the food came, we took it outside to eat in the weak, clear sun. You asked what I would do while you worked, and I told you I would read and wait until you were done—I wanted you to drive me up to the observatory in the afternoon.

We drove back to the A-frame, and you set up at the kitchen counter while I went to lie on the sofa under a blanket. I stacked books in my lap and checked emails on my phone. There was a message from my supervisor, asking me how the Mulholland archive had been, and hoping I'd had a happy Thanksgiving, an email which I did not know how to respond to, and so didn't. There were several emails from the university, one from my health insurance company, and then an email from an unexpected name. *Camila Vargas, subject: Lovely to meet you.* She said she hoped our trip had been wonderful, assuming, I suppose, that it would be over by now. She hoped to keep in touch, she said, and I should feel free to call her sometime and talk about my project, if I thought it would be helpful. The email was sent from her official university address, but in the body of the email she included her phone number, as though she really meant it. Hearing from Camila made me feel reassured—maybe I had not made a fool of myself in front of her. And maybe I was on the right track. I paged through the Dos Passos book I'd bought the day before, then decided on the memoir, which would, I thought, be useful for my research, and which I could, at the very least, tell my supervisor about.

The book began with the description of a memory. Katie Lee remembered walking barefoot in a stream. The stream ran through a side canyon she had chosen to explore that day, the River muttering behind her. She was in love with the place. The way the red sandstone curved, and the willows hung over the water, and the way the herons nested in the cliffs. The stream she was walking along led to a pool, and on the other side of the pool stood a ruin. Lee took off her clothes and put them on the edge of the bank, held her camera above her head, and swum through the ice-cold water to the other side. Naked but for the camera slung around her neck, she climbed hand over foot up the moki steps to the ruin of a house. The wooden beams were still in place, and petroglyphs decorated the stone walls. The grinding stone belonging to the Anasazi woman who once lived in that house was resting by what once was the door.

Lee wandered naked in the ruined house that day, knowing it would soon be gone. Not long beforehand, she had been running a boat down the Colorado through Glen Canyon, and as she came towards Lee's Ferry she looked up. When she took out her binoculars, she saw that the little moving dots along the rim were surveyors. They were going to dam the canyon.

The man who decided to build this particular dam, Floyd Dominy, had been there the day that the flood gates on Hoover Dam were opened. It had made him a lover of dams. The future director of the Bureau of Reclamation had stood on the transformer deck, just as we had, and looked westward from the concrete edifice. The dam was, he thought, something greater than the pyramids, something greater than the Parthenon, or any of the wonders of the classical world. Because it was not a monument to cultures that had risen and fallen, not some monument to the dead. The dam was a monument to the living. Nothing, he believed, had ever been more important than what human beings were doing on the Colorado River: subjecting nature to the will of man. Dominy dreamed of a staircase of reservoirs backing up the Colorado all the way from the Rockies to the Mexican border, a never-ending supply of water. The dam at Glen Canyon would be his crowning glory. He didn't care about petroglyphs, or sacred sites, nor hippie bleeding hearts.

Lee was one such bleeding heart. She went back to the River, month by month, as the concrete was poured. She saw the side canyons disappear as the artificial lake they named Powell began to fill. She saw the young men on "salvage archaeology" missions, removing pottery, documenting petroglyphs and houses, and all that was left by generations of Zuni, Hopi, Navajo, and Paiute people, the descendants of the Anasazi who had lived there centuries ago. The house Lee had walked naked through, along with thousands of others, was drowned beneath the water.

One day, after the dam was finished, Lee was on the River and stopped for a moment to look down into the water. A sunbeam hit something familiar below. She dived off the side of her boat and swam down. What she saw in the water was that canyon she had walked in naked, not so very long ago. She was swimming hundreds of feet above it.

I knew that since Lee had written her memoir, the canyon had begun, gradually, to undrown. As the waters had receded, hundreds of those houses had emerged from the waters. Some petroglyphs newly exposed on ancient rocks had been drawn over with Sharpied cocks and balls. Ancient Puebloan pottery washed up on the shore alongside cans of beer thrown into the water. And it was around this time, when I was thinking through the many types of loss collected in that canyon, that you came into the living room to ask me how important it was to me that I see the observatory.

Why? I asked, putting the book down. Are you still on the call?

It's over, you said. But Kenneth emailed me while I was on it.

I am not sure whether the two of you had been in conversation since we'd seen him, or whether his email was utterly unexpected. From what I understood, Kenneth had changed his mind since seeing us on Saturday. Talking to us so intimately seemed to have cracked him open. He thought we could be trusted, and he suggested that, if it was on our way, if we were not yet en route to Utah, and if we had time, then it would be permissible, perhaps even meaningful, if the two of us came out to the site of *Negative Capability*. We could go only on the proviso that you didn't report back to your boss: we were being invited as friends and private guests, not as representatives of the Foundation. Kenneth thought your boss was a fool. A man who, with his money and legacy, didn't know a thing about art in any real sense, only what cultural cachet it afforded him. Kenneth felt that the project needed to be protected from your boss, who he thought to be the worst thing to befall the Foundation in its long, admirable legacy. Now that Lawrence was gone, Kenneth believed that the director's primary aim was to get the work accessible, and make public at last the great unfinished masterpiece that Lawrence Greco had left behind. He imagined your boss had already prepared the press release: *"Negative Capability" now completed! Open to tourists! Book a ticket! Make a trip!*

I sat up and pushed the blanket off my legs. You said yes, right?

Of course I did.

Will that be okay? Hiding it from your boss?

Are you okay not going to the observatory?

Of course, I said. Of course! Let's go. Now.

We drove down the mountains through the ponderosa pines, tracing our way back to the red rock country, the temperature rising as we lost altitude, from forty-six to sixty-three by the time we passed by Slide Rock and the Creekside Whirlpool and the rainbow trout farm. We drove back through a landscape of red dust, the names of the plants on the road telling the story of its severity: crucifixion thorn and catclaw acacia and broom snakeweed. Then a right down a road only named by a number. We drove past a sign warning, "Primitive Road: Caution. Use at your own risk." Ahead of us the flat land rose steeply into red mountains, clouds banking over the horizon and blocking out the sun.

We arrived at a heavy iron fence, where we saw Kenneth waiting in his Ford truck. He was wearing the same red-dusted pair of Nike Gore-Tex running shoes, and a different pristine Adidas sweat suit, this one in bright blue with red trim on the arms, neck, and hem.

Hello, he called out. I'm glad you've come!

He didn't move towards our car, rather we watched him walk to the fence, unlock it, and open the gate. He waited until we'd driven through to lock it behind us. We looked out across the same featureless plain we'd driven through, barely even punctuated by the stray gnarled form of a juniper or the spiny fingers of cholla. As we trundled along on the dirt road towards a shed and some parked earthmovers, I could see you clutch the steering wheel more tightly, brimming quietly with anticipation. Does this all belong to Kenneth now? I asked.

No, you said. This site, when Greco got it, he had a twenty-year lease. But that was in the '80s, when he first started it, and he couldn't keep it up. So the Foundation stepped in when the lease was expiring, for the work, so that it could continue. He's been building this my whole life.

So where is it? I asked you. Looking around, I could not see anything that looked any different to the desert all around us.

You told me it was beyond the shed, and that it couldn't be seen from where we were—it went down, right into the ground, not up. *Negative* capability, get it?

Kenneth beeped the horn of his truck behind us and motioned to you to pull over. We parked the rental car by the earthmovers. We need to walk from here, Kenneth called out in his clear, high voice.

It wasn't far. He led the way. He walked surprisingly quickly given the stiffness of his hips, and kept his hands always clasped tightly behind his back.

Have you always lived out here? I called out.

Near here, he called back. He slowed, and we walked together. He pointed back east towards the approximate location where their house was. That's where we live, he said, and I noticed that he had, not for the first time, referred to their "we" in the present tense. He had used it talking about *Impossible Princess* as well. As though Greco were still alive, still living in their house and listening to Kylie Minogue, as he always had. It was a slippage between present and past tense I recognized from conversations with your father, and a tendency I now see in myself.

This was Lawrence's favorite place, Kenneth said. This land here. Nobody ever comes out here. We were silent for a moment as we walked, nothing but footsteps crunching on rocky soil. Then Kenneth said that during that first year with Greco in the desert, after Kenneth had abandoned the city for good, a car drove by not far from their house. They were in the yard, but the desert there was flat, and they could see a car coming for miles. Kenneth pointed out the approaching car to Lawrence and he jumped up, dark-tanned, buck naked, and he disappeared inside. Came back with a gun. Trained the barrel on the car as it sped by in the distance. The car didn't drive any closer, and probably never even knew it had a gun trained on it. But Lawrence wanted to make sure, Kenneth said, and after that he had a fence put in, the same fence, I thought, that we had seen only half an hour ago as we had driven past. Kenneth wondered, sometimes, what would have happened if the car had, in fact, approached their gate. If the driver had needed directions, say, and saw distant human figures to ask. At the time, he had experienced a moment of profound fear.

When did you stop being afraid? I asked.

No, honey, Kenneth said. You don't stop being afraid.

We returned to silence, and he picked up the pace, walking ahead of me once more. There were dark clouds on the horizon. A wind rushed across the plain. I could hear it in the rasping and rattling of the creosote and the amplification of the scrub-jay's call. I caught on the edge of my vision, as we walked down the path, a shock of lightning in the far distance. Branches of light splintered and cracked, but I didn't hear thunder. I wondered whether the bolts would reach us, and remembered, for a moment, what it had been like to fly over lightning in February, the utter strangeness of flying above a deadly storm.

The sky was enormous. How was it possible that its vastness was so physically palpable here, in the desert? When after all, it was the same sky all over.

Kenneth! you called out. Wasn't it here? Am I crazy?

Nearly, he called back. I'm afraid you're going to be surprised. He kept walking, scuffing up clouds of red dust with his Nikes. We all were. I looked down to find my own boots were coated in dust.

That's when the depression came into view.

It was no hole or crater, although it was vast, and lower than all the earth around it. It was low, but no perfectly mathematical spherical hole. There were no mirrors, no tunnels, no chambers. An earthmover was parked on the opposite edge of the depression. This was not what it was meant to be at all.

You stopped as though startled. Kenneth? you called out. There was a note of anxiety in your voice, as though you were hoping he might offer reassurance.

Kenneth's voice came drifting back to us over the wind.

There was a flash flood about a year before Lawrence passed, he called out. It was a disaster. Destroyed years of his effort. All the mirrors cracked—every single one of them. He always knew it was a risk, obviously, out here. Building it the way that he was. He sent the crews away and wouldn't let them clean up. Then, after a week or so, it didn't seem to him like such a disaster anymore.

We drew closer, as Kenneth began to walk us into the enormous depression where the hole that had so famously characterized *Negative Capability* once had been. What we were moving through looked more like a scar on the landscape, a remnant of what had once been there rather than the product of thirty years of work. The spherical shape was still in evidence. But the hole was gone.

What happened? you asked Kenneth.

Remember, no telling the boss, he said.

You nodded.

He decided to fill it in, Kenneth said, looking around. I think he realized that there was something more beautiful about attempting to restore it. He knew it wouldn't be the same, not the same thing as the project he originally conceived. Not the thing on the websites and in the articles. It would be something else entirely. Don't worry, he said.

He had no need of worry. You were calm. It was hard not to be. The lightning continued to branch on the horizon, the wind moaned, and yet everything was quiet.

Don't worry, Kenneth reiterated. Lawrence documented it. There are photographs. Photographs from all the way through. But when

Lawrence got sick, he wasn't finished. He knew they'd go ballistic at the Foundation, would never let him do it if they knew. So he asked me to help. Now it's just me out here every day, doing what he made me promise I'd do for him.

We looked down at the depression, at the negative space erased. The absolute vastness of the enterprise.

You drive that earthmover? I asked, pointing to it in the distance.

Kenneth nodded. That's the one.

It's incredible, you said.

Kenneth seemed to relax. I'm glad you can see that, he said. I'm glad you think so.

Can we walk around it a little? I asked.

Of course.

Stepping across that expanse, lower than the ground, cocooned, almost, by the landscape, I felt overcome by something I have felt neither before nor since. A peace, maybe. An acceptance of my own smallness. And that smallness felt appropriate, it felt okay. How to describe an intense aural experience of quiet? A quietness that made of me a creature, as quick and fleeting as a jackrabbit. You walked behind me, and your footsteps seemed to be the only sound at all.

How do you feel? you asked me. You walked a few steps until you were standing beside me and took my hand.

The sky has exploded, I might have said, and the heavens are falling down on me, and though I know this is not the truth, it is the capital-T Truth. Although I didn't say that, not really.

I think I said, Quiet.

We stood there holding hands for some time. Kenneth lingered on the edge of the depression, and from where we stood I could no longer see any tangled thatches of creosote or prickly pear stretching out to the distant mountains. I could only see the sky and Kenneth, in his blue sweat suit stained red by the desert floor. He looked terribly far away from down there in the negative space, and for all his frailty he looked strong, like the kind of figure one might want to install on the rim of the Grand Canyon to conquer any stray notion that down there lay something like annihilation. He was keeping watch over you and I, and keeping watch over this immensity, a life's work, a work of love.

My boss is going to flip out, you said.

Will you tell him?

No, you said. He'll find out eventually. Right now, this is just for us.

7

A Rebuke of Glamping—Glen Canyon Dam—When the Water Falls Below the Intakes—The Bottomless Pit—A River of Milk and Honey—Dancing in the Bathroom—Many Margaritas—The Rain Follows the Plow—John Wesley Powell—A Surfeit of Pillows—Uranium Mining on the Land of the Navajo Nation—Where Radiation Nests—Hands—Monument Valley—Bad-Luck Crystals—Bluff—Greenhouse Vegetables—Zabriskie Point—Why the Revolution Failed

I s there fog ahead? I wondered, as we drove out of Flagstaff the next morning. Everything appeared suddenly so gray. We passed a boy in a hooded sweatshirt, biking on the side of the road, casually moving along the incline. Something about the boy on his bicycle struck me as eerie, although I couldn't have said, precisely, why. I had woken from nightmares during the night, and then listened to those strange howls in the ponderosa pines growing sheer up the face of the mountain behind us, everything in that early morning hour drenched in the sweat of omens and auguries. I was in a mood to read meaning into everything I saw through the window as we headed north towards Utah.

We overtook two successive cars with boats hitched to trailers at the rear, and then began our ascent. The road was winding and carved its way between steep red cliffs. And then all at once it leveled out, and we found ourselves high above the desert floor, all traces of fog burnt up in the light. In the notebook in my lap, I jotted down the words, "I feel like we're ascending to a meeting with God." The sudden sublime swells of feeling kept overcoming me, like a physical thump to the middle of my chest. The mesas were mineral-banded like seashells are, and at the lookouts along the highway we passed picnic tables where women were selling Navajo jewelry and buffalo jerky. There was a gray haze across the edge of the western horizon, not fog but something denser and lower, more sinister. From the fires, I thought. The smoke was still traveling.

We passed a sign for "Shash Diné." It was, I saw when I swiped open my lock screen and looked it up, a Navajo glamping hotel. We had seen places like this on Airbnb when we had been trying to book accommodation. Cabins, hogans, and bell tents outfitted with bedding and solar lights and fresh drinking water. You had said you liked the idea of staying in a hogan, but I had argued that in the mornings it would be terribly cold, and so we had booked a room at the Page Boy Motel; one star, Lake Powell Boulevard. I had, to be honest, been affronted that you wanted to stay in a glamping hotel. Not only was the word so silly, but the entire concept smacked of the corporate whimsy of the early 2000s. Fundamentally apolitical happenings like guerilla knitting or silent discos, co opted to sell people iPhones and Magnum ice creams. Glamping embarrassed me, and it embarrassed me that you found it an attractive concept.

When we got to the dam's parking lot my phone had run out of battery, and so you offered to record the tour for me. You opened VoiceNotes, pressed record, and hid the phone in your pocket. On the recording I can hear the scrape of the microphone against the fabric inside the pocket of your jeans, and then the voice of a woman asking us please to not photograph the security guards stationed all over the dam. Some, she said, were more particular than others.

She asked us where we were all from. North Carolina! she exclaimed. Great! The UK! Wow! Moldova! Welcome!

When she asked you where you were from, you said, Phoenix.

She didn't say anything about Phoenix.

Yeah, you said in reply to her silence, and then issued a small hoot of laughter. Phoenix was too local, perhaps, and too unremarkable to be welcomed from. We were standing side by side and maybe she assumed that being your wife, I was also from Phoenix, because I was not asked where I was from.

I, myself, am from Page, the guide said, directing us into the dam. She explained that her family arrived when the dam was being constructed in the 1950s. She led us into the heart of the structure, showing us the new rotator blades, turbines, and magnets. A little boy on the recording asked questions about cement, about electricity, and about whether he would soon be allowed to see the River. When we eventually got to the top of the dam, I can hear as I listen back now the sound of your whistling, as you peered over the sides and down towards the water.

Wow, you said quietly.

On the recording the woman explained that the last time the lake was full was in 1986. The drought has been ongoing since 1999.

Then you asked, very politely, What will happen when the water gets so low that it doesn't flow through the dam anymore?

The woman's voice betrayed a note of anxiety. There's a plan for that, she said. If the water falls below the lowest intakes, they won't be able to make power at the dam anymore. But the water will still be able to get through.

There is audio of more questions being asked and other concerns being raised. An Australian woman complained about her—our—government's inability and unwillingness to transition to cleaner energy sources to avert climate catastrophe. Hydro-electric and solar and wind power, she said, listing solutions. I said nothing during the tour, particularly not to the Australian woman, because I didn't want to get into a conversation with someone who would recognize my accent, who might ask me to back her up, when I knew next to nothing about what was happening in the country of my birth, and was ashamed.

After the guide said her goodbyes, there followed a few moments of silence, and then my voice, at last, whispering furiously in the gift shop. Telling you that there was a very real danger the dam would reach deadpool in the next few years—that was the word to describe what will happen when the water sinks below the intakes. That the "Law of the River" was doomed from the beginning. I was furious at the tour guide, who had said that the water ran through seven states and Mexico and then into the sea, when it hadn't reached the sea in years. I said there were proposals—had always been proposals—for decommissioning the dam at Glen Canyon. The flooded land could never be restored, but maybe it could be redeemed. The cottonwoods would always be waterlogged, the petroglyphs always once-drowned, but there would be something on the other side. Something to hold out hope for.

Then there is audio of you asking me, placatingly, whether I would like to adopt a bat.

We must have been looking at a display of plush bat puppets, because on the recording you read from the tag that bats in the Southwest are killed by white-nose syndrome, climate change, and wind power development. "All profits go to bat conservation efforts."

Thirty dollars for a bat seems like too much, you said.

Then there came the sound of the creaking of a rotating display of "Sherriff" pins, all with different names. You were holding one that said "Sherriff Carl."

Will you get it for him? I asked.

No, you said, it's not really his sense of humor.

You put it back on the rack. Then you said, If my mom were still alive, I'd get it for her. They have a Sherriff Lynda badge, spelled her way. She'd have been into it.

There followed an exchange between the woman behind the cash register and me, as I purchased a John McPhee book about the geology of Utah and Nevada. The woman said to me, I like your coin purse. Very vintage.

And I can hear, in the recording, that I was not polite to her. I was dismissive, my—Oh, thank you—filled with disdain. I must have been terrible company that day.

How do you feel? you asked me as we crunched across gravel towards the car.

Kind of sick, I said to you on the recording. And really sad.

That is where it stops.

* * *

We drove out of the car park, down the main road of Page, and I put my own phone on the charger. I suppose it was unsurprising that everything in town looked new. Nothing was older than any of our parents. We looked along the main road for somewhere to eat. Options were sparse, and the pressure to decide fast was amplified by the roar of six lanes of traffic, everyone else seeming to know precisely, confidently, where they were headed.

We parked the car outside a restaurant called El Tapatio and headed inside. We were seated in a walled booth painted with vivid illustrations of flowering prickly pear and an adobe village. I ordered a mango margarita, which came in a salt-rimmed glass the size of a baby's head. You took a photograph of me with the margarita, and it is only looking at the photo now that I realize you had arranged the picture such that the rays of the sun painted behind me seem to emanate directly out of my skull. In the photograph I am smiling, I look pleased and a little arch about the sheer size of my drink, but I have dark circles under my eyes, and my jaw looks stiff, as though beneath my smiling lips I were clenching my teeth.

We ordered a bowl of guacamole and chips, a vegetarian enchilada, and chicken fajitas. I love these old, kitschy Mexican restaurants, I told you when you asked if I was happy.

When you went to the bathroom, I ordered a second margarita. While I waited for you, I stared out the window into the lot, where only one or two cars were parked. I supposed people had other things to do, Tuesday lunchtime after Thanksgiving weekend. Other people with other lives. My thoughts roiled. The night before, when the dropper full of melatonin had sent you to sleep, I had stayed awake, still fizzing with the experience of visiting *Negative Capability*, or what was left of it. I had left you in bed, rifled through my bag for the books I'd accumulated, discarding the Dos Passos and the Katie Lee memoir, and finally settling on the Charles Manson biography you'd bought for me in Los Angeles. I started from where I'd left off, and read until late in the A-frame's living room, until I was tired enough to go back to bed and sleep. But I didn't sleep for long.

In my dream I was in a bottomless pit. What I understood, on the other side of waking, was that the dream was a regurgitation of what I'd read. Because there was a bottomless pit in Manson family lore. It was where they planned to hide out when the race war arrived, the one Manson had prophesized would imminently engulf America in the late 1960s. Shortly before falling asleep, I had read a chapter describing the point at which he told his Family that it was only out in the desert where they would be safe, in a city of refuge located in a bottomless pit.

Manson's vision of the pit was drawn from a mangled Hopi story, which told that humans first emerged on the earth from a hole in the ground. It was from this hole that man entered this, the fourth world—the three previous worlds were made a mess of. It was said that the location of the origin point was a spring on the Little Colorado River in the Grand Canyon. This place, Sipapuni, was where death and life met in the one place. But in Manson's garbled stories there was no Colorado River. He was born and raised in West Virginia—all deserts looked the same to him. He preached that the bottomless pit could be found in Death Valley, maybe simply because it was so much more proximate to L.A. than any of the other deserts. After the famous murders, it was to Death Valley that he sent his Family, telling them the time had come to hide. They squatted by a ranch, where the heat was blistering in the summer of 1969, the reprieve of early evening marred by the awakening of the rattlesnakes. The city of refuge would be accessed through a hole into the earth nearby, he said. Manson set his Family to looking. Down there, they would find warmth and light. A river of milk and honey would flow. There, they could become whatever they wanted to be, and nobody would die or ever grow old. Some of the girls, true believers, swore they must be close to the source because they could feel they were beginning to sprout fairy wings from their shoulder blades.

In the dream I had the night before, the river was white and ran between high canyon walls streaked with long sickly seams of honey, oozing into the steady burble of the milky waters. The whole place was lit dimly, sunlight peeping through a slot in the rock above. It was only when I looked upwards that I began to be scared. I suddenly realized that through that slot lay the real world where I once had lived, but there was no rope, no ladder, nor any way to get out. It was then that I saw a hand come down from up high, holding the lid of a saucepan, a lid that perfectly fit the hole to the bottomless pit. As the hand put a lid on the sky and blotted out the light, and as I realized I was underground and alone, I began to scream. I woke up struggling to get those screams out of my mouth, smothered and sweating beside you in bed. But you didn't wake up, and I didn't tell you about the dream. I lay awake listening to those howls in the mountains above the house, and I slept maybe an hour more before the alarm went off and we had to leave.

As I waited for you to come back from the bathroom—you were taking a very long time, and I had ordered, while I waited, another margarita—I wondered whether the dream's origin point was that depression in the desert we had stood in the day before, several feet below the ground's surface, looked over by a man destroying a masterpiece as an act of devotion. *Negative Capability*, Greco had named his life's work, and love itself was surely a kind of negative capability, one in which the boundaries of the self are forced open to incorporate the other, the limits of the heart reaching ever outwards, into the perilous territory of uncharted emotion. *You have absorb'd me*, Keats once wrote to his lover Fanny Brawne. *I have a sensation at the present moment as though I were dissolving.* Being snuffed out by a saucepan lid in a bottomless pit beside a river of milk and honey; surely that was not so very different? And as my mind spun in circles around these thoughts, I realized that I was, three margaritas in, no longer sober, and that everything I could see in front of my eyes was wavery, even though it was still the afternoon. When you came back our food had already been served.

Were you dancing? I asked.

You showed me a video, one of several you had recorded in that session, in which you set your phone on the sink of the Mexican restaurant's bathroom, stepped back, then began to dance in a frenzied, fluid way, something between Ian Curtis and Merce Cunningham. You had been making these videos since the very first days of our dating. I had grown used to it by then. Used to the long periods alone at bars or restaurant tables, with a drink and my phone, waiting for you to return from the bathroom, while you were recording your performance. I recall the night your parents first told us that they suspected your mother had cancer, during a holiday dinner at a Williamsburg restaurant when they'd been visiting the city. After the announcement, you had excused yourself to go to the bathroom, and in the fifteen minutes you were gone I sat there in the excruciating small talk of appetizer options and "Is the music too loud?" with your mother's suspected tumor looming over everything, wishing you'd come back and hating that you'd left me there and knowing that you needed, right then, to be alone. You had recorded your furious dance against the green textured wallpaper of the Williamsburg restaurant's bathroom to a piped-in song by Sylvester, and texted me the video, the vibration of my phone on the table the sign that finally you were done, and you would soon return to the table.

When we left the restaurant, we walked past a statuette of a horse erected by the door, standing up on its hind legs, and I ran my hand across its copper flank. Do you want a pony? you asked.

A seal, I said. Or a whale.

I told you I wanted to walk for a while through the town before the light was completely lost. We headed east along the main road past a store selling essentials. "Liquor Fishing Guns Ammo Archery," read its windows. Cars sped by, making it too loud to speak. It wasn't a good walking town. A block or so past the restaurant, a museum came into view.

Oh, a fun, kitsch museum, I said to you. It will be fun! Look, it's even got a boat.

No need to say the word "fun" twice, you said.

You steered me towards the doors, past the boat moored on bricks outside the entrance. On a noticeboard outside, a flyer advised visitors that the lowering water levels in Lake Powell made it treacherous to launch boats. "The water is estimated to be between eight and ten feet deep and buoys will be placed that say, 'Shallow Water—Cross at Own Risk.' As the lake levels continue to drop, red and green navigational buoys will be pulled out and replaced with orange floats."

The woman inside warned us that she was closing soon, but we said we would be quick. The museum was dedicated to John Wesley Powell—the namesake of the lake. It was small, and as old and dated as the exhibits at Hoover Dam. Along the walls of the dioramas were pasted watercolor illustrations of Powell's diaries, as though depicting a scene in a nineteenth-century adventure novel. Closer to the glass were positioned hand-crafted figurines of Powell, standing in his britches, and holding a tin mug with his one hand. Canyon walls rose high above him, peeling away at the sides where the glue had lost its adhesive quality. Further along, I stood for a time before an exhibit on Glen and Bessie Hyde. They had been married in Twin Falls, Idaho, in 1928 and planned to honeymoon on the River. They began their trip in a boat Hyde constructed himself, neglecting to fit it with life preservers. The couple got down to the South Rim of the Grand Canyon okay. They bought groceries and gave an interview to a man from the *Denver Post*, who thought it was neat that Bessie might be the first known woman to run the River from the confluence of the Green River down to the Grand Canyon. They took off from the South Rim one November morning, and a few weeks later their boat, camera, and Bessie's diary were recovered smashed up among the rocks in Lower Granite Gorge. Their bodies were never found.

I took a photo of a sign towards the end of the museum's journey-path, a flyer that said, *The Future of Glen Canyon Dam: What will happen? How long will it last?* In the phone's photo editor I circled in black with my finger a paragraph that explained, *Some kind of national emergency (an invasion by enemy forces or a pandemic) might trigger a withdrawal of personnel from the dam. But even this eventuality has been planned for.* You found me circling the photograph on my phone's screen, led me to the door, and called out, Thank you very much, to the docent.

Outside, I couldn't help but approach the boat. It was roughly sixteen feet long, a green wooden craft tucked under a wooden structure to keep the sun from fading it. I reached out to touch the wood with my fingertips. The boat was a replica of the one Powell had used to explore the River in 1869. The replica had been built by Walt Disney Productions and used in a river running sequence in a 1940s film. The Disney Corporation had kindly donated it to the museum.

Was it fun? you asked.

Well, I said, the thing I found weird was that the main thing I knew about John Wesley Powell was that he said there would never be enough water in the West to sustain a sizable population. We made our way to the sidewalk, and I tripped over a small stone. I listed, nearly falling into the road.

There wasn't a single thing about that in the museum, I continued.

Okay Miss Two-Margaritas-with-Lunch, let's try and walk in a straight line, you said. You didn't know I'd really had three.

I'm not drunk, I insisted, as you put your arm through mine and steered me down the path. I just wanted you to know, I explained, that the museum was wrong. If nothing else, I knew about this, had done all the requisite reading. Powell had understood that there wasn't enough water in the desert.

There was, in the late nineteenth century, a popular theory that the rain followed the plow. Meteorologists conjectured that white settlement had permanently changed the rainfall patterns in the United States. Maybe it was caused by newly planted trees which jostled up moisture in the atmosphere. It could have been that plowing the soil exposed increased dampness to the sky. All people needed to do was keep settling, keep moving west, and soon the whole continent would be greened. For a time, it became popular to dynamite the air to make it rain. And this, it was thought, might be a solution to the question of water.

Powell had headed the first settler expedition to run the full, dangerous course of the Colorado River. Back when the River straining against its canyon walls sounded sometimes like a bone saw. Men died. But he had seen the full dimensions of the only River that ran through the West. When he got back East, he published his report.

He began by explaining that the greatest reality of all in the West was drought. Further to that, not enough water ran in the River to irrigate the land. Ideally, you needed a reservoir of water, a dam in a good location, and the only way to do it would be a communal agreement, with benevolent Big Government oversight and an agreement to share resources. When "the rain follows the plow" revealed itself to be wrong, planners turned to Powell's irrigation theories with an evangelical devotion, building dam upon dam. And the dams worked. Cities grew. Farms were irrigated. And the groundwater shrunk away and the rain stopped falling.

None of this was ever meant to be here, I said, and it can't keep on the way that it is, waving my hands about, using the biggest words I knew, sounding completely lucid, sounding as though all the sentences were making sense. But as I spoke I found that I was unable to unbuckle my own shoes without your help.

You told me to keep my shoes on. That it was not time, yet, to take them off.

We were nearly at the motel, and you told me we would get to bed soon, that you'd find me something for dinner to sop everything up, all of that tequila, which wouldn't normally, you thought, have made me so drunk.

I don't want dinner, I said. I'd like more tequila, though. I put my hand in my tote bag and fumbled around for the battered pack of American Spirits somewhere down at the bottom, and held them in my hand without pulling them out.

You sighed. And then you said, almost as though to yourself, Sometimes I think you get excited about catastrophes. Like you're excited about the idea of everything falling apart.

In the morning I woke up on the very edge of the motel room's bed. Between us were two pillows, and I could see you were hugging another. There was a pillow beneath your head and a pillow across your forehead and eyes. You were sleeping soundly. How many times had I woken to find you obscured by pillows? When we first started dating, I thought the pillows you needed to get to sleep were quite sweet, like a remnant of the little boy who liked building forts and playing hide-and-seek. But the longer we had been together, the pillows struck me as increasingly odd, as though they were a symptom for some other greater dysfunction. I had been alarmed at the satisfaction I had felt, in previous days, arriving at Airbnbs and motel rooms where there was not a surfeit of pillows, forcing you to sleep without them. As though I thought in some perverse way that the discomfort would do you some good. But at the Page Boy Motel, there were lots. Outside, through a crack in the blackout curtains, I could see the sun rippling on the cool blue water of the swimming pool, and hear the sound of the cars roaring by outside.

Looking at the map, I realized that to get north we had to drive south. My planning had gotten sloppy. I had assumed that from Page we could drive northeast into Utah, but when I looked at the map there was an eerie absence of road directly north of us. No big towns, no highways. It may have been completely impassable, and certainly couldn't be done in the Hertz rental car. After you woke up, I told you about my mistake. You asked to see the map.

Let's go through Tuba City, you said.

So that's the way we went. We took off from Page, buying coffee and corn-syrupy muffins from a gas station for breakfast, eating them from our laps in small pinchfuls. Passing out of town we drove clear into the horizon under a glaring blue sky, where clouds smeared the firmament like toothpaste spat into a sink. For a while we drove behind a trailer, watching the sad nodding of a horse's head through the slim gap in the siding. Something I thought was a red-tailed hawk glided in circles over the road. I shifted in my seat, and dug into my bag for ibuprofen, swallowing the last two tablets in the bottle. My head hurt. Occasional cramps rumbled through my abdomen. I wasn't sure what was going on any longer. I counted the days in my head. Three weeks since my period had been due, which would make me, if I was in fact pregnant, seven weeks along. I thought about the tequila I'd drunk in Page the day before. Like the worst kind of tabloid harlot, an unfit mother. No greater villain than that.

Around us spread the great expanse of the plateau. We were speeding across traces of ancient shorelines to the sounds of *Another Green World*. For millions of years the earth here had shifted, risen, and fallen against an ocean. And then the ocean receded, and the land was heaved up into the elements. Mountains were carved from rainfall. Domes and rock tables were whittled away by wind. Rock that had accumulated as bits of pebble and sand, bound by silica and lime, disintegrated into the dust that covered the leather of my boots. Outside Tuba City soft sandstone swelled over the road, glowing pink in the sun. We stopped for gas, filling up beside an overweight man wearing a turquoise necklace which grazed the collar of his shirt and talking to a sunburned, aging hippie in surf shorts and bare feet about college football playoff rankings.

The town we drove through was quaint and quiet. Some houses were boarded up and crumbling, as they were all over the Southwest.

As we drove, you told me that the Phoenix news was always reporting on conflicts happening in Tuba City, or at least they were when you were growing up. Because, among other things, the government had allowed uranium mines to poison groundwater in the Navajo Nation, of which Tuba City was the largest town, and the de facto political center. In fact, most of the uranium in the country could be found in the Navajo Nation.

Was it around here where the government tested bombs? I asked you, looking out to the horizon line as though I might see a mushroom cloud.

I think they did, yeah, you said. A lot of the land is sacred, too. But not to the government, I guess.

In my mind's eye I saw a landscape all red dirt and blue sky, tens of bombs dropping at once and the flames coiling up. All that radiation moving in clouds, evading fences and state lines. I remembered, then, reading a book many years ago by Leslie Marmon Silko, in which she described the open-pit uranium mines constructed on the land of her people, the Laguna Pueblo, when she was young. She recalled, not long after those first desert nuclear blasts, observing men roaming around open land with Geiger counters slung over their shoulders, clicking away as they searched. When the mines opened, elders declared that none of their people should assist a desecration by working there; to enter the body of the earth would be to violate her, because the earth was sacred above all things. Those were drought years, though, and people needed work. They went to the mine anyway, but many men refused to enter the shafts. Instead they worked in the open pit, where they breathed in the radioactive dust and took it home on their skin.

And then one day, at a mine called Jackpile, two workers sent to inspect the radioactive waste piles found a peculiar shape in the rock nearby. The shape was that of an enormous snake, the length of five grown men. Its mouth was open, and it was looking west. And what was stranger was that, although the snake looked as though it had been there since time immemorial, the men inspected the waste piles twice a week, and knew that they had never seen the snake before. It had emerged from the earth in a matter of days.

People traveled from far away to see the snake in the radioactive residue, and around its body people left pieces of coral and turquoise, cornmeal and shell, to feed its spirit. Barbed wire was hitched between some posts to protect the snake from clumsy visitors, and to try and demarcate to outsiders the significance of the emergence, among the radioactive waste, of a newly sacred place. The snake was taken as an affirmation of what is self-evident: the persistence of the earth, even when it's blasted and dug up. The state highway was rerouted, eventually, away from the snake, and whether it was still there or not in the remains of the uranium mine I wasn't sure.

The piles of radioactive waste were left there, out in the open, even when the mines closed. The dust became airborne. It flowed into the water, it found its way into the plants and the animals, into everything that lived on the land. Radiation nested in the bones and the lungs, accumulating over time. I wondered whether what happened here was just as bad as every monstrous thing I'd ever heard about the catastrophe of radiation. The way every form of life is implicated—from the disintegrating thyroids of horses near Chernobyl when the reactor exploded, to the worms which switched from asexual to sexual reproduction, and the entire forest of pines scorched red, which first shed their needles, then died, and collapsed. And that was only what was observed. What about the slower forms of destruction, those we didn't think to keep track of, those that take a longer time?

See, you said, and pointed to a sign along the side of the road. "Talk with your doctor about uranium, radiation, and your health," it said, behind a layer of red dust. We were already halfway out of town. The sun was high overhead.

We passed into an eerie landscape of short grass and lonely rock outcrops, occasionally spotting a hogan or a boarded-up house. We stopped, because you were hungry, at a Sonic drive-through, where

"Rockin' Around the Christmas Tree" was being pumped through the staticky loudspeakers into the lane between ordering and pickup. You ordered a slushie and Tater Tots to share, and when you passed me the bag, I pointed out a note attached, reading, "Your Kayenta Sonic Drive-in will be OPEN Thanksgiving Day!"

That was five days ago, I said.

You made a humming noise of concurrence. I feel like we've put nearly a thousand miles on this car you said, reaching across and picking the Tater Tots from the bag in my lap, feeding them into your mouth. Is that possible?

I have no idea, I said. You know I still don't understand miles.

You tried to explain again. That it was easier if you thought about the distances you were allowed to drive according to speed limits in an hour.

But, I told you, my brain would simply not retain this information, would leak it the same way I'd leaked Fahrenheit and ounces and quarts. We passed a Burger King with a small black dog loitering by the entryway, seemingly without an owner. The roads were cracked, flaking, like sunburnt skin as it's peeling. A sign we passed detailed the benefits of testing for pre-diabetes. You told me to change the album, and I put on *Broken English* by Marianne Faithfull, which seemed like it shouldn't fit the mood of the landscape but did. We passed a conveyor bringing something down from the Peabody Kayenta Mine, something dark.

Is that coal? I asked you, pointing to the conveyor.

I don't know, you said. I don't know what coal looks like, really. Is it black?

I think so, I said, but we were already passing by. I looked up to the hills where the conveyor led, and I thought of all the tiny prehistoric plants, shellfish, the delicate architectures of bacteria and algae and coral, all submerged, compressed, crushed down under the weight of years, penetrated with drills, blasted from the sandstone, the topsoil removed, heaved into the light. You can wind back the story so far into the past. Your hands on the wheel of the car, driving us north towards Utah. Your hands on my hips in the house in Encinitas. Your hands in your pockets at Seven Magic Mountains. Your hand holding mine the day we were married. Your hands exist in all these moments, all these times, all at once, when I remember them. When you were gone, in those first few days, I lay on the couch and I did not go to work and I did not eat and sometimes I began drinking at noon, or earlier, because I didn't want to be awake, and I would try to ward off any thought at all, because anything at all could trigger collapse. Your hands especially. What would I do without those hands? If I happened to recall your fingers, your bitten fingernails, your knuckles on the wheel, I might be struck with the realization that the absolute photo-realistic intimacy with which I knew those hands would fade over time if you did not come back, and such a memory could send me into spasms of crying. I was terrified of losing anything I had of you, any shred of memory that was mine. It was appalling to wake up in a silent apartment, an apartment without you in it.

I could see the shape of Monument Valley on the horizon long before we were anywhere near it. The shape of the tall red buttes was as familiar as New York City, from all the films I instantly realized had used it as a location. Horses grazed behind fences, and I saw a stall along the side of the road selling apples, but many of the stalls advertising "Navajo Handmade Jewelry" were closed for the season. We turned in to the entrance where a woman manned the booth, a woman who looked cold and stiff, wrapped in her puffer coat and ear warmers. She handed us a flyer and directed us with her finger towards the prescribed route, trying not to stray too far outside the three walls of her plywood shelter.

I thought we could hike a bit or something, I said.

Oh, I didn't, you said. It's sacred, I'm pretty sure. Or there are places here where deities live, and other ceremonial places. Would you want a bunch of tourists being able to roam all around your sacred spaces taking photos? It'd be like trashing a synagogue.

We drove along the gravel road while I took photographs through the car window with my phone. But taking photographs reminded me that I was a tourist, and I felt ashamed. People had stopped in their cars along the route. From the window I could see that a teenage girl had paid money to sit on a horse and had donned a Stetson like she was a female John Wayne in leggings and Adidas sneakers. You pointed ahead to a family jumping into the air on the count of three, and another girl on the edge of a small escarpment with her arms held out as though to encompass the enormity of the butte.

There's something so sad, and mediated, about this, you said. Nobody can really experience it properly. You can just experience everybody else taking photographs.

It was, I agreed, like landscape as theme park. But just because we weren't taking group photographs didn't make us any different, I thought.

A familiar-looking overlook appeared ahead on the trail, and large signs directing us towards it described it as John Ford Point. We followed the line of cars up, and you said, Should we get out here for a bit?

When I opened the car door a cold breeze seemed to barrel across the plain, even though it was midday, and the sun was high above us. A line of stalls were set up near the parking spots, and places where you could pay to have your photo taken like John Wayne. Maybe I'll get something for my mother, I said. Do you mind if I do?

If you want to.

Buying a dream catcher and a necklace, I asked the owner, an elderly woman in a big purple parka with her long braids tucked into the hood, whether she would be here much longer, through December. I couldn't imagine how she could bear standing up here, exposed to such bone-chilling cold.

We're here all year round, she told me, unless the weather is too bad. Rain or snow.

It snows here? I asked her.

Sometimes, she said.

Walking back to the car I passed a large black dog trying to get the attention of the two teenage Navajo boys who were sitting by the edge of the tent, sharing a cigarette, watching a clip from a Dave Chappelle stand-up special on one of the boy's phones. I found you leaning against the driver's door, looking anxiously at your emails.

What's wrong?

Nothing, you said as you opened the door and got back into the car. You exhaled deeply and affected a stretch. Your hips were tight.

It's just that my boss wants to talk on the phone, you said. I asked if he could wait a few days until we're back in New York.

About anything?

No, I think it's just he wants to talk, but you never know. It's just going to be weird, if he asks me about the Greco project.

Just do what Kenneth told you, I said. Pretend like it never happened.

Right. I can't stop thinking about it. That's all.

Talking to your boss?

No. Just what it felt like to be out there. To be there on Monday.

We had arrived back at the highway and drove by a family stopped by the side of the road, standing beneath a sign saying, "Welcome to Utah: Life Elevated," posing for a photograph. Approaching a roundabout, I asked you to turn left and towards the Trading Post. I need to pee, I explained. In the bathroom I found that there were spots of blood, again, in my underwear. I put a layer of toilet paper over the crotch, a kind of makeshift panty liner. I did not know what else to do. In the other stall, I heard a woman making a phone call in Italian, the speedy staccato of her speech sounding unexpectedly reassuring over the tinkling of urination.

Outside, I found you by the gift shop. I drifted towards a case filled with rocks and crystals. They were pretty: hunks of petrified wood, purple amethyst, and the crystallized sugar of geodes. What do you think? I asked. Should I get something?

You reminded me of the crystal that we, or rather I, had received as a gift the year before.

Moving from bar to bar on New Year's Eve, we had met a new, and as it turned out short-lived, romantic interest of the lanky Arkansan photographer I lived with before I moved in with you. The girl had had a horrible year. She was glad it was ending at last. She was already drunk, and she had been troubled when I accidentally spilled wine onto her jacket which, she said, was made of monkey fur. I had asked if monkey fur was not illegal.

She sneered and said, Who cares?

As we were leaving she offered me a cigarette, and said she wanted to give me something. I've carried this crystal around in my purse all year, she said, and I want you to have it. May it bring you positivity and happiness.

It struck me as an extraordinarily kind gesture, and I put the crystal in my own bag. I did not believe that crystals had any kind of metaphysical or supernatural powers, but it was pretty, a pale rose-colored quartz. We took a cab to meet other friends, and in the back seat you kept your hands to yourself, imposing a kind of coldness between us because you had seen that I had been smoking a cigarette, and you hated it when I smoked. You hated the taste of my mouth after I'd had one, and you hated it with the panicky fear of a child who still believes that bad actions make bad people. When the cab stopped and I got out, my purse fell out of my hand and hit the bitumen, propelled forward, and fell down into a grating below. An hour later, my phone fell and its screen smashed to pieces.

What enormous bad luck in one night, I commented.

Do you still have the crystal? you asked.

You reminded me that the girl had said her year had been awful, and that she had carried the crystal in her purse through it all. Whether

I believed it or not, the next morning we went to Enid's for brunch, and while we waited for our food, I took the crystal out of my purse, and left it on the window ledge we were seated beside. I'm half expecting Enid's to burn down, you said.

It didn't burn down, but it did close, right around the time things began to get really bad.

I put the crystal back in its place, and we left. When we were back on the highway you were silent for a while, with Captain Beefheart & His Magic Band occupying the silence between us.

This land just shouldn't be America, you finally said.

What do you mean, I asked. Like, the way that it looks?

No, you said. It shouldn't be considered America's. It should be Navajo. It should be their country.

I nodded. I didn't know how to respond, or what to say. Well, I said after a while, we're in Utah now.

We ate a late lunch at the San Juan Trading Post near Mexican Hat, and took off north, the light already beginning to thin into blue. We passed the sombrero-shaped rock along the side of the road that gave Mexican Hat its name, and by the time we'd reached the outskirts of Bluff the light was gone; we were driving in complete darkness.

There seem to be a lot of churches in this town, I commented.

Yeah, well, what do you do out here but fear God? you replied. Why did you want to stay in this town?

Because it's near Bears Ears, and Canyonlands, and kind of near Moab.

But I had supposed that the town was bigger, or more substantial. Maybe we would find that it was, in the daylight, but it seemed in the dark like a near ghost town. A bush on the side of road as we turned into the street we were heading to looked, illuminated by our headlights in the dark, like a ghost of the Virgin Mary. Her hands were held out to us in supplication.

When we arrived at the Airbnb we found that it was better and larger than I had expected. It was, in fact, an entire house, with a fully functioning kitchen, a large bedroom, and a full greenhouse at the back, filled with vegetables and herbs. The visitor book in the living room said we were welcome to use as much as we wanted of the vegetables, and so I began to plan a meal. We would just need to go down to the store. There was a restaurant in town, but it was closed for the season. Much of everything around here was closed for the season, it seemed. I had not realized how out of season we were, when I had planned the trip.

The store was really a gas station. The only vegetables for sale were onions and a brown head of lettuce. I picked up spaghetti, and an onion, although not the lettuce. You emerged from an aisle with packets of chips, gummy bears, peanut M&M'S, and a box of Hostess cupcakes in your hand. At the register they sold fresh cinnamon rolls, the *Navajo Times*, and seven different kinds of jerky. We bought one of everything. As we walked back to the house in the frosty quiet you said that I should try having some of the weed you still had left over.

How do you still have any of that left? I asked.

Honestly? You paused, then said, Brandon gave me a bunch at Thanksgiving.

How much?

I mean, we won't run out. I think it would help you, you said. We can watch a movie and you'll just relax. I really think alcohol is terrible. I always feel so bad the next day, even if I only have a little.

From the greenhouse out the back I picked tomatoes and red chard and some fresh green basil. It was odd to stand in a greenhouse with nothing but darkness on the other side of the walls. I wondered whether this house used to belong to somebody's mother, once upon a time. How else could you explain the presence of the greenhouse? There was no garlic in the greenhouse that I could find, although would I have known what garlic looked like from what grew above the soil line? I took what I had, and what I could identify, and found a chopping board in a drawer by the stove in the kitchen. I slid your mother's engagement ring from my wedding finger and left it on the side of the sink, so that I wouldn't damage the setting, and began chopping vegetables while water warmed to a boil in a saucepan. You paged through the visitor's book and offered me the vape pen, and you told me as I inhaled that they had mined uranium here as well.

Is the drinking water okay?

Doesn't say anything about that. I guess it's okay?

While I chopped, you asked what time I wanted to leave in the morning. When I asked why, you said that you might like to try and wake up early and go for a walk before we set off. Alone. It was, you said, something you'd been texting with Brandon about. He had sent you an instructional video, something he had been trying, and which he said really helped him. Helped with what, you didn't say.

I said that sounded fine. We had barely been apart from one another for the entire trip, except when I went running.

You set up your laptop in front of the big-screen TV in the Airbnb's living room, and you searched around for movies. Should we watch something filmed in Monument Valley? I asked.

We should watch something from the desert, you said.

You searched around. I said I'd watch whatever you wanted, and when I brought over the food in the chipped blue bowls, you had settled on an option. The film opened on a meeting of Black Panthers and college students debating social revolution. It was the late 1960s. Were they willing to die? A man stood up and said he was willing to die, sure. But not of boredom. He walked out. *That bourgeois individualism*, a Panther said, *is going to get him killed.*

You handed me the vape pen, and I held on to it. I took big, deep inhalations, trying to get it down as far into my lungs as I could. I felt a strange pulsing in my abdomen. I did not know what it meant. I was tired, I told you. You encouraged me to have more. In the film, executives for a property development company were evaluating the ad for their new desert utopia. *Enjoy the full relaxation of outdoor living. Bask in the desert sun by your own private pool.* Cut to a view of happy, thin white people, recreating. *Breathe the unpolluted air of the high desert.*

Take your son quail shooting in the wide-open spaces. Who knows, you might even bag a mountain lion. Become an independent man. Forge a life of your own like the pioneers who molded the West. And wasn't that exactly the kind of milk-and-honey life one would hope to find in a bottomless pit, in the middle of a desert? A place where everyone looked like you, loved like you did, and soon grew fairy wings from their shoulder blades.

Back in the city, the bourgeois individualist stole a plane, took off over Los Angeles, and flew into the desert. Meanwhile a long-haired beauty was driving on her way to the desert utopia. The plane and the car converged over the highway. When they met a few moments later he asked where she was headed. *Phoenix*, she said.

Why Phoenix? he asked. *There's nothing in Phoenix.*

You laughed at that and asked if you could have some of the vape pen.

No, I said.

You laughed at that too, and you let me keep it. The bourgeois individualist told the girl he was in trouble. He got in her car, and they drove out to Zabriskie Point, a vast alien landscape, like a heaving ocean suddenly frozen and turned to sand. The long-haired beauty offered him some weed. They began to touch each other, and then they began to have sex. I took more and more of the vape pen, big gulps of it down, the sour, repulsive taste of the weed coating my mouth like swamp gum. The sex scene had turned into a hallucinatory orgy. All of Zabriskie Point was covered in coupling bodies.

This is why the revolution failed, I said, but I did not elaborate when you asked me to.

You laughed. I've never seen you so high, you said. You're so fun like this.

I always knew it would be like this, the bourgeois individualist said after orgasm.

Love? asked the woman.

The desert, he replied.

I put my head in your lap, taking more into my lungs. My eyes strangely placed in my head, as though I might like to take them out and give them a rub with a sleeve. The bourgeois individualist decided to take back the stolen plane. When he got into L.A. the police were waiting, shots were fired, and he was killed.

A short while later, having arrived at the utopian desert community, the long-haired beauty stood staring silently at the concrete walls. And as though to suggest that her staring was the catalyst, the building exploded into flames. Black smoke coursed into the air. Debris tumbled slowly downwards to the sound of Pink Floyd: wires, wood chips, Wonder Bread, pool chairs, hardback books blooming like flame-flowers from the bookcases. And then the screeching music cut, the long-haired beauty smiled, and in a light that could have been caused by fire or a desert sunset, she got into the car, turned the engine on, and took off into saguaro country.

Are you crying? you asked me. My jeans feel wet.

I nodded. Yes. I had not even realized that I was.

8

Holotropic Breathwork—The Pineal Gland—Text Messages Sending
Green—A White-Tiled Shower Floor—Clots in the Shower Grates—
Ibuprofen—Sinclair Gas Sign—Proud Gateway to Bears Ears—
Bluff Pioneer Cemetery—Rock Circles—Desert Burials—A Future
Child—Alliterative Names For Girls—The Art of Women—Georgia
O'Keeffe's Fear of Water—Lost Bodies and Boats Discovered
in Lake Mead—A Hamburger, Rare, with a Pickle and Fries

When I woke up in the morning it was seven o'clock, and the light was just beginning to slip itself through the closed blinds of the bedroom. I had an imprecise awareness of having heard an alarm sounding, but when I came to consciousness it was because you had dropped your boot, and the sound of the thud against the floorboards startled me awake. You were already dressed, sitting on the end of the bed and tying your shoelaces.

You're going out? I asked.

Yes, you said softly, just for an hour maybe. You whispered your words, as though I might still be coaxed back to sleep.

Where are you going?

Remember, I told you? I'm going to drive out a bit and do that thing I was talking about. What time do we have to check out?

Noon, I said as you stood up, and the distribution of weight on the bed shifted. Is it meditation? I asked.

Basically, you said, sliding an arm inside a jacket sleeve. I'll be back well before we have to leave. Then you looked closely at me, as if for the first time. You okay? you asked. You don't look great.

I'm not feeling that well, I said. I'll go back to sleep. I turned over and listened to the sounds of your leaving: the car keys and the swish of the fabric of your jacket, and the thud of boots on the floor as you walked down the hall. I heard you slam the car door and the growl of the engine as it began to recede down the road.

I wondered what manner of meditation Brandon had recommended. I hadn't said so, but it seemed to me slightly daft and performative, to go out into the desert to meditate in the wilderness.

The kind of *Simon of the Desert* stuff that seemed more suited to film than real life. Years later, I opened your laptop and read through your emails, and I found the email that Brandon had sent you right after Thanksgiving, the one which included the directions you had followed that day. "Breathwork," was the email's subject line. Which was yoga class stuff, I thought. I'd done breathwork, or versions of it, on Saturday mornings in Greenpoint. Lying on the hardwood boards of a converted warehouse with fifty other people, listening to the whoosh-whoosh-huh of the collective breath, so forceful that it seemed to shake the floor. You had been in regular contact with your brother over that last week since we'd seen him, and I suppose you were talking to him about all manner of things you weren't speaking about with me.

Brandon, in his email to you, had explained that he had lately been attending workshops, all-male affairs, to try and deal with some of the emotions he had been feeling "post-Mom." He wrote to you that at one such workshop he had been introduced to Holotropic Breathwork. It had been initiated at the end of a weekend full of various large group conversation sessions and small group sharing sessions, meditation, hikes, and ice baths. Brandon had told you that he had had psychedelic experiences in these workshops he'd been taking. Or maybe it would be more accurate to say that they were profound spiritual breakthroughs. More than anything else, they had helped him with his grief. In Brandon's notes, he told you that you needed to start by lying down. Hands by your side, stay comfortable. Start by taking breaths in through the nose and out through the mouth. Eventually, drop the nose. Become all mouth. After a little while, let the inhalations become deeper, and make them quicker. Begin to take two inhalations, and one exhalation. It feels unnatural because it is, he wrote. It's not hyperventilating, Brandon wrote to you, although it had felt like hyperventilating to me.

Brandon's email explained to you that when a person did Holotropic Breathwork, their blood became flooded with oxygen. Brandon told you that the flood of oxygen would prompt the pineal gland to release DMT. He didn't explain what that was, so I looked it up, and found websites suggesting that if one could activate the pineal gland this way, through breathwork, one could have an authentically natural psychedelic experience. The body was the only way to solve anything, Brandon wrote to you, because it was where all the problems had started. He felt convinced that it was the only way to release *the trauma of Mom*, although he did not specify in his email whether he meant the trauma of her death, or the trauma that was a by-product of being a mother's son. He told you that what you would find was that over time the part of your brain that experienced anxiety, grief, and guilt would be silenced. It had worked for him. He suggested that you do it in a quiet place, where you could be as loud as you wanted, *away from Eloise.*

Maybe you had somewhere in mind when you left that morning. I never asked. I wouldn't know about Brandon's instructions until years later. I was distracted by the pain in my abdomen. Getting out of bed, I went to find my bag, where I remembered having a bottle of ibuprofen, only to recall once I opened it that I had taken the last pills the day before, in Page. I wished I had asked you to buy me painkillers from the store before you'd left. It hadn't occurred to me, as you were leaving, that I would need them.

Returning to the bedroom, I saw that there was a circle of blood on the striped yellow sheet on which I had been sleeping. It was not a lot of blood, maybe the size of a Reese's Peanut Butter Cup. I climbed back into bed and pulled the covers over my body and considered that perhaps even allowing myself to believe that I was pregnant, even for a few days, had been the trick. The thing that had brought the illusion to an end. Now there was the familiar, dull thudding in my abdomen, right behind my pelvic bone. And a sharper, more intense pain which I had to breathe through. I needed ibuprofen. I lay down on top of the circle of blood. I didn't go to the bathroom, didn't try to clean myself up. Not yet. I was waiting for something, although I couldn't have told you what it was. It was not long after you left, about twenty minutes, when things began to escalate. The pain worsened. A knot behind my pelvic bone, the deep-set place where the cramping came from every month, but never before like this. I wondered whether it hurt so much because I was paying attention to it, and so tried to distract myself by reading news articles on my phone, but distraction failed to keep it at bay. The cramps came in waves. It was like being on a boat smacking across a bay; during those seconds when the bow rose above the water, I felt no pain, but the moment didn't last, and inevitably I was, once again, brought swiftly down to the water's hard surface. I sat up slowly, left the bed again, and crouched down to rummage first through your bag, and then mine. Neither of us had any extra painkillers. But then I found that it did not seem possible to leave the crouch I had assumed on the floor. The idea of stretching my body out to its full length felt suddenly unbearable. If I were to stand up, everything, I thought, would seize up into a white-hot obliterating *something*, a something I did not want to try to countenance. The idea of walking to the general store for some ibuprofen by then seemed utterly impossible. I could at least, I thought, clean myself up. I pushed a hand between my thighs to feel the crotch of my black leggings. It was wet with what I knew was blood. I knew I needed to relocate to the bathroom. A little blood on the by-the-night sheets was okay, but not this much. Not at the rate it was coming out of me. I heaved myself out of the crouching position on the floor with a clenched-teeth scream, overcome by the excruciating pain that ripped through me as I stood. It took me a moment to steady myself, and then I walked towards the bathroom, keeping a hand against the wall to stay upright. I took my phone with me. I texted you, clutching the doorframe with one hand, asking you to please get me some strong painkillers on your way back, because I didn't feel well at all. I hit send, but the blue message stayed there on the screen, without being marked as "delivered." A few moments later, when I'd reached the bathroom and checked our message thread again, I saw that it had sent through as green. Maybe your phone was out of reception, I thought. In the bathroom I took the leggings off and kicked them into a ball and sat naked from the waist down on the toilet. There was a lot of blood. It had smeared the tops of my thighs, which was unusual. I tried to wipe it away, but it was of a hue and texture and volume that toilet paper could not handle. I looked at my phone again, where I had placed it on the edge of the sink. I picked it up. I called your number. I was scared, you see. I wanted you to come back. I did not want to be alone. But the call went to voicemail, and I hung up. You never checked your voicemail, so there would be no point in leaving one. I sat my phone on the ledge by the shower, so that I would see it if it lit up with your name, and then I took my top off and threw it into the same pile as the leggings, then turned the hot water on. I sat on the floor of the Airbnb shower holding my legs to my chest, leaning my chin on my knees, and let the warm water fall over my bent head and cascade down my back. Only then did it feel a little better. The shower floor was tiled in a bright white diamond pattern. Against the clean expanse of the shower, the clots coming out of me were easy to track. This was not my bathroom, and this was not my shower, and we were meant to drive into the Utah canyonlands later that morning, and already it was eight o'clock, but I was there, and couldn't have moved an inch.

Clots. Tens of them. They were of a strange consistency, like pieces of raw liver. Maybe the size of a dime, and occasionally the size of a quarter. I watched them emerge on the shower floor beneath me, and then, caught by the water, slowly drift towards the drain. They collected over the grate, unable to fit through the metal holes, and I thought about pushing them down as sometimes I push wet pieces of carrot down the kitchen sink when washing up dishes, but I couldn't bear to touch them. I wanted so much for you to come back.

I sat there in the shower for half an hour with the hot water coursing down my shoulders, until the pain began to ebb. When I eventually stood up and turned the taps off, dried myself, made sure the drain was clear, collected my toiletries, and then set down several folded layers of toilet paper into a clean pair of underpants, I checked my phone again. You still had not replied. You had been gone for more than two hours by then. Once dressed, I walked into the living room, collecting our things as I went. I put the dishes from the night before in the sink and tidied away the junk food wrappers still on the coffee table from the night before, beside your closed laptop. I centralized all our belongings in preparation for departure. I rinsed a cup in the sink, filled it with water, and then took a long drink, only remembering, when the aftertaste hit, what you'd told me about uranium. A glint of light caught my eye, and I only noticed then your mother's engagement ring, still resting on the counter from where I'd left it the night before. I reached for the ring and held it between my fingers, the sapphire and the smaller diamonds swooping to frame the stone. How you'd cope if I lost it, I wasn't sure. I slid it back down the ring finger of my left hand. Would I have preferred to leave it behind? Why did it feel so much heavier, more awkward, to put it back on? Why had I said yes when you'd asked me to wear it, knowing how much the symbolism might cost me?

I walked slowly towards the store, where I found ibuprofen in an aisle adjacent to the produce baskets filled with brown lettuce and onions. I took four pills, still standing there in the aisle. I couldn't wait. I bought pads for the first time since I was fourteen. I knew one was not meant to take so much ibuprofen at once, because it risked damaging the liver, but I did. I had no concern in that moment for any of my other organs. I paid and walked out into the car park, beneath the tall green Sinclair Gas sign advertising the prices for unleaded and diesel, and as quick as I could across the highway, even though there was no passing traffic to speak of. The houses built along the dusty streets were surprisingly grand. Many of them seemed to have been built in the nineteenth century, made of stone, and many-storied. On the lawn or by the front door of just about every house I passed was a blue-and-pink sign saying, "Proud Gateway to Bears Ears."

I was nearly back at the house when I felt my phone vibrate, and I reached for it, thinking as I did that it would be you, but it was only an automated message sent by campus security, alerting us to a burglary in a residential building near the university. It was almost ten o'clock. The light in the house's living room was dim and wintery, a bleak emanation filtering through curtains and shuttered blinds which made me feel nothing but hopeless. Walking to the store had tired me. I closed the door, and as I turned to flip the lock, I saw your phone sitting on the hall table next to the front door. I called out your name. But even as I did, I could see that the car wasn't parked in the front. You still weren't back. I reached down to your phone and pressed the home button. Nothing happened. It was off. I realized then that you hadn't even taken it with you. You had placed it so carefully on the hall table that I understood immediately you had not forgotten it. You wanted to be unencumbered by it. We had had so many fights about your phone; your feeling that it was a suck on your time and headspace, a parasite of some kind, that you would prefer to be without, even as you spent so much of your time scrolling and swiping on it. You viewed the phone as an addiction. Sometimes you got so angry with it that you would put it in a drawer of the kitchen or hide it under the bed when you left the house. Or you would put it in your bag on "Do Not Disturb" mode, so that even if I called or texted, nothing would show up on the home screen, and nothing would light up or vibrate to unsettle your train of thought. I remembered nights when you had not told me you were going out, when I had gone to sleep only to wake up at three in the morning and realize you still weren't home, and I would be paralyzed with terror, trying to text you, or call you, and you wouldn't reply, and so when you eventually came home you would find me edgy and weepy and ready to yell at you, because I had not known where you were, and what if something had happened, how could I contact you? You argued that you deserved your autonomy, to not be at my beck and call, and I agreed with you. I didn't want to surveil you, nor to be a burden. You promised you would always be safe, that you would always come home, and that I could trust you.

When have I ever hurt you? you would say.

I was angry when I saw your phone there on the hall table, and I had rarely felt so all alone.

I sat down on the couch where we had watched the film the night before. I stared at the television on the other side of the room. The silence was profound, nothing but the low electronic hum of the refrigerator motor, and the occasional trill of a thrush in the elm by the front door. All I could do was wait. I clutched my phone, as though I suspected you might still call. I opened the lock screen and checked my email, checked the news, scrolled through Instagram, but no distraction was adequate. I reopened my emails and searched for the message that Camila had written to me on Monday morning, then tapped the blue digits of her phone number, before I'd really thought about it. The phone rang. I don't think I even really expected that she would answer, but she did.

If she was surprised, she didn't let on. She spoke as though she had been expecting my call. She said that she was at the university, and had just concluded her office hours, which had been busy, a parade of students with papers due in the next fortnight beginning to panic and asking her for reassurance. I told her that I had been delighted by her email and hoped she could speak to me about my doctorate, once we were done with the trip. Ideas she might have for further research, maybe, or a possible solution to what I might do and where I might go when I was finished with it. She was surprised because she had, as I had correctly guessed, thought we were back in New York.

I'm in a small town called Bluff, in Utah, I told her, expecting perhaps that she would be impressed. As though the smaller the Southwestern town, the more gravitas it would lend my Southwestern credentials.

But she knew Bluff. Had eaten at the San Juan Trading Post just like us, and told me about a woman essayist who had written about the town's lawns. I spent a summer there once, she said, on a self-styled writing retreat. Instead of going home to my family after college.

I was pleased that she was speaking to me in the language of personal anecdote. As though she was denying my appeal for a mentor and a teacher, and insisting instead on a casualness produced by the equalizing effects of unveiled intimacies.

As she spoke, I stood up, walked down the hall, and began to bring the rest of our things into the living room. I did this slowly. The cramps had begun to die down now the painkillers had kicked in, but each time I bent over a dizzy spell overtook me, blackening the edges of my vision before I straightened. Camila asked if I had seen the cemetery on the edge of Bluff. I told her I had not. I had to admit that I hadn't seen anything more than the street between the Airbnb and K & C Trading Post on the highway.

You should take a walk to the cemetery, she said. The cemetery was the best thing in town. At the time of her stay, she told me, Camila had been into taking photographs on an old 35mm film camera, and she still had one of the photographs framed, somewhere in her house. A picture of the headstones and piles of rocks. The town had been settled as a Mormon outpost, she explained to me, around the time that the Saints in Salt Lake City were trying to push out into new territory. There were never very many of those early Mormon settlers, and most of them were buried in that graveyard. It was hard country in that part of Utah, and little wonder so many of that colonizing party had died so soon, and often so young.

The reason she had gone to the cemetery so frequently to take photographs, she said, was that it was unlike any other cemetery she could remember visiting. The graves were marked in the ordinary way, yes, but nearly every grave was also marked by a mound of stones, in roughly the same length and width as the deceased body below. For babies the mounds were small, and almost perfectly circular. Adults were marked by longer rock heaps. The circles were constructed out of stones from the surrounding bluffs, which I imagined must have been frightening to harvest; there could always have been a snake hiding beneath a stone. Indeed, Camila said she sometimes saw rattlesnakes on her walks, although more often gopher snakes and whiptail lizards, when she was walking through the cemetery in Bluff. Creatures sliding behind a crop of stones or slipping back into a crack of earth.

When I asked if she knew why the bodies were buried beneath mounds of stone, she said that was how people used to bury the dead in the desert. It was sometimes quite simply too hard to dig into the ground. Have you seen that earth? she asked. It takes a lot to dig a hole, let alone one that deep. The rocks cover up the body. They let you know whether it's been disturbed. But it's an imperfect practice, she said, especially if it's done quickly.

Camila's ex-husband, an immigration lawyer, had told her stories about those who had come through the desert, up from Central America and across the Mexican border, by bus to Mexico City, onwards to a tiny Sonoran town in the middle of nowhere, and then by foot across the border into the U.S.—people who told stories about the bodies left behind in the desert. Those who got cramps, who grew too exhausted or too tired, those fallen by injury or snakebite. Bodies they'd see the traces of. Bones that looked like human kneecaps, or the curve of a jaw. Often, those traces of bodies were not from people abandoned on the desert floor to die. They were people buried by their loved ones on the trail.

People have always buried bodies beneath stones in the desert, thinking the piles of rocks will keep the body safe. But the problem with that, Camila continued, is that rocks retain heat. The sun heats them during the day, and so the warm body buried beneath decays even faster. Vultures arrive. Then coyotes. This was such an unexpected and strangely intimate turn in the conversation that I suppose I might have told her what I thought might be happening to me. But I didn't know what was happening. Or, rather, the word sat just on the far side of articulated thought. Not even my inner voice could utter it. Because maybe I was being melodramatic. Maybe nothing very bad was happening, had happened, was still to come; how could I even discern the edges of the event? If I had, in the space of the last week, passed from believing my period would come, to something else, I had not progressed any further than that in any meaningful sense, because I was waiting to see what I thought about it. And until I knew how I felt about it, how could I tell you?

I thought back to the beginning of the year, to those days after your mother had died, when I was standing in that Phoenix strip mall while you spoke to the jeweler and asked for the return of her engagement ring. When I had cried that day, watching the pregnant couple across the way wedge a stroller into their car, it was in part because the reality of our own future child was so strong. So absolutely real. Sometimes when we were being silly and giggly, we had spoken that child into being. Always with an alliterative name, just like yours. Leonora Levin. Lachrymose Levin. Lovelorn Levin. Lolly Levin. We had so many imaginary daughters. If what was happening to me on the trip had happened a year beforehand, before the death, I don't think that I would have hesitated to tell you. Instead, I was all hesitation. You were out in the desert trying to exorcise yourself of grief, and I had no idea when you would come back. You could have driven all the way to Colorado by now, and we were due to check out of the Airbnb in an hour, and I was sitting on the brown tartan couch I had, only the night before, laid down on and cried while watching the end of *Zabriskie Point*, and now all I could do was wait and keep talking to Camila.

So I told her about *Zabriskie Point*, and I told her that I had cried. She was surprised, because in her memory it was a terrible movie. I agreed with her that I thought it was, probably, a terrible film. But there was something moving about it. Both the orgy in the desert, and the scene of absolute destruction at the end. She told me that there were better movies to watch about the desert, and better art made about the desert. Look to women's art, Camila told me. The art made by men about the American desert is all ideological, it's all so tediously imperial. She told me I should instead watch *Desert Hearts*.

I hadn't seen it, I told her.

Women make better art about the desert, Camila repeated emphatically.

Georgia O'Keeffe? I asked.

I guess, she said, although I could tell that wasn't who she had in mind.

But I knew about Georgia O'Keeffe, and suddenly remembering a story I had heard, I wanted nothing more right then than to talk about her. The urge to tell Camila about Georgia O'Keeffe became, in that moment, the next best thing to telling her what had happened in the shower. If I could not say aloud what I thought had just happened, I could approach the feeling from side-on, like a crab scuttling back towards its shelter. I reminded Camila that Georgia O'Keeffe had lived in Manhattan with her famous photographer husband before she moved out to the New Mexican desert. In the city she had lived in a skyscraper, which seemed antithetical to her myth as an artist of vulval flowers and animal bone, I supposed, but the skyscraper was the only way she felt she could survive New York. From the twenty-eighth floor it was like living in her own personal eyrie, the boundless sky and all its moods open around her when she lay on the floor and looked upwards. Up there, she painted the sky, the unfurling stamens of flowers, the sinuous curves of waves, and the steady surface of lakes. Her work was drenched in the damp, fecund climate of the East, the intimacy and safety of its moisture.

And then, the year she was thirty-five, she was commissioned to paint a mural in the ladies' powder room at Radio City Music Hall. And something broke. She could not complete the painting in the powder room, and she walked off the job. A few days later it was noticed that she was having trouble speaking. She was tired, her head ached, and she fell into sudden bouts of tears. The crying jags worsened, lengthened, and she ceased to eat or sleep. And then things got very bad indeed, because after a week or so of this, she developed a morbid fear of water, and wouldn't drink a drop. She was institutionalized.

This woman who was known for being self-sufficient and formidable was all of a sudden fragile, deathly afraid of her husband, and unable to stop crying. When she got out of the hospital, she was still not strong, and could not go home to the apartment on the twenty-eighth floor. Nor could she bear to see her husband. She had been to the Southwest before, but this time she went out there changed, and alone. To recover. Driving one day through the landscape a little outside of Santa Fe, she discovered a place named Ghost Ranch. She fell in love with the hills and the red oxide cliffs, the bright and singing sky. For the rest of her life, she would spend the best part of every year in that place. When people mentioned to her their terror of the desert, of its barrenness and their feelings of alienation when they were in it, O'Keeffe instead spoke about the tenderness of the red curving hills. She said that sometimes as she was painting them, the hills looked so soft that she wanted to take all her clothes off and lie against them. And maybe that is why I have always loved the contours of her desertscapes, which are so bodily, so undulating and curving. When the animal bones she painted were thrown in contrast against the soft desert, they seemed to suggest that there was something much more intimate and absolute in this landscape than the forces of the men who had storied it. But the curious thing, the thing I wanted to tell Camila, was that before the breakdown, O'Keeffe had always painted water. Had painted its flux and ebb, its consoling surges and delicate rippling. But after she grew afraid of water in that New York hospital, the terror never quite went away. After the year that she was thirty-five, nearly all Georgia O'Keeffe's paintings were of arid landscapes.

I was slumped into the cushions of the couch telling her this story when I heard the sound of wheels on the gravel, then a car door slamming. I interrupted Camila, who was trying to tell me about artists she considered more interesting than Georgia O'Keeffe—Judy Chicago and her '60s-era *Atmospheres*, for instance, the haunted photographs of Graciela Iturbide. I told her that you had come home, and that I should go. We were running late. It was fifteen minutes until noon, and I had meant, although not really told you, to be well on our way towards Moab by now. Half the day was lost. I asked if I could call her again when I was back in the city, and thanked her. I tried to thank her with something that might go some way to communicating the gravity of my gratitude. How could she have known how desperately I had needed to be distracted? I didn't notice the confusion in her voice, nor the note of annoyance at my abrupt end to what was, without question, a bizarre and indecorous phone call to a woman I had imagined I had more intimacy with than I did. We said goodbye.

Hey, you said, standing in the open door.

You didn't take your phone, I replied.

No, I didn't want it to disturb me. But look, it's not even noon yet. Should we pack up?

I was worried, I said.

I'm sorry. You didn't need to be. I'm fine. I'm always fine.

You were gone a long time.

I know. I only realized how long it had been when I was on the way back and looked at the clock on the dashboard.

I stood up. A wave of dizziness darkened my eyes for a moment, but it passed. I took a step towards you. Can I have a hug? I asked.

You rushed towards me and hugged me tight, laughing into my hair as though I were behaving in a manner you found exceptionally sweet. I'm sorry, I know you were worried. Are you okay?

I don't feel very well, I told you.

Oh no, do you think it was the weed?

Maybe, I said, and pulled away from you. We began to load the car with our things, moving slowly. I didn't bother to properly pack my bag. It didn't seem to matter, so long as we could get everything into the car and get out of town. I had already figured out a new route. We could still drive through Bears Ears, but we wouldn't have time

to get out and walk around, not properly. Not that I felt well enough
to walk around.

I looked over to you, to see if you looked any different. And to my
surprise, you did. You moved gracefully, purposefully, and the expression on your face was happy.

Was it good? I asked.

You nodded. You told me you had driven sort of south and sort of
east, down towards the Four Corners where Colorado, New Mexico,
Arizona, and Utah meet. You had stopped on a shoulder in a place
where you could see no people and where few cars seemed to travel.
You pulled a towel out from the back of the car and set off walking.
You had walked into the stretch of land along the roadside, picking
around clumps of saltbush and tamarisk, just being quiet, and allowing yourself to be alone. You walked for a while before you came to a
good place and laid the towel out on the desert floor. You sat down,
and you stared up at the bright blue sky overhead. You began to take
slow breaths, in through the nose and out through the mouth. It was
tingly, you said, at first. And then after what felt like not very long
at all, something shifted. You felt an incredible release. You told me
that you began to laugh uncontrollably. You found that your hands
had begun to act on their own, twitching about, smacking the ground,
grabbing at the edges of the towel. Then you began to see a sort of
figure in the distance, and a bright blue light; the more you focused
on it, the bigger and more intense the blue light became. The quiet
was not quiet, or rather, the quietness was incredibly loud. Then you
began to cry. And it felt like all you wanted to do was scream. Brandon had said that you should let the body do what it wanted to do, so
you did. You screamed, you said, like you were an animal; completely
alone, and uninhibited. It felt like something was released in that
moment, like tar-black mucus being expectorated from your lungs.
Your hips rolled from side to side, your knees lifted, and eventually
the screaming turned to laughter. In those moments afterwards, when

you allowed your breath to return to normal, you felt truly and pro-
foundly at peace. You finished telling me all this as we stood outside
the house, our things in the back seat and the boot, and you were smiling so broadly that I was not quite sure what to do.

I'm sorry you were worried, you said. I really am. Do you feel better? Do you still want me to go get you painkillers?

No, I said, I'm okay. I went to get some on my own.

I told you I wanted to go to the bathroom before we left, and so
I unlocked the house one more time, walked past the linens and towels I had balled up to hide the bloodstains, left there by the door for
the person who would come to clean the house, and back towards
the bathroom where I had, a few hours earlier, not been able to stand
straight. I changed the sanitary pad. The blood had thinned. It was no
hemorrhage anymore, but I found nestled on the used panty liner several curdled, dark knots of blood, custardy in texture. I thought, in the
bathroom, about telling you. But how could I? When you were at last
at peace, and happy, when you had just described what you had been
doing that morning, how could I tell you that I had been here all the
while, miscarrying our child?

I zipped up my jeans, stood up, and pulled my jacket on. In the
bedroom I double-checked once more for anything we'd left behind,
and discovered, in the corner by the door, one of your notebooks and
a pen. I pocketed them, to hand back to you in the car. I didn't look at
what was written or drawn inside the notebook. Years later, I would
spend many hours in our apartment poring through your scattered
things, looking for clues. I would find many notebooks, but none of
them journals, none of them chronological, and none of them dated.
They documented only the scraps of thoughts you'd had. Some of
them mentioned me with just my initial, "E." Some of them mentioned
"B." Some of them mentioned your mom, but none of the notes read
like plans, and none of them suggested a possible explanation. The
police wanted to know if there was anything that might indicate a plan.
They were asking, I knew, whether there was a note, something that

might explain what had happened, or something that might explain that what had happened had happened for a reason. That you had disappeared by design. But I didn't find anything.

Much is the same, and yet so many things have happened since you went away. Not long ago they announced an emergency water shortage on the Colorado River. Lake Mead had begun to get so low that bodies were starting to resurface from the waters. They found one man who had been stuffed inside a barrel and shot; he had been underwater since the 1980s. There has resurfaced a swamp boat from World War Two, and countless human bones. Everything that was once buried rises up eventually, and I pay attention now, every time they find somebody new. So far none of the bodies in the Lake have been you.

I did see a doctor, of course, once we were back in the city. I was sent to an examination room in the hospital on 59th Street for an ultrasound. Everything looked normal, the doctor said. I wouldn't need dilation and curettage, and I wouldn't need surgery. I had probably lost it at about seven weeks. Some women, she said, don't even notice it that early.

It had been painful, I told her, and she nodded.

It often is, she said.

The worst of the pain, I thought, had probably lasted forty-five minutes, but it had felt like it had lasted hours, when I was down there on the floor of that shower. Pain does that, of course. It elongates time, or else it annihilates time.

What kind of story was this, then? I remember thinking when I emerged into the leafless, gray midday of 59th Street. A story with no real beginning, and no real ending.

I walked up Amsterdam to a diner near Lincoln Center, sat down and ordered an enormous hamburger, rare, with a pickle, fries, and a piece of cherry pie. I ate. I had not finished swallowing before I took another bite, and then another. I ate like I hadn't allowed myself to eat in years, until it began to hurt, until I began to hiccup as I swallowed the mouthfuls down. How was I to tell you, after it was all over? Why bother? What was the lesson of such a story? And why start at the beginning, when it was already at its end?

9

Palm Trees—Mary Pickford Window Shopping—Colorado City—
An Abortive Lunch—Are There Bears in Heaven?—Acid Trip—
Cherry Trees—Naming Colors—Controlled Burning in the Kaibab
National Forest—Jacob Lake Inn—The North Rim of the Grand
Canyon—No Longer Being Certain When and Where One Is—The
Flight of a Hawk—A Return to the Upper West Side—An Overlook at
Bright Angel Falls—Pinecones—The Return of the Desert Tortoise

The next morning I felt bright, showered, and well-slept. I had wiped clear from my mind the events of the day before, like so many lost notes written on a classroom whiteboard. The volume of the stereo was turned up loud; I sang along to every word of *Dig, Lazarus, Dig!!!* Leaving town, we passed a psychic, a museum dedicated to the pioneers, and a Dixie Palm Motel, before arriving at the turnoff which would take us south back towards Arizona. On the outskirts of town, we encountered sad, sprawling trailer parks named exultant things like "Zion's Gate." Everywhere, palm trees guided the way, even in the grounds of the trailer park. The palm trees had followed us all over the Southwest, from Las Vegas to San Diego to Phoenix, breaking up the ubiquitous vistas of horizontality; all the concrete, asphalt, and fibro paneling. When I saw palm trees broken and collapsing on the edge of towns, they seemed to signal the threshold of civilization, either the leaving of it, or its arrival.

Before this trip I had never thought to question where the palm trees came from, although when I thought about them properly, I understood that they couldn't—of course they couldn't—be native to the landscape. The long, spindly ones came from Mexico, the trees with bark like old pineapple skin were from the Canary Islands, and the kind that looked suited to being battered by a cyclone were native to Queensland. Not long before Kenneth passed away, I received an email from him about palm trees. After you left, he and I began to correspond, as though I were inheriting the relationship you had cultivated with him after Greco died. We were of a kind, Kenneth and I; that's what he said. By then Kenneth was ill—liver cancer, he was pleased to say. We would email silly stories every few weeks, gifting each other the kindness of distraction. Near the end, when he was quarantined at home with a live-in nurse, he wrote that he had been reading a book about old Hollywood. He loved the stories of all that old glamour, those days when women wore furs and men wore hats, and all Southern California was a film set. And did I know the reason why Sunset Boulevard in Los Angeles was lined with palm trees? Most of the streets in L.A. had originally been lined with pepper trees, he wrote to me, but in the 1920s the city's streets were widened, and the peppers cut down, to make space for all the new cars on the roads. When it came to the stretch of Sunset between Normandie and Fairfax, there were disagreements about what to do next. Mary Pickford was a silent movie actress and, at the time, the most photographed woman in the world. Pickford thought it was criminally inexcusable that so many trees had been destroyed, but she didn't want them replaced with identical peppers, which were feathery and shady and grew sometimes untidy. She advocated for the planting of five hundred Mexican fan palms along Sunset Boulevard. Their trunks would be narrow enough that Pickford would be able to window shop without ever having to leave the comfort of the seat of her car. Isn't it beautiful, Kenneth wrote, that the symbol of the desert city became the palm tree, just because Mary Pickford didn't want to have to find a parking spot?

He sent me the story about Mary Pickford not long after I had traveled back to Phoenix to visit your father, who was thinking of selling the house. I hadn't seen him since shortly after you'd left, and the rooms seemed even emptier, somehow. Ever more like a monument to the people he'd lost. The beans were still there in the pantry, the stolen street sign still arranged over your childhood bed, the television perpetually tuned to a mostly unwatched program. He wanted me to look through your things and decide on what I might want to take back with me. I stayed with your father for four days, and that first evening, while he tidied the kitchen to the background noise of *The*

Rachel Maddow Show, I walked through your mother's garden, by the paloverde with its wind chimes, past my lounge chair and the swimming pool, around the tortoise enclosure and the barbecue, to the far side of the garden where your mother had erected raised beds for herbs. I walked over the gravel to the hammock Brandon had strung up just before your mother died, filled now with decaying leaf litter from the wattle trees it was tied to. Everything looked as it always had. In that moment, it felt as though time hadn't passed at all, and that I could pull the pack of cigarettes out of the back pocket of my jeans, and I would once again be smoking in secret on the Saturday morning after Thanksgiving, while you cried in the bathroom about your lost noise-cancelling headphones. The sensation of collapsed time felt smothering, unbearable, and the only thing that brought me out of it was the realization that I could not hear the knock-knock-knocking of the woodpecker in the palm tree. When I looked over into the yard next door, I noticed for the first time that it was gone. The palm tree had disappeared.

When I asked your father at dinner, he told me the neighbors had torn the tree down when a trimmer died. Just about all the landscaping and tree-trimming companies used by families in the neighborhood employed undocumented laborers, paying them dismal wages as a result. No real safety standards to speak of. The man who died had scaled the tree and was yanking away the dead palm fronds, when he pulled at the wrong one. The old, desiccated leaves looked attached to the trunk, but in fact they were only bound to other dead fronds in a deceptive weave. A thick ring came loose, fell on top of the tree trimmer, and pinned him against the belt that was holding him to the trunk. The palm fronds were unbearably heavy and filled with dust and bugs. The man asphyxiated. It took hours for anybody to notice. The man had escaped calamity in El Salvador, traveled through Guatemala and up the length of Mexico, walked through that deadly desert, only to die unseen and trapped in the decorative palm fronds of some Camelback Vista yard, with nobody to hear him when he tried to scream. The family who owned the house had been upset by the death, and had torn down the tree, so as not to be reminded of it. I was saddened by the story, as well as saddened by the loss of the tree. I was saddened by anything that had changed since you left, because I wanted everything to be in place for you when you eventually came back. During those days when I was visiting your father, I opened the door to the tortoise enclosure for the first time since you had last led me in. The old tree was still there, as well as the large rocks and shrubs. It looked the way it always had. I was turning around to leave when I saw something move.

There he was: your tortoise. Sitting in the shade made by one of the rocks, camouflaged against the earth. I closed the door to the enclosure, rushed inside to the refrigerator, and found in the vegetable crisper a package of pre-sliced strips of red and green peppers. I hurried back, opened the door, sure that the tortoise would be gone, but he remained there, basking in the early evening ambient heat radiating from the rock. He was so much smaller than I thought he would be, and so ancient. I approached, and he remained still, looking at me. I crouched down. He didn't move. And so I opened the package in my hands and very slowly offered him a slice of red pepper. He moved his head, looked agreeable to the idea, and extended himself forward. He began to take bites of the slice I held between thumb and forefinger. I took my phone out of my pocket with my other hand and began to film him. I wanted evidence, I wanted to be able to show you.

Hey, Tortoise, I said as I offered another piece of red pepper. It's nice to meet you after all this time.

The red cliffs gave way to a landscape of small farms and cattle ranches. We passed empty land, occasionally impaled with a post, reminding passersby that this was private property. The radio played "Proud Mary" by Ike and Tina Turner, but as we approached the state line the reception began to get fuzzy. It was nearly lunchtime. Shall we try and stop here? I asked.

Sure, you said, but this town doesn't really look like a town.

Maybe if we turn? I wondered, peering out at what I thought was its center, hidden, as it seemed to be, from the highway. I think this might be Colorado City, I said. If it is, it's a Mormon Fundamentalist town. I don't know whether they welcome people stopping by.

Tall fences and long yellow grass hid the shapes of houses that lay beyond them. There's a Mexican restaurant over to the right, I said.

We drove into the lot and parked by a plastic playset. The A-board menu advertised burritos and chips, but the door was closed and locked, and it was not clear whether the place really was a restaurant. It certainly didn't look like one. What do we do? I asked.

Why don't we get off the highway and drive into the town? It's big enough, there'll be something in there, right? A flock of birds twitched unsettlingly on the plastic playset.

You turned the car around, and then took a left off the highway. We headed into empty residential streets towards the cragged sandstone pinnacles which towered on the outskirts, and we passed only one other car on the road. Through the windscreen I could see three women, all wearing their long hair in pouf-fronted updos. They were outfitted in the collared pastel dresses of Fundamentalist Mormon women I had seen on television, hovering outside a courthouse while their collective husband was inside, being tried for the sexual assault of children he had taken as polygamous wives.

I followed you into a bakery, where two women stood behind a counter under fluorescent lights. They did not look pleased to see us, but then again, they were dressed in ordinary sweaters and jeans; no pouf-fronted updos or long pastel dresses. In the windowsill, a wire tray intended to hold copies of the *Short Creek Observer* sat empty, beside three homemade ceramic gourds. *A Charlie Brown Christmas* played over the sound system. We ordered and paid for cheese and tomato sandwiches, and a coffee each, which I sipped at a laminated table on a laminated chair while I waited for our food. You left to go find a bathroom, and as I sat there, I listened to the conversation happening at the table behind me, two men and two boys, eating together what smelled like a rotisserie chicken. I thought they must have been a family. One of the little boys was expressing his anxiety about the prospects that a bear would get him one day in the woods.

Behind me I heard the grandfather ask, quite loudly, What happens when you die? This seemed like an odd thing to ask a child over rotisserie chicken.

When the boy responded, he said, Are there bears in heaven? Which did not seem like an answer.

The grandfather said, Yes, there's gonna be bears in heaven.

I wish there weren't, said the little boy in a small, dejected voice.

Two orders were called for men—all men—who had come in and paid after us. By now I had been waiting for fifteen minutes. The women behind the counter would not meet my eye, although the table I was sitting at was only a few feet away. I was, I realized, the only woman in the bakery who wasn't preparing food. I was not welcome here. You returned and sat, telling me the bathrooms were oddly situated, on the other side of a conference room. Like they hold meetings in there, you whispered. Our food still isn't ready?

No, I said. I leaned over and explained, also in a whisper, that I was beginning to think we weren't going to get our sandwiches.

We've paid for them, you said.

It wasn't much, though. Ten bucks for everything.

Our coffee was finished. I could see the women buttering bread behind the counter, but they weren't preparing the cheese and tomato sandwiches. I understood then that they had never intended to feed us.

Let's just leave, I said.

We walked out past the table where the two men and two boys sat. As we passed, I heard the grandfather ask, Do you guys attend that

Wednesday night youth night? The little boy who was afraid of bears was picking the last of the flesh from the carcass of the chicken and nodding his head.

I t was the story we told most often when we got back East, this story about the abortive lunch in the Mormon Fundamentalist town on the Utah–Arizona border. It worked well as a discrete set piece, one which crystalized our position as fish out of water. A story essentially silly, because it was about the failure to obtain sandwiches we'd already paid for, and even though we hadn't seen anybody behaving in a particularly remarkable way, it was easy to suggest that everything that happened in Colorado City was due to the essential oddness of a populace who were all, for the most part, members of an antigovernment, polygamous sect. It was easy to ham up and exaggerate, and it was easy to tell because the story was basically meaningless, disconnected from anything else that was authentically significant about our trip out West. Once we got back home and saw the people that we knew, we came to lean on these sorts of stories in front of others, as though we had begun to perform an alternate version of our relationship to the outside world. In front of your art world friends, in front of my university friends, we were bright and dynamic and quick. But as soon as we were alone, we were quieter, tense, and very often sad.

I think now that things got worse after you were fired. How could they not have? You were angry, and embarrassed, and around others you simply avoided talking about it. On my own, I could not conceivably tell that story with the efficiency and structure that I could tell the story of our not-lunch in Colorado City. If I were to have told the real story of your firing to anybody around me, I would have had to tell them about Kenneth, about our visit to *Negative Capability*, about the promise we had made, and how it had felt to stand out there in that desert with lightning branching on the horizon and the sound of that tremendous and terrible quiet. That story was beyond my capacity to explain it, and besides, it wasn't my story to tell. Because in the end, when Kenneth met with the board and revealed to them, finally, the artist's final vision—the erasure of the much-anticipated, mathematically perfect spherical hollow in the earth, the thoughtful destruction of all those tunnels, mazes, and, mirrors, of all those viewing spaces and chambers that no member of the public had ever had occasion to visit, the land-scar Greco had left behind instead—and when he handed over to your boss the photographs Kenneth was giving them in return for their financial investment and support, they immediately suspected you of being a collaborator in the deception. You had kept the secret for so many months. You were terminated by the end of the week.

We carried on as though it had never happened.

At that time—March, April—I was seeing our friends less and less. I was preparing for my exams. I was always working. I was mortified by the phone call I had made to Camila from Bluff, which I could see, months later, had been unprofessional and bizarre. I was dismayed by the chilly distance she had enforced when I had tried to ask her for help with my work. I could only, I decided, rely on myself for any help. I buried myself in work, as though the library books I borrowed might physically form a walled fortress around my still and studying body. I knew that I was not home as much as you would have liked. After all, suddenly you were always at home. I suppose you were lonely. It occurs to me now that you didn't quite know who you were without the Foundation, even though you had hated it, even though you often spoken of leaving, and even though you often asserted that you were glad that it was all over now. You didn't like the new work you had found. It was only part-time, and your lack of drive to find anything more sustainable, as well as the happy acceptance of more of your father's money, troubled me. I did not know how to say so, because why should your lack of drive to get a job bother me? It wasn't as though I had a job. But it did. More than once, you asked me to give you my half of the rent early, as though you conceived of our apartment as something you alone paid for, and my portion of the rent money something you were rightly owed.

You wanted the money, I suspected, to buy more and better-quality drugs. It was around then when, in the odds-and-ends drawer beneath the toaster oven in our kitchen, I began to find—among the tape and stamps and matchsticks—plastic baggies filled with weed, vape pens and cartridges, cookies, and tinctures. Sometimes I would come home late from the library and open the front door to find a glass of red wine waiting for me on the table, and a note you had written—sometimes telling me you loved me, sometimes a picture of a frail old man or a smiling baby boy drawn in black marker—but if I turned right and walked through our railroad apartment to its other end, you would be lying in bed, watching cartoons on your laptop in our bed, vaping with your new noise-cancelling headphones on, and if you didn't notice me enter the room I often wouldn't even say hello. Instead, I would walk back through the apartment to the living room, picking up the glass of wine and beginning to drink on that same gray couch your mother had brought you, and there we stayed, you in the bedroom, me in the living room.

You'd figure out I was home, eventually, when you needed to go to the bathroom, or sometimes I'd come to bed to find you already asleep, the laptop still open and playing *Rick & Morty* in the hollow you'd made between your legs and your chest. Your therapist referred you to a psychiatrist, who wrote you a prescription for Lexapro, and then increased the dosage, and then increased it again. I was hopeful about the prescription, at first, but it didn't change the amount of weed you smoked. You were often in bed before you began taking the Lexapro, but after the prescription kicked in you were bedbound as though you were ill. You couldn't get a clear thought out anymore. You couldn't get through the day without a nap, all of a sudden like a child or an old man. The medication had taken the edge off, but it didn't help so much as numb. It didn't affect the crying jags, or the times when you hit the walls, or yourself. It didn't change the three-hour fights that left me weeping on the bathroom floor.

You said that weed helped. It didn't seem to bother you that you couldn't remember what I'd said to you most evenings, or that you'd already told me a story, or watched whole episodes of television shows you couldn't recall because you'd been so stoned. Everything was framed in terms of help. Weed helped, Mariana helped, breathwork helped, intermittent fasting helped, acupuncture helped. Did I?

I was always in the living room, reading or studying for my exams. But I found that, over time, you began to resent the reading, as though I had abandoned you, as though reading were some kind of betrayal. And so you would come into the room I was sitting in, and you would dance. Watch this, you'd say, and put one leg out, one arm out. I would hold my face in a stony rictus and watch the confused expression appear across yours. Because I had always been charmed by your dancing. Even *I* wasn't sure why the dancing now made me feel so panicked, and so harassed. All I wanted was to read, and I read with an absorption and fervor I'd rarely felt since your mother's death, because for the time I was reading I was incapable of hearing the thoughts in my own head.

Somebody, maybe it was Mariana, maybe it was Brandon, told you that microdosing was what you needed if you were feeling what other people might call "depressed." One night in April you came all the way uptown and met me outside the library. You had brought me a cookie from Levain, and as I took a bite, you asked me if I would go with you down to Bed-Stuy to run an errand. The cookie was a bribe. And so I read a book on the A train for over an hour, and when we got off at Nostrand you led me through the streets to a building where a rat was in the midst of escaping a trash can. We walked up four flights of stairs, to an apartment where all the blinds were closed. The door was opened by Jase, a bespectacled, over-stuffed white man in his thirties, who shuffled in his tracksuit into another room, while we watched his roommate play *Red Dead Redemption* beneath a framed poster from the TV series *Angel*. Jase came back with a package and handed it to you. From then on, the tabs of acid Jase sold you sat in a vial of vodka in our refrigerator. The vial was there long after you left. I only recently made myself take it out of the fridge and wash it down the sink, after which I found myself clutching the edges of the kitchen counter and shaking until I began to cry. You micro-dosed every second morning, before coffee, and well before food, as you no longer ate before two in the afternoon. This was to give your body the time to return to zero blood sugar, you said. I knew all about that. That's how I'd been eating, on and off, for years. You said the microdosing helped as much as the weed, and Mariana, and breathwork, but some days I knew you'd take the whole tab that you bought from Jase, days when I wasn't at home, when I was in the library. I was in the library as often as I could be.

And then, when my exams were over in May and the cherry blossoms were in the last of their bloom, you told me you wanted the two of us to spend the day together, and that it would mean a lot to you if we could take acid. You did not fully understand my resistance to taking psychedelics, but I agreed, in the end, that we would take a half tab each and go to the park.

The problem began when we decided to take the tabs at home, in our kitchen, immediately after breakfast. It began to kick in on the G train, and then seemed to reach its highest point when we transferred at Hoyt-Schermerhorn to Nevins Street and kept going. All that sound. The bumping of sweaty bodies in that overheated train car. It was, in a word, unpleasant, now that all my senses were heightened, and you, meanwhile, were too attentive to how I was handling it not to absorb my agitation as your own. When we got off the train at Grand Army Plaza it didn't matter how beautiful the park was; we were not having a nice time at all. I agreed to walk down the southwestern side of the park towards Windsor Terrace, and the walking did seem, for a while, to restore a sense of pleasantness. But everything was heightened.

Let's name colors, you said as we walked along the path.

This was a joke from way back at the beginning of our relationship. When I was upset or worried about something, when I did not know what to do, you'd suggest that we name some colors. We would walk, and point to them in the landscape: blue, teal, mauve, pretty pink, very gray, rusty red, green. So we named colors that we could see along the western edge of Prospect Park. I held your hand, and my mind slowed down, and I let myself notice the landscape around us, with its springtime trees so green and fecund they looked like they might drip, or ejaculate. There was a cherry tree nearby, newly planted, and beneath the tree were fallen blossoms. I noticed that the blossoms had fallen over handwritten signs, bunches of flowers, and votive candles. I crossed the road and walked over to the memorial. You followed me.

These are pretty trees, you commented.

I agreed. I paused. I thought about not saying it. But I did.

This, I think, is where that man self-immolated last year because of fossil fuels, I finally said.

I didn't look at you, and you were silent a moment, but then you groaned—a loud, violent cry of frustration. I turned my head to see that you were walking away. Why? you yelled. Why do you have to tell me these things?

I often think of that moment now you're gone. Why? Why do I have to tell you?

We drove southeast from the state line, through the Kaibab Paiute Indian Reservation towards the town of Fredonia. Soon we began to see smoke. What at first I thought was haze began to take on a darker form the closer we traveled towards it. There's a fire, I said to you, as if you couldn't see. I thought that it was almost possible to see the outlines of people moving on the horizon, but figures did not come any closer no matter the distance we covered. I asked if you could see the same thing.

You're seeing ghosts everywhere, baby, you said, and put a sooth-ing hand on the back of my neck.

It's probably a controlled burn, I said, more to myself than anything else. It was the last day of November, and there wasn't any breeze. We passed the Grand Canyon Motel—"We have TV!"—which a roadside sign said had closed three weeks earlier. Fredonia seemed falling down and boarded up, but it was hard to tell whether this was because every-thing, like the motel, had closed for the season, or whether something alarming had happened to empty it out. As we gained elevation and entered the Kaibab National Forest, we were the only car in sight, and the flat desertscape evolved into that of pinyon pine and juniper. Logging trucks drove past us loaded with freshly cut tree trunks. The plumes of smoke were enormous by then, billowing out to the east as we drove southward. The atmosphere took on the fire-lit quality of my childhood Christmases.

Are we driving straight into the fire? I asked.

It looks that way, you said.

The road curved, and ahead of us we could see a truck stopped on the shoulder. You asked whether we should pull over too, and I said, Yes. On the ridge a middle-aged white man was watching the smoke plume out of the pines. He was taking photos on his phone, just like I was. It was beautiful, the real danger being distant. The quiet was intense, punctuated by nothing but the calls of the sparrows. The air smelled of smoke and burning pine needles. The mountains looked dark, almost black in the glare; the road surface uneven. Frightening. You and I would not know what to do, in a place like this, if something went wrong.

We got back in the car and kept driving, past trees growing lonely among tree stumps, orange and blue stripes of paint marking the trunks of those bound for cutting. Small plumes of smoke appeared on the sides of the road, and then flames, lapping at the base of the trees. There was no wind to whip them up. And yet it filled me with terror to see fire in the forest. I think this terror had something to do with my sense that fire was spreading the world over, like a contagion. Fires were still burning in California. They had burned, months earlier, in Montana, Nevada, Oregon, and Utah. They had raged through Greece. They had burned across the moors in Yorkshire and Lancashire, and were already beginning to rage down the east coast of Australia towards my childhood home. Fire bred more fire, and I was afraid sometimes of seeing every place I had ever loved destroyed by flames. Such a notion took hold of me as we drove through the forest, while flames licked the sides of the road, and the smoke smothered the contours of the horizon, and darkness descended. Through the dense throng of smoke I could make out only flame. I could no longer see the shape of any tree or feature of the landscape, unless it was burning. The smoke was in my hair, on my fingers, in my lungs. It was everywhere.

You kept driving, and eventually the worst was over, and the smoke began to thin. There was no movement, no sound, not a breath of wind. This, I thought, will be what it's like at the end of all things. You put your hand on my thigh and held on. And eventually all that was left was the smell of smoke, which lingered long after we had left the flames behind.

We stopped for lunch again and parked among logging trucks. The patrons of the Jacob Lake Inn—"Elev. 7925 Café Motel Curios Store"—were all loggers and forest workers, sitting in the restaurant in their workwear and eating cheeseburgers and blueberry pie à la mode. You found us seats at the counter and ordered while I went to the bathroom.

I needed to change sanitary pads. There was barely anything coming out of me anymore, only a darkish stain, and occasionally something brown, spiderwebbed and membranous. I had nearly succeeded in putting the events of the day before out of my head, but here was the evidence of the something that had happened. And in that moment, confronted with the materiality of the thing between my legs, the worry flooded through me. I was alarmed at how efficiently I seemed to be not thinking about it. But it never again occurred to me to tell you about what had happened. I flushed, unlocked the door, and washed my hands. In front of the mirror, I adjusted my hair and re-applied concealer to the dark patches under my eyes. I look so tired, I thought.

Returning to the café I detoured through the curio shop. I lingered for a moment, and, disregarding the lesson of the New Year's rose quartz, I bought three rocks, deposits of hematite, augite, and feldspar, which the woman at the counter told me had come from the North Rim. These were not the only rocks I came away with from that trip. I have them laid out around me now, arranged on the windowsill above my desk. There are pieces of limestone-dappled granite, pieces of dolomite and quartzite, pinecones, shells, and the rocks I bought at Jacob Lake Inn that day. Look, I said to you when I returned, showing you the rocks. I'd been gone so long that my sandwich was already cold. Aren't they pretty?

After we had paid and left, we passed a fire service truck lighting up the grass around the Inn with a handheld flamethrower. It was hard to tell sometimes whether the stretches of land had been logged or burned. We approached a sign saying that Highway 67 was closed during the winter. "Road into the North Rim Closed on December 1 due to Winter Conditions," said the sign.

Is it closed? you asked uncertainly.

I don't think so, I said. I think that happens tomorrow. December first is tomorrow. I guess this is the very last day we could come. I had no idea.

Imagine if we'd driven all the way here and the road was closed? you said.

Well then I would have been mad at myself, I said.

We drove past a mint-green barricade which would, on Saturday, descend across the road. Once we'd passed the official entrance to the North Rim, we left the burning-off behind, and descended into a road swaddled by towering Douglas firs. Along the side of the road grew stretches of bright green grass. "Do Not Cross the Meadows" read a sign. A few moments later we saw two deer emerge from between the trees and begin to graze. We were the only car on the road, and we were, I knew, already late. It was nearing three o'clock. The light wouldn't hold out much longer.

Are those pines dead? I asked you.

I think they've just lost their leaves, you said. Like the trees in Flagstaff. Aspens lose their leaves.

Aspens. We must be so high up for there to be aspens.

Very, you said, and reached across to hold my hand.

When we eventually reached the end of the road, parking was easy. We drove right up to the visitor's center, and you stopped the car by picnic tables overlooking fir trees and the striated troughs of the vast emptiness of the canyon.

I had never seen anything like it.

I had never seen anything so immense. So quiet. So infinite.

We locked the car and began to walk towards its edge, to the handrails that took walkers down to the paths around the rim. We don't have time to go down into it, do we? you asked.

I don't think so. The sun is going to set in an hour and a half or something.

It's okay, you said. I'm happy up here.

I followed behind you as we walked along a sandy path towards an outlook. We were so high up that the clouds seemed touchable up there, fluffed across the sky like spilled cotton balls. It was hard to imagine ever leaving, or that a place existed outside of this one. It was the only real place on earth, and I had no thoughts in my head at all. The only thing I could hear was our footsteps, and then suddenly, piercing across the canyon from the branch of a ponderosa pine, a hawk screamed and then took flight. In that moment between the hoarse scream of the hawk and its appearance, I was filled with a sense of panic, as though the small creature quaking inside me knew by instinct that the bird of prey had seen me, wanted me, that it was coming. For that elongated moment I saw every needle in the pine, every rock along the path, and every possible way to run. I could hear the flapping of the hawk's wings with a crystal clarity. I watched it take off over the chasm beneath my feet, and followed its path as it traced the curve of that endless absence.

When we reached the lookout I followed you, climbing up onto the ridge that hung over the canyon. You sat down, and so did I. We were the only people in sight. How was it possible to be at the Grand Canyon, and so alone? The longer I sat, the more I was able to imagine myself as the very last person left at the end of all things, alone there with you in the wake of a future calamity. I put my hand on your thigh, afraid of losing you. I was not sure any longer when and where I truly was. The waning sun bathed the land below us in brilliant gold, and down there in the absence I imagined I could see movement. There, I thought, I once was home. I have known such moments at other times in my life. A few months ago, I decided to sell the gray couch your mother had bought you. I had always hated it, and its coffee stains were a constant reminder of times I prefer not to remember. When it was gone, I bought a blue velvet couch from a man on the internet, who was selling it for cheap. I rented a U-Haul and followed the blue route on the map as I drove north; since you left, I have learned to drive. I knew that I was going to the Upper West Side, but it did not dawn on me until I was close that the man from whom I was buying the couch lived on the same block you had lived on when we were first dating. As I followed the road across Manhattan, I imagined what it would be like, any moment now, to turn left from Broadway, and to see the green awning of the old, familiar building. Where we first had sex, where you first made me dinner, where I once waited for you in the snow when your cab from the airport was heading home, where we sat out blizzards together, where you played me The 13th Floor Elevators for the first time and we danced, where your mother once moved all my underwear into a bag in a separate closet when she was visiting, where we watched the evening hours of *The Clock*, where you put books in the freezer to kill bedbugs, where I had mono, where you had pneumonia, where I once gave myself whiplash by brushing my hair too forcefully, where you installed a pull-up bar in the hallway you never used when I was home, where my coat lived alongside yours in the closet, where I learned to roast a chicken, where we had our first fight, where you once left me naked and napping in bed while you went to a business drink and then rushed home to climb back into bed with me in the blue light of a springtime dusk. And I wasn't thinking about any of it very seriously, not really, as I approached the street, counting the numbers upwards as I reached the 70s, past the Bank of America where I opened my first U.S. account, past Fairway where a woman always stood with a sandwich board protesting their rodent problem, past the Beacon Theater where we had seen Patti Smith and Nick Cave & the Bad Seeds, and as I turned left I became no longer certain when I truly was, because I knew in that moment, with every fiber of my being, that I could reach into my pocket, pull out my keys, open the door beneath the green awning, take the elevator to the fifth floor, turn left, and fit my key in the lock. There you would be, standing there, the year that we met, and I would fall into your arms.

I have vertigo, you said.

I put an arm out and placed it across your chest. Don't lean over, I said. Below us the canyon was beginning to turn red in the setting sunlight. Be careful, I said. It's a long way to fall.

That's what's so strange, you said. You paused a moment and listened to the silence.

Do you not like it?

No, no, no. It's amazing. I like it. I'm just sitting with this feeling of falling. Not trying to fight it.

I felt vibrations start up against the skin of my wrist. "Reminder to move," said your mother's Fitbit.

After a little while we stood up and followed a path to the right. We walked along a trail following the signs to Bright Angel Falls, along the transept to a wooden lodge. A plume of smoke snaked up from the northwest. It did not seem to come from the fires we had passed.

Do you think it's from the California fires? you asked me.

We kept walking, past tiny wooden cottages looking out over the canyon. You pulled out a joint and lit it, and then offered me some. I took a puff, then three more, commenting that the cottages should be let out as artist's retreats, not closed for the season. I bent down and salvaged two pinecones from the forest floor. I would take the pinecones back home, I thought, along with the rocks. I would have pieces of this place forever, and never forget that once I was alive here.

This is what weed does, you said, looking back at me.

Does what?

It makes you want to take two pinecones when reasonably you'd only need one.

No, I need both.

You put your arm around me as I caught up with you. Sure you do, you said.

We came upon a building with a few benches arranged in front of big open windows to view the scenery. We climbed up the stone steps and I leaned against the ledge, surveying the canyon. When I turned back, you had sat down in the square of golden-hour light the setting sun was casting. You look so beautiful, I told you.

Thank you, you said, then adjusted the hair over your forehead. I walked over and put my arms around you. For several moments we held on to each other, and I settled my head into the crook of your shoulder. When I stood up, ready to leave, or at least walk somewhere else, you told me to wait.

Go down the stairs, you said. Then start filming, and make sure I'm not in the frame when you get to the top.

Okay, I said, but it was as though all the brightness and beauty of the afternoon had been bleached from my field of vision. Because I did not feel like being part of another performance. I could not bear for this place, of all places, to be rendered artificial and abstract in one of your video pieces. But I didn't say anything. I walked to the bottom of the staircase, turned the camera on, and held up my phone.

The camera follows the steps up from the path to the viewing platform. The film settles on you, and you begin to wave, but there is no element of surprise. You're simply a man waving from a bench atop a staircase. From behind the camera my voice, sounding annoyed, says, It doesn't work.

Why not? you ask.

You're right there. There's no way for the camera to catch you suddenly.

Shoot the wall. Come up the stairs faster and shoot the wall.

There's no way to not see you when I'm coming up.

You point at me in the recording, growing frustrated. Shoot the stairs—you pointed to the left—then the wall.

The camera descends back to the bottom of the stairs, then stops.

The next video is longer. I've aimed the camera down. There is an awkwardness, as I turn at the top, angling the camera up to the wood-beamed rafters, and then across to the viewing window, where the sunlight filters through a juniper tree. I can hear myself breathe. Then the camera turns, quickly passing across the wall, and settles on you, sitting on the bench. You are wearing your black jeans and black sneakers, the blue down jacket you bought when we went to Montreal for my twenty-sixth birthday. You are smiling and waving. The camera stays on you for five seconds. And then I turn, into the blue sky and fir trees, and make my way back down the stone steps without you.

Since you left, I have spent a long time looking at the things left behind. Videos like that one. Your notebooks. Your bank statements. All your clothes. The books on the bedside table. I've tried to leave everything where I found it. Sometimes at night I reach out, half-asleep, thinking you're still there, and when you're not, when the sheets are flat and husbandless, I begin to cry. At first I would wear your dirty T-shirts to sleep, the smell of your sweat and skin a comfort. But after a while the T-shirts began to smell like me, like my skin, and my sweat. I wasn't sure anymore that I could really smell you when I lay alone in our bed. That's when I began to know that you were really gone, and that I would need to let go of the idea that you might come back.

10

The Route to the American Airlines Terminal at JFK—Hair Grown Long—Disappearance—An Unnamed Road off NV-165—Thomas Merton—Underlined Pages—A Bison in a Meadow—A Motel without Television—Static Electricity—Vermilion Cliffs—Cliff House—Tumbling Boulders—Wanting It to Look Like a Real Western—Lee's Ferry—Paria Beach—Drinking the Water—Turquoise—A Smooth White Stone Thrown into the River—Making Dinner

This is what I know: at first, it was just the fact that you stopped taking your medication. You didn't tell me you had stopped, not for some time. You were popping the pills from the packs each morning and washing them down the sink. When you did finally tell me, you said that the medication made you feel like you were encased in fog. You had lived in that fog all year, through your thirtieth birthday in the summer and mine in the fall, through the Thanksgiving your father spent with us in Brooklyn, which you could barely remember, and through my mother's visit at Christmas, when she had taken me aside in the kitchen and asked me, quietly, what was wrong. So when you stopped at New Year's as we entered a new decade, you told me that it felt like wresting control back. You were being positive, you said, as though a simple assertion of positivity would conquer all ills. You felt that you would soon be on top of things again. I didn't know that quitting medication without a tapering-off period was dangerous.

By February you'd been off the pills for a month or more. You had plans to fly back to Phoenix to visit your father for the second anniversary of your mother's death. I couldn't come with you, but then again, you hadn't asked.

I walked you downstairs to the street to wait for the Lyft to collect you. We stood under the leafless ash tree, and I held on to parts of you as we spoke and waited. I held on to the blue jacket you bought on my twenty-sixth birthday in Montreal, and your nail-chewed fingers, and your neck. I held on to you. And then the car arrived, and the driver hopped out to load your roller bag—a small one, only carry-on sized—and you turned to me. I kissed you, and you held on to me very tight, and you said, I love you. I said, I love you too, and I put my palm to your cheek and stroked the rough surface of your beard, and I inhaled your smell, and then we let go, and you got into the car. The car drove away, up to McGuinness Avenue, where it idled at the red light, and I kept watching, kept waving, until the light turned green and the car turned left, where it would join up with the BQE, merging onto the Long Island Expressway, looping in a circle in Flushing Meadows, sending you south down the Van Wyck Expressway to the American Airlines terminal at JFK. That's the last time I saw you.

Your father told the police he had noticed nothing out of the ordinary. For three days you ate dinner with him every night, you helped with chores, you made visits to Home Depot and Costco, and you took his car to get serviced. You drove out to see Brandon, who wasn't doing so hot, you told me in text messages. You sent me pictures of the tortoise eating sheets of iceberg lettuce. You sent a picture of your childhood drawings, with the one I was fond of placed right on top. *My name is Lewis, I am seven. I have two tortoises. They are good tortoises. My state is California. I don't have anything more to say.* You sent me a video of a bug skimming the surface of the swimming pool, and another, longer video, where you ran into frame and began to dance, with the same jerky, uncontrollable motions as the routines you performed in restaurant bathrooms, only this was in the driveway of your childhood home. Your hair had grown so long, I remember thinking. Almost as though I hadn't been paying attention to you. How had I missed it? I've watched the videos and looked at the photographs you sent me that week so many times since, trying to find in them a message. A meaning.

When the car came back from the mechanic, you asked your father whether you could borrow it for the day while he was at work. He said that was fine—your father would drive your mother's Suburban, which even now he hasn't sold. He didn't ask where you were going. You had told me in a text message that you thought it might be nice to drive out to Sedona, to try and have lunch with Kenneth. Kenneth, when asked later, was alarmed to hear about this message. Kenneth had not heard from you in months, he said, not since you were fired. When he learned that you had disappeared, he set out across the vast track of land where the gash had been re-filled, and from the window of his truck, he looked for any signs of you: the car, your backpack, your wallet, the zipper from your jeans, the buckle of your belt. He didn't find anything. Nobody found anything.

The police took their time—young men can just take off, they told me. But you hadn't texted, and you hadn't phoned, and all my calls went to voicemail, all texts went straight to green. You'd turned your phone off, or it had run out of battery; nobody was sure. It took a few weeks until they found the car. It was parked on an unnamed road off NV-165, a road which terminates on the Nevada side of the River. The windows were closed, the door was locked, but you were not inside. The police tested the car but found no trace of mud, nor blood. None of your things were there, not even a backpack. They searched the area but came up with nothing. I flew down to Phoenix, and I spent the month there, sleeping in your childhood bedroom once it had been searched, waking up in the morning to the blinding desert sun peeking through the blinds. I read the books you'd left behind on the desk which doubled as bedside table. *The Invention of Morel*, and *The Man Without Qualities*, and *Dhalgren*, and a slim book by Thomas Merton on the teachings and sayings of the desert ascetics that you'd borrowed from me. Both of us underlined our books, although you wrote notes more often than I did, in your jagged, left-handed scrawl. We both underlined in pencil, and it was sometimes hard to tell which of us had made notes in any one book. One morning I went outside to sit on the lounge chair with a mug of coffee balanced against my legs. There was a faint rustle of leaves in the paloverde by the wall and the tinkle of wind chimes your mother had hung in its branches. A knock-knock-knocking sounded from the palm tree in the yard next door. I began reading Merton's prologue, where he discussed the value of paying attention to those mythic men who had exited society and retreated to the desert to be closer to God, like Simon in the Buñuel film, who had spent his life atop a plinth in the middle of Syria. One of us had underlined a paragraph:

We must liberate ourselves, in our own way, from involvement in a world that is plunging to disaster. But our world is different from theirs. Our involvement in it is more complete. Our danger is far more desperate. Our time, perhaps, is shorter than we think.

I have so many things I want to ask you. Was it you who underlined the passage? What did it mean? Did you believe in it? Did those pages articulate something that you couldn't say out loud? In my mind, I am always asking you, talking to you. Still. Even now.

The sun set quickly as we drove north towards the exit of the Grand Canyon National Park, the way we had come. The sky turned pink and purple, then began to darken. With the setting of the sun came the cold, and in the blue light of dusk the dew that had been invisible on the forbidden meadow became white and turned to ice. We passed a family of deer by the road, and then, further on, a bison, grazing alone. The smoke from the burn-offs still floated in the air, and the last threads of sunset cast the strips of paint on the road a shade of sickly yellow. It was hard not to focus on them ticking by behind us as we sped on. I had the sense that the loneliness and eeriness of the landscape was only being kept at bay by the heating inside the car, the coolness of the water in the bottle I held between my thighs, the familiarity of one another and the music we were playing.

I wonder if people have been murdered on this side of the Grand

Canyon? I said, looking out at the darkening forest stretching out on either side of us.

Yeah, you said, I was just thinking this would be a good place for a guy to get rid of his wife.

That's a very incriminating thing to say.

You may bring it up at the trial, you said.

We passed a sign as we entered the more heavily wooded parts of the forest: "Do not report. Prescribed fire in progress." Soon, all was dark.

When we eventually reached the crossroads and turned east down Highway 89A, I began to get nervous. Neither of us had been able to get reception on our phones for hours. The map, when I opened it, was a featureless expanse of gray across which a blue dot blinked, going nowhere. What if we miss it? I asked.

It'll have lights on, you said. There are literally no other houses or motels out here. It'll probably have the only lights we'll be able to see.

You were right. We saw the motel from miles away, hurrying towards us in the dark.

You parked the car in the lot, but as we made to get out, I was suddenly struck with the suspicion, and then the conviction, that when I opened the door I would place my foot squarely on the coiled body of a rattlesnake. I couldn't say now where this fear came from. It is easy to read portent into bad vibes and hunches with all the benefit of hindsight, but in the moment, it might have meant nothing at all. In the landscape of memory, stories can be read into everything: the knock-knock-knocking of a woodpecker, the relentless repetition of a Christmas carol, the impossibility that every dog we saw that November was named Max.

No, no, you said to me with your hand on the driver's-side door handle. There are no snakes here. It's too cold for snakes.

The temperature had dropped below freezing. The car's thermometer read thirty-two.

I opened the door and climbed out without looking down. You were right, of course. There were no snakes. My breath made a cloud of mist in front of me as I followed you towards the lit-up window across the lot. In the angling store which doubled as the motel check-in, a gruff woman in a blue Hawaiian shirt took our details.

The restaurant's only open for another hour and a half, she said. And the televisions don't work. If you want to complain about it, you can take it up with the boss in the morning at 6:30 on the dot. She barely paused for breath.

That's fine, I said, that's no trouble. I took the key she had passed me. Where do we find the Wi-Fi password? I asked.

Oh no, there's no Wi-Fi, she said, and laughed bitterly.

The room was wood-paneled, with orange woven lampshades screwed into the walls on either side of the bed. I took my shoes off, then flicked the light switch. A horrible shock shot through me, and I yelped. What was that? I asked.

It's static electricity, you said. Maybe because you're standing on the carpet with your socks on?

Why would it do that?

I don't know, you said.

When you came to bed and took the synthetic red quilt off the bed, you got zapped by static electricity as well.

What's wrong with us? you asked.

I don't know, I said, and then put my arms around you, snuggling into your warmth.

The morning was a revelation. The darkness of the night had masked the sheer scale of the flat emptiness around us. As I looked out southward from the motel porch, there was nothing but blue sky and land giving way to the white glow of the horizon line. Behind the lodge rose sheer sandstone cliffs, threaded through with intense red oxide and blue-tinged manganese. The night before, I had seen nothing but the light reading "Motel," and I'd had no idea we were staying right on the edge of the Vermilion Cliffs. I stood in the car park taking pictures on my phone, and felt you come from behind and hold me. You put your arms around my waist and leaned your chin on my shoulder.

I checked us out, you said.

A pay phone outside the angling shop rang twice, then stopped.

Weird, you said into my hair. Ghosts?

Undoubtedly ghosts, I said.

Are you happy?

Very happy.

Snakes didn't get you.

Nope.

Murderers didn't get you.

Nope.

Safe and sound.

Should we walk a little? I asked. Just to see? Before we have to leave?

Marry me, I should have said.

It was an odd place to be a pedestrian, but it was the only road going, and we walked along its edges where the red dust stained the tarmac. After only five minutes we came to a parked car, an old, half-ruined house, and three women selling Navajo jewelry. An elderly couple in matching beige shorts were engaged in conversation with the women. There were many large, precarious boulders scattered around, which were of the same red sandstone as the rough bricks of the house. I took a photograph of a metal hook buried deep in one of the rocks, then circled back when the couple returned to their car. I was looking at the necklaces arranged on the fold-out table, when I heard you ask the women, Excuse me, did I hear you tell that man that this place had been reconstructed?

Oh yeah, said the jewelry seller. Some of it. The house.

The house, the woman told us, used to be a kind of restaurant.

A couple got it into their heads that they would sell food to passing motorists making their way towards the Grand Canyon's North Rim. But after the Trinity test in 1945 and those first published images of mushroom clouds and the shadows of atomized human beings etched ghostly in stone, the woman who ran it began to be afraid. She was certain the sounds she could hear in the night were nuclear bombs exploding in the desert. They did it in New Mexico, after all, and they did it in Nevada. What was to stop them from doing it here? She would lie in bed, and she would imagine the way the ground would tremble when a bomb hit. The radiation burns on her dog's flank, the litters of eyeless newborn kittens, the white light followed by utter darkness. The land would shake. The whole house would rattle. And weren't those vermilion cliffs above their heads sure to start cleaving off? Wouldn't they come tumbling down? After years living in fear of those boulders, the couple left. The restaurant didn't find new owners. It didn't take long for it to look like the ruin it was now.

So that's what the other rocks are? I asked. They were the rocks that fell? Did they test bombs here?

The jewelry seller laughed. No, she said. I thought they'd been here forever too. But I learned not too long ago those rocks were moved here for a movie set. She turned and pointed towards a ledge behind her. See those hooks up there?

I nodded. I could.

Well, the Hollywood people, they came out here from L.A., when Westerns were the big thing, and they strung a bunch of cables through there—she pointed, tracing her finger downwards to where we stood—and wrenched the rocks down. There. So they'd look better, I guess. More stagy. I think it was the 1950s.

It was, said a second jewelry seller. She had been listening. All those big rocks were dropped in from somewhere else. The film crew wanted it to look like a real Western.

In the real West, I said.

I guess, she shrugged, and laughed.

We walked back to the motel. The Hawaiian-shirted woman in the angling store had told you we could get coffee at Marble Canyon Lodge a little way down the road. We put our things in the car, got in, and began driving. What if we miss it? I asked.

I mean, I think we'll see it, you said. There are no other roads. Stop being afraid of missing stuff.

We took off down the road towards the big blue sky, the sides of the highway dotted with yellow-flowering shrubs on this, the first day of December. We passed the jewelry sellers by the big boulders, and overtook a city-clean car moving slowly, considering stopping to see the necklaces and dream catchers. I scanned the radio stations while we drove, rolling past "Rockin' Around the Christmas Tree," then gave up and silenced the radio. It was pleasant just driving. The sun expelled the chill of the evening before, and it was around then that you took a left. I asked why, as I had not directed you to do so.

Let's just check it out, you said.

I looked back and saw the sign. Lee's Ferry.

Lee's Ferry—the artificial halfway point of the Colorado, according to the law of the River. It's the last "wild" section, I told you, and the only part that is meant to look anything like it did before.

We drove along through red cliffs and fallen boulders, austere and deadly—beautiful—above us. How do you even describe landscape like this? I asked you. It's beyond words.

I don't know, baby. Maybe it's okay to not be able to describe it.

We followed the road along, between the cliffs, and I was surprised when I noticed parked cars and campers, people who had stayed the night. I do not know what I was expecting at Lee's Ferry, but I was not expecting what I saw. Rounding the last bend, with the car park to our right, I saw in front of us, through the red-dusted windscreen, a beach. And beyond the sand, the brilliant turquoise River running wild.

Let me out, let me out, I said, reaching for my seat belt.

You killed the engine, and I opened the door, rushing from the car park down to the sand, coming to a stop at the edge. I knelt. I put my hand into the aquamarine waters of the Colorado River, into the water that had cleared Glen Canyon Dam and was making its way down to Hoover. I cupped my palm, and I drank. The water was terribly cold. I felt an icy sensation in my throat and down into my chest as it moved through my body.

I stood up, and from the corner of my eye I noticed a man emerge onto the beach with his dog following close behind. The dog's barks echoed off the canyon walls. I could hear the roaring of the rapids from somewhere further along around the bend, and the lapping of the water along the shore. You caught up with me. We walked along the beach, hand in hand, through the bits of river weed and sticks and rocks that had washed up over the decades. The dog galloped along the beach, elated by the scene, joyous in his movements. Max, called the dog's owner, don't go too far. Max the dog turned, obedient, and trotted back towards his master along the sand.

They're pretty rocks, I said, pointing at the collection of stones on the River's edge. You bent down and reached down to hold one in your hand. It was blue, and so soaked with water that it looked alien, as though no organic substance could have possibly produced it. It was dappled green and gray.

What is it, I asked. Is it moldy?

No, you said, with some reverence. It's turquoise.

Oh wow, I said, and went to grab it from you.

I'd like to keep it, you said, holding it close.

Oh.

I need it more than you, you said to me gently. I wouldn't exist without this River, but you would.

You pocketed the turquoise and kept walking. That piece of turquoise sat on your desk for the longest time, a talisman like any other. You took it with you on trips, for luck, and you took it to Phoenix when you never came back. I never found it in your childhood bedroom. You must have had it with you.

We walked now, surveying the stones. I picked up pretty, dappled rocks, brilliantly colored because still waterlogged, and put them in the pockets of my cardigan. You knelt by the water's edge, and I couldn't see what you were looking at exactly, until you showed it to me in the palm of your hand. The stone was pure white, without flaws. Smooth and lovely.

Do you want this? My mom would have liked it, you said.

Your mom and I liked different things.

So should I throw it back in the River?

I paused. I did not want you to do that. I looked around us, at the pure, flowing water and the towering red cliffs. You could make it a ceremony for her, I said. You could give it back to the River. She was raised on this River too.

You nodded. That's true, you said.

You turned and faced the River. You closed your eyes, as though a child in silent prayer, and both of us grew very quiet. The rumbling of the water, the wounded whine of a grackle, the sound of wind trapped by rock. You threw the white stone into the River.

Hello, Lynda, you screamed, as the stone plunged into the water. Your mother's name echoed off the canyon calls.

Hello, Lynda, I shouted.

I hope you're okay, you shouted.

Thank you, I shouted.

I miss you, you shouted.

You put your arms around me. We stood there together on Paria Beach and held one another. It's so beautiful, I said.

I'm with you there, starling.

A great swelling of feeling in my chest, expansiveness. The sublime.

I loved the River, that landscape, for one real reason. It made you. You were of it. My husband. And now, at the end of it all, what is left? An engagement ring, a "Reminder to Move," some North Rim pine-cones and beach-foraged stones. Limestone, sandstone, quartz. They are here, and you are gone.

Sometimes when I am cooking, when I am folding laundry, when I am marking student papers at my desk, or reading, or brushing my teeth, something will hit me. Memories from times when we were happy, and times when we were not. And there are some days when I almost believe in your absence. Hours when I am living in the present tense of my life. Hours when I almost forget. But then I remember again, the pain washes back, and I go under the wave into the dark water and drown.

Tonight, I am standing in our kitchen. The spices are stacked higgledy-piggledy along the shelf over the stove. It is spring, and there is ivy growing up the side of the fence below the kitchen. The window is open. At the restaurant on the corner, they are playing languid ragtime jazz music, full of clarinets. The kitchen is the same as it was when you got in that car to the airport. The grapefruit seg-ments from the tree facing David Lynch's house are still frozen in a Tupperware container in the freezer. The same photographs are pinned to our refrigerator—the photograph of you sitting in your mother's lap, a photo of me as I tentatively pat a wallaby, the strip of black-and-white photo booth shots taken at the Flagstaff restaurant along Route 66. The receipt for the dollar and twenty-nine cents we made on the poker machines the day we got married. We never did cash it.

The fridge is full. The pantry stocked. The kitchen tiles are swept and mopped. The cabinets washed down. Even the trash can is clean. Plates are stacked in order of size, glasses are nested inside others of their own kind, the spoons and forks and knives all have their places. I am standing at the stove, and I am stirring. Rice, wine, butter, onion. Tomatoes and zucchini and cheese. It won't be long now until dinner is done. It's a beautiful night, and I am barefoot. The sun is coming down over the maple tree. I am still waiting for you to come home.

Notes on Sources

8   The "writer of the West" is Joan Didion. The essay in which she speaks of dams and swimming pools is called "Holy Water" and is collected in *The White Album* (FSG, 1979).

10 The diorama presentation at Hoover Dam is based on a transcription from a video recording I made in the Old Exhibit Building at the Hoover Dam Visitors Center on November 15, 2018.

13 The land around the Hoover Dam is connected to the creation stories of many people, including those of the Hualapai, Mojave, Hopi, Zuni, and Navajo peoples, but the story about the grieving chief is a Southern Paiute story and adapted from *Anthropology of the Numa: John Wesley Powell's Manuscripts on the Numic Peoples of Western North America, 1868–1880,* edited by Don D. Fowler and Catherine S. Fowler (Smithsonian Institution Press, 1971).

27 The book Eloise reads in the hotel room after her wedding ceremony, *Lonesome Dove*, is by Larry McMurtry (Simon & Schuster, 1985).

34 The description of the 2018 Camp Fire is drawn from *Fire in Paradise: An American Tragedy* by Alastair Gee and Dani Anguiano (W. W. Norton, 2020).

42 The description of how a person might theoretically die from heatstroke is derived from the very useful article, "What It Feels Like to Die from Heatstroke," by Amy Ragdale and Peter Stark, published in *Outside*, July 18, 2019. The description of what comes afterwards, and all details about bodily decomposition in

desert environments, is derived from *The Land of Open Graves* by Jason De León (University of California Press, 2015).

43 The apocryphal story about highways used as runways during the Cold War was drawn from *Killer on the Road: Violence and the American Interstate* by Ginger Strand (University of Texas Press, 2012).

45 The Buñuel film referred to is *Simon of the Desert* (Criterion Collection, 1965). All quotations are taken not from the original Spanish but from the English language subtitles supplied by Criterion.

50 The books about death Eloise references are *A Very Easy Death* by Simone de Beauvoir (translated from the French by Patrick O'Brian, Pantheon Books, 1965), *The Book of Mutter* by Kate Zambreno (Semiotext(e), 2017), *The Cancer Journals* by Audre Lorde (Penguin Classics, 1980), and *Illness as Metaphor and AIDS and Its Metaphors* by Susan Sontag (Picador, 2001).

50 The book titled *Dying* is by Cory Taylor (Tin House, 2017).

50 The Roland Barthes book referenced in Section 2 is *Mourning Diary* (translated from the French by Richard Howard, Hill & Wang, 2009).

54 The *This American Life* story referred to is included in episode 540: "A Front," and makes up Act Two, "The Border Between America and America," reported by Debbie Nathan, and first broadcast by NPR on November 21, 2014.

55 The description of the formation of Salvation Mountain was drawn from information derived largely from salvationmountain.org.

66 The piece Eloise and Lewis saw at the old Whitney Museum of American Art is *16 Sculptures* by Travis Jeppesen, which was part of the 2014 Whitney Biennial.

68 The poem Eloise describes in Section 3 is "Meditation in Lagunitas" by Robert Hass, included in *The Apple Trees at Olema: New and Selected Poems* (Ecco, 2011).

69 The section on William Mulholland is derived from information

included in the books *Cadillac Desert: The American West and Its Disappearing Water* by Marc Reisner (Penguin Books, 1993) and *Water to the Angels: William Mulholland, His Monumental Aqueduct, and the Rise of Los Angeles* by Les Standiford (Ecco, 2015). *Cadillac Desert* was a crucial foundational text for much of this book.

75 The book Lewis buys for Eloise is *Manson: The Life and Times of Charles Manson* by Jeff Guinn (Simon & Schuster, 2013).

78 Information on "Nature Boys" and eden ahbez is derived from the excellent book *Sun Seekers: The Cure of California* by Lyra Kilston (Atelier Éditions, 2019).

91 Much of the information about the Colorado River once it crosses the U.S.–Mexico border is drawn from *Where the Water Goes: Life and Death Along the Colorado River* by David Owen (Riverhead Books, 2017).

98 The sections in the book on Keats' idea of "negative capability" and its implications were inspired by a reading of *Keats's Odes: A Lover's Discourse* by Anahid Nersessian (University of Chicago Press, 2021).

99 The Coen Brothers film referred to is *The Ballad of Buster Scruggs* (Netflix, 2018).

102 The volume of Elizabeth Bishop that Eloise reads is *Edgar Allan Poe & The Juke-Box: Uncollected Poems, Drafts, and Fragments,* edited and annotated by Alice Quinn (FSG, 2007).

103 The biographical information about Elizabeth Bishop, including all quotations of correspondence, was derived from the biography *Elizabeth Bishop: A Miracle for Breakfast* by Megan Marshall (Houghton, Mifflin, Harcourt, 2017).

104 The Miguel Hernández poem referred to is named "Elegy," and the Robert Lowell poem is titled "Obit."

109 The Anthony Bourdain episode quoted from is titled "Antarctica," which is episode 9 of season 5 of *Anthony Bourdain: Parts Unknown,* first broadcast on CNN on May 28, 2017.

119 The books Eloise refers to reading on the lounge chair are *We Have Never Been Modern* by Bruno Latour, translated by Catherine Porter (Harvard University Press, 1993), *Vibrant Matter: A Political Ecology of Things* by Jane Bennett (Duke University Press, 2010), and *Hyperobjects: Philosophy and Ecology after the End of the World* by Timothy Morton (University of Minnesota Press, 2013).

131 Much of Brandon's rhetoric is drawn from information derived from multiple episodes of the podcast *Conspirituality*, hosted by Derek Beres, Matthew Remski, and Julian Walker.

142 The information about the five stages of grief and Elizabeth Kubler-Ross, the woman who named them, was sourced from an episode of the podcast *Radiolab* broadcast on July 23, 2021, titled "The Queen of Dying," and produced by Rachael Cusick, for WNYC Studios.

154 Kenneth and Lawrence Greco's plan for their afterlives was inspired by a reading of *To Be a Machine: Adventures Among Cyborgs, Utopians, Hackers, and the Futurists Solving the Modest Problem of Death* by Mark O'Connell (Doubleday, 2017).

165 The *Guardian* article referenced by Eloise is "Crisis in Our National Parks: How Tourists Are Loving Nature to Death" by Charlotte Simmonds, Annette McGivney, Patrick Reilly, Brian Maffly, Todd Wilkinson, Gabrielle Canon, Michael Wright, and Monte Whaley, published online on November 20, 2018.

167 The book by Katie Lee that Eloise reads is called *All My Rivers Are Gone: A Journey of Discovery Through Glen Canyon* (Johnson Books, 1998).

168 The description of Floyd Dominy's thoughts and feelings are derived from things he said in videotaped interviews included in the 1997 PBS documentary *Cadillac Desert: Water and the Transformation of Nature*, by John Else and Linda Harrar.

182 The John McPhee book Eloise purchases is *Basin and Range* (Farrar, Straus and Giroux, 1981).

184 Information on Charles Manson and the bottomless pit was derived from *Manson: The Life and Death of Charles Manson* and *Helter Skelter: The True Story of the Manson Murders* by Vincent Bugliosi and Curt Gentry (W. W. Norton, 1994).

185 The quotation from Keats' letters can be found in *So Bright and Delicate: Love Letters and Poems of John Keats to Fanny Brawne* (Penguin Classics, 2009).

187 The section detailing the expedition of John Wesley Powell and prevailing American theories about rainfall in the late nineteenth century was compiled from readings of *Cadillac Desert* and *Beyond the Hundredth Meridian: John Wesley Powell and the Second Opening of the West* by Wallace Stegner (Penguin Books, 1992).

192 The details about uranium mining on Indigenous American lands are drawn from Dina Gilio-Whitaker's book *As Long as Grass Grows: The Indigenous Fight for Environmental Justice, from Colonization to Standing Rock* (Beacon Press, 2019).

192 The Leslie Marmon Silko book is titled *The Turquoise Ledge* (Viking, 2010), and it is from her work that the description of the stone snake discovered by the Jackpile Mine is drawn.

193 The effects of nuclear radiation on plants and animals are drawn from the book *Manual for Survival: A Chernobyl Guide to the Future* by Kate Brown (W. W. Norton & Company, 2019).

201 The movie that Eloise and Lewis watch is *Zabriskie Point*, directed by Michelangelo Antonioni (Metro-Goldwyn-Mayer, 1970), and all italics are direct quotations from the film.

208 The description of all-male workshops and Holotropic Breathwork was inspired by an essay by Barrett Swanson called "Men at Work," published in *Harper's*, November 2019.

214 The "woman essayist" Camila refers to is Ellen Meloy, and her essay on lawns appears in *Seasons: Desert Sketches* (Torrey House Press, 2019).

218 The anecdote about Georgia O'Keeffe's relationship to water

comes from *Georgia O'Keeffe: A Life* by Roxana Robinson (University Press of New England, 1989).

228 The details about palm trees and Mary Pickford are drawn from Jared Farmer's book *Trees in Paradise: A California History* (Heyday, 2017).

238 David Buckel died on the morning of April 14, 2018, in Prospect Park. The email he sent to the news media shortly after setting himself on fire read, "My early death by fossil fuel reflects what we are doing to ourselves."

253 The books belonging to Lewis which Eloise refers to having found are *The Invention of Morel* by Adolfo Bioy Casares, translated from the Spanish by Ruth L. C. Simms (NYRB Classics, 2003), *The Man Without Qualities Vol 1* by Robert Musil, translated from the German by Burton Pike (Vintage, 1996), and *Dhalgren* by Samuel R. Delany (Vintage, 2001).

253 The slim book by Thomas Merton is *The Wisdom of the Desert* (New Directions, 1960).

OTHER SOURCES

Edward Abbey, *Desert Solitaire: A Season in the Wilderness* (Touchstone, 1990)

Thom Andersen, *Los Angeles Plays Itself* (Mubi, 2003)

The Way of a Pilgrim: Candid Tales of a Wanderer to His Spiritual Father, translated from the Russian by Anna Zaranko (Penguin Classics, 2017)

William Atkins, *The Immeasurable World: Journeys in Desert Places* (Faber & Faber, 2018)

Jean Baudrillard, *America* (translated from the French by Chris Turner, Verso, 2010)

Simone de Beauvoir, *America Day by Day* (translated from the French by Patrick Dudley, Grove Press, 1953)

Ernest Becker, *The Denial of Death* (The Free Press, 1973)

John Berger, *G* (Bloomsbury, 1972)

Julia Blackwell, *Time Song: Journeys in Search of a Submerged Land* (Pantheon Books, 2019)

Charles Bowden, *Some of the Dead are Still Breathing: Living in the Future* (Houghton Mifflin Harcourt, 2009)

James Crump, *Troublemakers: The Story of Land Art* (First Run Features, 2016)

John d'Agata, *About a Mountain* (W.W. Norton & Company, 2010)

Mike Davis, *Ecology of Fear: Los Angeles and the Imagination of Disaster* (Vintage Books, 1998)

William deBuys, *A Great Aridness: Climate Change and the Future of the American Southwest* (Oxford University Press, 2013)

Donna Deitch, *Desert Hearts* (The Samuel Goldwyn Company, 1985)

Bernard Devoto, *The Western Paradox: A Bernard Devoto Conservation Reader*, edited by Douglas Brinkley and Patricia Nelson Limerick (Yale University Press, 2001)

John Dos Passos, *The U.S.A. Trilogy: The 42nd Parallel / 1919 / The Big Money* (Modern Library, 1937)

Roxanne Dunbar-Ortiz, *An Indigenous Peoples' History of the United States* (Beacon Press, 2014)

Umberto Eco, *Travels in Hyperreality* (translated from the Italian by William Weaver, Harcourt, Brace, Jovanovich, 1986)

American Indian Myths and Legends, selected and edited by Richard Erdoes and Alfonso Ortiz (Pantheon Books, 1984)

Legends and Tales of the American West, edited, told, retold, and illustrated by Richard Erdoes (Pantheon, 1991)

Nick Estes, *Our History is the Future: Standing Rock Versus the Dakota Access Pipeline, and the Long Tradition of Indigenous Resistance* (Verso, 2019)

Mark Fisher, *Ghosts of My Life: Writings on Depression, Hauntologies, and Lost Futures* (Zero Books, 2014).

William L. Fox, *Michael Heizer: The Once and Future Monuments* (Monacelli Press, 2019)

Sigmund Freud, *Beyond the Pleasure Principle*, edited by Todd Dufresne and translated from the German by Gregory C. Richter (Broadview Editions, 2011)

Diana Fuss, *Dying Modern: A Meditation on Elegy* (Duke University Press, 2013)

Eduardo Galeano, *Genesis: Memory of Fire Volume 1*, (translated from the Spanish by Cedric Belfrage, Nation Books, 2010)

Amitav Ghosh, *The Nutmeg's Curse: Parables for a Planet in Crisis* (University of Chicago Press, 2021)

Ruth Wilson Gilmore, *Abolition Geography: Essays Towards Liberation* (Verso, 2022)

Greg Grandin, *The End of the Myth: From the Frontier to the Border Wall in the Mind of America* (Metropolitan Books, 2019)

Vince Guaraldi Trio, *A Charlie Brown Christmas* (Fantasy Records, 1965)

Dave Hickey, *Air Guitar: Essays on Art and Democracy* (Art. issues Press, 1997)

Obi Kauffman, *The State of Water: Understanding California's Most Precious Resource* (Heyday, 2019)

Ben Knight and Travis Rummel, *DamNation* (Patagonia Inc., 2014)

Jon Krakauer, *Under the Banner of Heaven: A Story of Violent Faith* (Anchor Books, 2004)

Chris Kraus, *Video Green: Los Angeles Art and the Triumph of Nothingness* (Semiotext(e), 2004)

Lapham's Quarterly: Water XI, no. 3 (Summer 2018)

Ken Layne, *Desert Oracle Volume 1: Strange True Tales from the American Southwest* (FSG, 2020)

Brenda Lee, "Rockin' Around the Christmas Tree," written by Johnny Marks, from the album *Merry Christmas from Brenda Lee* (Decca, 1958)

David Lynch, *Lost Highway* (October Films, 1997)

The Sonoran Desert: A Literary Field Guide, edited by Eric Magrane and Christopher Cokinos (The University of Arizona Press, 2016)

John McPhee, *Encounters with the Archdruid* (Farrar, Straus and Giroux, 1971)

Andrew Needham, *Power Lines: Phoenix and the Making of the Modern Southwest* (Princeton University Press, 2014)

PBS NewsHour, *Tipping Point: River on the Brink*, A PBS Newshour Special, November 11, 2021

James Pogue, *Chosen Country: A Rebellion in the West* (Henry Holt, 2018)

Roman Polanski, *Chinatown* (Paramount Pictures, 1974)

Jedediah Purdy, *After Nature: A Politics for the Anthropocene* (Harvard University Press, 2015)

Stephen Pyne, *Fire: A Brief History* (University of Washington Press, 2019)

Hugh Raffles, *The Book of Unconformities: Speculations on Lost Time* (Pantheon Books, 2020)

Laura Raicovich, *At the Lightning Field: An Essay* (Coffee House Press, 2017)

Jahan Ramazani, *Poetry of Mourning: The Modern Elegy from Hardy to Heaney* (The University of Chicago Press, 1994)

Lauren Redniss, *Oak Flat: A Fight for Sacred Land in the American West* (Random House, 2020)

Robert Smithson, *The Collected Writings*, edited by Jack Flam (University of California Press, 1996)

Rebecca Solnit, *Savage Dreams: A Journey into the Hidden Wars of the American West* (University of California Press, 1999)

April R. Summitt, *Contested Waters: An Environmental History of the Colorado River* (University Press of Colorado, 2013)

David Treuer, *The Heartbeat of Wounded Knee: Native America from 1890 to the Present* (Riverhead Books, 2019)

Simeon Wade, *Foucault in California: A True Story—Wherein the Great French Philosopher Drops Acid in the Valley of Death* (Heyday, 2019)

The Oxford Handbook of the Elegy, edited by Karen Weisman (Oxford University Press, 2010)

Lawrence Weschler, *Seeing Is Forgetting the Name of the Thing One Sees: Over Thirty Years of Conversations with Robert Irwin* (University of California Press, 2009)

Eric Dean Wilson, *After Cooling: On Freon, Global Warming, and the Terrible Cost of Comfort* (Simon & Schuster, 2022)

Acknowledgments

Thank you to my editors, Laura Macaulay, Brigid Mullane, and Hana Park, for the insight and care they took in helping me shape this book. I am especially grateful to them for working collectively, across multiple oceans and time zones, on the manuscript.

Thank you to everybody at Pushkin, Ultimo, and Simon & Schuster who have spent their time, labor, and resources on bringing this book into the world.

Thank you for the belief, support, and counsel of my agent, Anna Stein, and to Lucy Luck.

Thank you to Christine Allan and David Blackah for putting me up in a time of crisis, which allowed me to write the first sentences of what became this book, and to Jane Cochrane for the weeks in Vaison-la-Romaine, where the first draft was completed.

Special thanks to the Staatsbibliothek zu Berlin Potsdamer Straße, the New York Public Library's Rose Main Reading Room, the Burke Library at Union Theological Seminary, and Columbia University's Butler Library, where most of this book was written. I am ever grateful to you all for providing silent, studious spaces to think in.

This book would be a poor shadow of itself were it not for the wisdom and kindness of those who read all or parts of this novel as it progressed: Gabriel Flynn, William Kherbek, Vijay Khurana, Rob Madole, Landon Mitchell, Daisy Sainsbury, Emily Waddell, Alexander Wells, and Elvia Wilk. Thank you all.

Thank you to Amina Cain, Macarena Gómez-Barris, Leslie Jamison, Kevin Killian, Amarnath Ravva, and Claire Vaye Watkins, with whom I had invaluable early conversations before I knew what form this book would take, which were more impactful than any of you probably knew.

Thank you to my Columbia students in the Fall 2022 semester class Writing Nature in the Age of Climate Change, for thinking through so many of the questions that informed this book alongside me.

Appreciation and gratitude and endless love, above all, to my husband, Vijay Khurana, whose mind and affections make me a better writer and person with every passing day.

About the Author

MADELEINE WATTS is the author of *The Inland Sea*, which was shortlisted for the 2021 Miles Franklin Literary Award and the UTS Glenda Adams Award for New Writing. Her novella, "Afraid of Waking It," was awarded the Griffith Review Novella Prize. Her nonfiction has been published extensively in *Harper's Magazine*, *The Guardian*, *The Believer*, *The Paris Review Daily*, *Literary Hub*, and *Astra Magazine*. She has an MFA in creative writing from Columbia University. Born in Sydney, Australia, she lives between New York and Berlin.